UNDERGROUND DRUID

A NEW ADULT URBAN FANTASY NOVEL

M.D. MASSEY

MODERN DIGITAL PUBLISHING

1

The scents and sounds in the Lower Ninth Ward spoke of the sorts of dangers that kept tourists away after dark. There were gunshots, sometimes near, sometimes far, beating out a syncopated rhythm that said, "enter at your own risk." A couple argued a few houses down; the wife accused her man of stepping out, a charge which he vehemently denied. From the sounds of it, he'd be sleeping on the couch with one eye open tonight. And behind me, a group of youths debated whether to mug me or leave me be. They finally decided I was a homeless drifter, and not worth their time.

Smart choice.

I ignored them and kept moving, because I was on the hunt as well.

I cast a cantrip to enhance my senses and took a long whiff of the dank night air. An anemic breeze carried the savory, spicy smells of someone cooking jambalaya, along with the acrid odor of a junkie smoking meth. I smelled cheap perfume from the girls working the corner a block ahead, and the sweet, skunky scent of the blunt they were passing around. Underneath it all lurked the sultry, decaying funk of Lake Pontchartrain to the north, and the earthy, silt-laden aroma of the Mississippi River to the south.

There were other odors on the breeze tonight, but only one spoke to my reason for being here.

Fae.

And also, vampires. *Just my luck.*

I'd come to New Orleans on a tip from a Vodoun priestess back in Austin. Janice—or Madame Rousseau, as she was known professionally—had recently helped me on a case involving necromancy. She'd heard that I'd helped rescue a group of children from a fae sex trafficking ring, and wanted to help bring the culprits to justice. After doing some digging, she'd contacted me two days ago with a lead on one of the ring-leaders, a feldgeister named Claw. He was the last of the fae who were immediately responsible for abducting the kids, and the only link I had to the shot callers behind the operation.

Claw had also planted an arrow in my chest. I still owed him for that one—but I was mostly here to get a lead on his boss, a nasty harvest deity known as the Rye Mother.

I'd searched for him for weeks with no luck, ever since we'd exposed the feldgeister gang to the Pack. They'd been posing as 'thropes for years, using fae magic to fool the Austin werewolf pack in a bid to oust the alpha, Samson, and take over. Their plan had been to use the Pack to expand the Rye Mother's influence into Austin, right under the noses of Queen Maeve and the Cold Iron Circle.

I'd spoiled their party. Only wish I'd done it sooner.

When Janice had told me Claw was hiding out in New Orleans waiting for an extraction, I'd dropped everything and headed to the Big Easy. My plan was simple—track him down and beat him until he gave me every last piece of info he had on the Rye Mother and her operations. That included where to find her, so I could finish what I started. She'd caused way too much pain and misery to get off scot-free, and I wouldn't rest until I'd stomped her ashes into the earth.

After spending an entire day crisscrossing the city, I was finally closing in on Claw's hideout. And while I couldn't figure out why the Rye Mother hadn't portaled him out of here already, I wasn't about to look a gift horse in the mouth. Maybe she'd abandoned him since he'd been exposed, or maybe she just didn't want to piss Maeve off any more than she already had. I didn't know and didn't care. I just wanted the chance to beat him senseless and then burn him to cinders, the same way I'd done with his brethren.

That was the plan... so long as the vampires didn't get in the way.

But I'd cross that bridge when it damn well presented itself. Right now, all I cared about was tracking down Claw before he got wind that I was on his tail. I took another long whiff of the night air, then course-corrected based on the wind direction and his scent. He wasn't far—maybe a block or two at best.

I kept to the shadows as I crept between the ruins of houses destroyed by Katrina, some of which sat right alongside new homes that had been built to replace the wreckage. It'd been well over a decade since the hurricane had destroyed the city, and sadly this neighborhood still hadn't recovered.

I tracked Claw's scent to an abandoned housing complex that reeked of mold and rot. Amidst crumbling buildings that had been tagged in a montage of spray paint and lost hope, the trail led me to a building that remained mostly intact. I took a sort of grim satisfaction in knowing that Claw was living under such wretched conditions.

Oh, how the mighty have fallen.

I staked the place out from an adjacent building, watching for any sign of the fae's presence. A dim light shone from a second-floor window, barely visible even at this distance. The smell of cooking food wafted from the building, blending with the odor of mold spores and rotting wood. Intermingled with those smells was the stink I'd come to associate with Claw and his kind. Freshly-plowed earth, hay, and fae magic.

I loosened my sword in its scabbard and press-checked my Glock to make sure I had a round in the chamber. I spent a moment readying myself to shift, unlacing my boots and setting them off to the side. I kept the rest of my clothing on, because everything else I was wearing wasn't worth saving. Then, I drifted out of the shadows of the building's interior, crossing the overgrown lot as quickly and silently as possible.

Claw was as good as dead. He just didn't know it yet.

I WAS JUST ABOUT to enter the building when I heard them approach. Six humans, coming from three different directions. *Shit.* I was dressed in a ratty old overcoat and watch cap I'd bought off a bum for twenty bucks, plus I'd rolled around in a nasty pile of alley trash before entering the Ward. Either my disguise wasn't good enough to fool these folks, or curiosity was about to kill the cat.

Two men approached in the open to my right, while four more snuck around either side of the building. I could hear them tromping around in the dark—and if I could hear them, so could Claw.

"Hey, man, got a light?"

I hung my head and took a deep breath, letting it out slowly before I pushed off the wall and turned to face them.

"Really, that's your opening ploy? 'Got a light?' I mean, shit, you may as well tell me you're about to mug me."

Two youths stepped out of the shadows and into the moonlight. Both were dressed in ratty gangster attire—wife beaters, baggy jeans, tennis shoes, ball caps, sports jerseys, and hoodies. I didn't have the heart to put a beatdown on them; it was obvious they'd already been through enough.

The lead youth shrugged. "A'ight, so you know what's up. Go ahead an' cough up whatchoo got in those pockets, and maybe we don't fuck you up."

I looked up and saw movement in one of the windows. *Damn it, I've been made.*

"Guys, I really don't have time for this." I dug in my pocket and pulled out a wad of small bills, tossing it to him. "Here. That's all I have."

He picked it up, thumbed through it, and shook his head. "Not enough. Not nearly enough."

The other four toughs emerged from either side of the building and moved in to surround me. I rubbed my forehead and growled with frustration. "I am telling you, I really don't have time for this crap. Besides that, you're about to step into some seriously bad shit—the kind you don't want to be involved in. Please, fellas, walk away."

The leader laughed. "Uh-uh, that's not how it works. Now we gonna show you how it is 'round here."

Just as the boys began to tense for an attack, something large and four-legged exploded out of the window above us. It leaped over our small group, landing a good fifteen feet past us and breaking into a sprint.

Claw.

"Loup garou!" one of the youths cried out. "Ain't got no time for that shit."

I opened my coat and showed the leader the sword and gun at my hip. "I'm here for him, not you. Now, are you going to let me pass, or not?"

The leader's lip curled in a scowl. "Go. We gonna let 'dem night runners deal with you."

"Much obliged, gentlemen!" I yelled as I took off at a run after Claw, who now had at least a half-block head start. But I knew how to slow him down. The feldgeister may have looked like a giant wolf in the dim light, but he was made of plant matter... and that made him combustible.

I drew my pistol and fired off two tracers at him. The magnesium-laden rounds ignited as they left the barrel of the gun. One hit Claw in the hindquarters, forcing him to slow in order to bite and snap at the wound to extract the round before he caught fire. I never broke stride. Claw visibly slowed his pace as he ran off into the night.

I was gaining on him now, but I held my fire. I needed him alive.

I was no more than fifty feet behind him, close enough to hear his footsteps as he ran. He was massive in this form—the size of a small pony, and made from a twisted tangle of vines, branches, grasses, and leaves that moved and articulated like flesh and bone. But more dangerous than his size was his magic. As a feldgeister—a field spirit—he had command over plant life, and to some extent, the earth. If Claw happened to pass through one of the nearby empty lots, he'd command the vegetation to trap me. I couldn't let that happen.

I slowed down to take more careful aim this time and fired off a three-round burst. *Bingo.* One round hit him in the ankle, crippling him. If that wound had been made by anything else, he'd be able to heal immediately. But as I'd learned from my battle with Claw's brothers, fire was their weakness. He wouldn't heal from that gunshot wound anytime soon.

Claw howled and stumbled, then caught his balance and ran three-legged into an alley between two abandoned houses. I skidded around the corner, and what I saw made me chuckle. A rusted-out shipping container blocked the alleyway at an angle

—debris that had likely been left by Hurricane Katrina. Claw was boxed in.

I passed the pistol to my other hand and drew my sword, whistling the theme from *The Good, The Bad, and The Ugly* as I closed in on him. He backed up, favoring his injured leg, and growled menacingly.

"Claw... fancy meeting you here. I just came down to New Orleans for a few days to enjoy some crawfish, jazz, and a hurricane or two, and whaddya know? I find out my favorite piece of shit roggenwölfe is here on vacation too."

His voice was a throaty rumble as he replied. "You can fuck off, druid. Go back to your junkyard, before you get hurt."

I tsked softly as I spun my sword in lazy circles. "Now now, Claw, no need to be rude. I'm just here for a little chat. You tell me where I can find the Rye Mother, and I won't burn you to a crisp like I did your brothers."

He shook his massive, leafy head. "Uh-uh. I told you to fuck off, and I meant it."

I took a deep breath and cracked my neck, left to right and back again. "Alright, I guess this means we do this the hard way."

I took a step forward as Claw coiled to attack. And that's when the vampires showed up.

———

THERE WEREN'T JUST a few of them, there were over a dozen— higher vamps, every last one of them. They were an assorted crew of bloodsuckers, all of them dressed like tourists out for a night on the town. I assumed that was their version of hunter's camouflage. Vamps in the Big Easy didn't play nice like my friend Luther's coven did back in Austin.

I typically found vamps to be weird and creepy, and these were no exception. Some dropped down from nearby rooftops, landing like cats. More sped in from various directions, skidding to a stop near their coven mates in a loose semi-circle behind me. Others jumped on top of the shipping container, cutting off any hope of escape in that direction. They posed, preened, and hissed, trying to intimidate me. *Yawn.*

I'd known that the coven was tracking my movements, so it was no surprise to me that they'd shown up. I'd been catching their scent on and off since shortly after sundown. I figured they'd made me for a hunter and were curious what I was doing in their territory.

These vamps ruled New Orleans. Long ago, they'd established a foothold here and chased out the fae, the 'thropes, and the Cold Iron Circle. Not that the odd fae or 'thrope didn't live here—they just weren't allowed to organize or challenge the authority of the local coven.

And what a coven they were. Luther, the leader of the Austin vamps, had warned me about them. He'd also cautioned me about coming here to track down Claw. Obviously, I'd ignored his warning—but the risk was worth it.

Now, I just had to convince them to let me go free with Claw in tow.

A tall, dusky vamp in a sports coat jumped down between Claw and me, facing me and leaving his back exposed to the fae. That almost made me like the guy. He wore a dark dress shirt left unbuttoned to expose a lean, hairless chest adorned with several gold chains. The vamp had diamond stud earrings in both ears and sported creased dark slacks and shiny black dress boots.

The vamp smiled at me, flashing his incisors. He was trying to intimidate me. It wouldn't work. Claw growled and swiveled his head to keep an eye on the vamps above and behind him.

"What have we here—a hunter and his prey? Or perhaps it is the opposite, no? The question is, what are a hunter and a fae creature doing in our city, without the coven's permission?" He spoke with just a hint of the local patois, but his accent sounded more Caribbean than Creole.

I kept my pistol at my side as I spoke. "My business is with the fae and the fae alone. Last I checked, humans don't abide by the rules of the world beneath."

The vamp tsked and tilted his head. "They do if they are hunters, operating in my city."

"Your city? And you are?"

He chuckled and took a slight bow, sweeping one arm to the side and the other across his waist in a grand gesture. "Remy DeCoudreaux, at your service."

I nodded. "Colin McCool."

Remy stood straighter and clasped his hands behind his back. "Your reputation precedes you, Mr. McCool. And, as such, you can understand why I might be concerned that you're operating in my city. One hears things, you know."

"Such as?"

He frowned slightly. "Such as that you work for Queen Maeve. That you have ties to the Austin Pack. That you're close to Luther and have friends within the Circle as well. And, that you have a strange habit of surviving violent encounters with creatures who are much older and more powerful than you."

I shrugged. "Just lucky, I suppose."

Remy blinked slowly and smiled. "I've observed that luck is most often a product of skill and talent... wouldn't you agree, Mr. McCool?" When I failed to offer a response, he continued. "I see you're a man of few words. So be it."

He gestured at Claw, who had been strangely silent during this entire exchange. "Whatever business you have with the fae here, it stands to reason that you're operating as an agent of one of the Austin factions. And that, I cannot allow. So, the question remains... do I kill you both, or is there something to gain by killing one and allowing the other to go free?"

"The Rye Mother will pay dearly for my safe passage," Claw growled.

Remy nodded slowly. "I'm sure she has some interest in the welfare of her children. But, then again, she has many children, no? And from the looks of you, I think perhaps she has abandoned one of her offspring for the sake of the rest."

I took a deep breath and let it out slowly. "I need him alive. And believe me when I say this is not a threat, but simply a statement of fact—you do not want to attack me or attempt to do me harm."

That remark elicited a great deal of murmuring from the rest of the vamps present. Remy raised a hand to silence them. "Mr. McCool, you are outnumbered, outclassed, and many miles from anyone who might offer you aid. Tell me, why should I not kill you where you stand?"

I rolled my shoulders out and cracked my neck. "I could tell you, but you wouldn't believe me. So, I'd rather just show you."

Remy snorted and took a short step back. "Be my guest."

I sheathed my sword and holstered my pistol. Then I removed my gun belt and scabbard, dropping them to the ground. Next, I removed my Craneskin Bag and set it on the ground as well. Then I stood, looking Remy in the eye as I ignored the snickers from the peanut gallery around us.

I shifted, instantly transforming into my half-Fomorian form. Since my battle with Claw's brothers, I'd been practicing a lot and had gained much better control over my ability to change. Lately, I'd managed to shift into something closer to my full Hyde-side persona. The clothing I was wearing stretched at the seams as I gained a foot in height and at least seventy-five pounds of mass. My skin thickened, bones rearranged and hardened, and my teeth and nails lengthened to jagged points.

Shifting allowed me to access the power of Balor's Eye as well, although it still hurt like a motherfucker to use the Eye's powers. Despite the discomfort, I allowed a trickle of the Eye's power to seep out of my eye sockets, just enough to set my eyes glowing a fiery crimson red. If there was one thing every vampire was afraid of, it was fire; so I assumed that magical laser heat vision would rank pretty high on their "oh hell no" list.

Remy's eyes narrowed. "So, it is true. I'd heard the rumors, but I didn't believe them." He rubbed his chin with a thumb and forefinger, then snapped his fingers. Immediately, the vampire coven dispersed.

Once they were gone, he stepped close to me and spoke. "Still, I cannot allow this trespass to go unanswered. You've left me in a precarious position, druid."

I cleared my throat, a low rumble that sounded like a growl in this form. "Tell your people that I owe you a favor, one you can call in at your discretion."

He raised an eyebrow. "Will you honor this arrangement at some future date?"

"I will, so long as your request does not require me to violate my own morals."

Remy flashed a wicked grin. "It's settled. You may go, and take the fae with you. But be advised: if you betray me, I won't go after you. It'll be your loved ones who pay the price."

He was gone in a blur. "Fucking vampires," I muttered. I turned to Claw, my eyes glowing enough to illuminate the alley. "Claw... I believe you and I have some business to discuss."

2

A fter slapping some cold-forged iron cuffs on him, I took Claw to an abandoned warehouse and proceeded to interrogate him. Although "interrogation" was probably too strong a word, since he started blabbering as soon as we hit the door to the warehouse. Apparently, he'd been hiding out in New Orleans due to a deal that the Rye Mother was supposed to have had with Remy. So, once Remy turned him over to me, he figured his only chance would be to cooperate with me.

Claw spilled his guts to me about the Rye Mother's operations, as well as her current whereabouts. According to Claw, she had cells of her offspring embedded in major cities all over the United States. In each city, she had a group of feldgeisters—her children—either operating in the open or posing as members of the local ruling faction.

Fae were notorious for being masters of illusory magic. This included the use of glamours, see-me-not spells, and other mystical tricks that could be used for disguises and subterfuge. With the right spells, the fae could pose as virtually any supernatural creature or human—just as Claw and his brothers had done when they'd infiltrated the Austin werewolf pack.

"You're telling me the Rye Mother has crews in every major city in the US that are trafficking children just like you lowlifes were?"

Claw hung his head and nodded. I'd made him change back into his humanoid form, which unfortunately meant that he was naked. I hadn't let him return to his hideout to get dressed, since I was worried he might trigger some sort of panic spell or charm. Right now, he was sitting on a stack of wooden pallets wrapped in an old tarp, shivering in the cool fall air. He looked kind of pathetic, but I couldn't dredge up a speck of pity for him.

It's not just that I wanted him to feel uncomfortable; my paranoia was quite justified. You never knew what the fae might pull on you. He might've been hiding a spell to let the Rye Mother know he'd been captured, or an invisibility charm to allow him to escape—or even a summoning spell that would call up another fae creature to fight on his behalf. After all the trouble I'd gone through to track him down, there was no way I'd allow him the slightest opportunity to escape.

Besides, I was gonna kill him anyway.

Claw wiped his nose with grubby fingers and sighed. "I know this is the end for me, druid. I'm willing to tell you everything if you promise to make it quick. I'm tired of running and hiding and having to look over my shoulder all the time. I just want it to be done."

"I bet you wish you would've killed me back in the mine when you had the chance."

He shrugged, pulling the tarp tighter around him. "It wasn't in the plan. Sonny was dead set on destroying Samson, and that meant making him think you killed his daughter. If it had been up to me, I'd have ripped your throat out right there. Can't change the past, though. No sense thinking about it now."

I tapped the barrel of my pistol on my knee. "Tell me what you know, and I promise you won't suffer like Rupert did."

I'd purposely mentioned Rupert, because I knew it'd scare the shit out of Claw. Rupert had been in charge of the place where they'd been keeping the abducted kids. Many of those children had been raped and horribly tormented while they waited to be sold or transported to Underhill.

When I'd seen what had been done to those kids, I'd tortured Rupert until he was a bloody, unrecognizable mess. Not for information—but just because he deserved it. After I'd carved him into hamburger meat, Maeve had sent Rupert back to the Rye Mother via portal.

I'd intended him to be a message that said, "I'm coming for you."

Considering what he'd done to the children we rescued, what I'd done to Rupert had been way too lenient. I'd killed Claw's brethren too, because they'd either abducted kids or hired others to do it for them. I'd also tracked down every human who had worked for Sonny, whether they had actually kidnapped any kids or not.

They had all suffered the same fate. Every last one.

Claw chewed on his lip until it bled, and I sat in silence watching the blood trickle down his chin. Being on the run all these weeks had obviously taken a toll on him, and he was starting to crack. I needed to play it cool, so I could get all the info I could while he still had his wits about him. If I played it too hard, he might do something stupid and force me to kill him prematurely.

The feldgeister's eyes were wild and frightened. I tossed him a bottle of water. He drank it greedily, gasping after downing half the bottle. He nodded once. "I'll tell you everything."

Claw spoke for the better part of forty-five minutes, and I only had to interrupt him a few times in order to get him to clarify the odd detail on the Rye Mother's operations. He gave me everything—names, locations, timetables, the works. I recorded everything on my phone as he spoke. Later, I'd transcribe it into notes and share that info with faction leaders in every city where the Rye Mother operated.

But, according to Claw, it wouldn't do much good.

"She's gone back to Underhill, where she thinks that you can't get to her—and she's taken all the kids she has with her. She's powerful, but she's also afraid of you. She figures she'll head back to the Underrealms for a few decades and wait for you to get killed or die of old age. Fifty years is a blink of an eye to her. After you're gone, she'll be back and running things just like she always has, supplying children to the unseelie fae in Underhill."

I scratched the back of my head with my pistol. "Well, that's where she's wrong. There's no place she can go that I won't follow. We have business, she and I—business that's unsettled. And I plan to square up with her long before my days on this earth are done."

He looked at me like I was crazy, then threw his head back and howled. "Wow, druid, I gotta hand it to you—you sure got some balls. I'm not even gonna bother asking if you're serious about going to Underhill. You won't last five minutes there—but hell, I gotta admire your willingness to kill yourself over a bunch of throwaway kids."

I tapped my index finger on the slide of my pistol. "See there, Claw? That's why you fae will never figure us humans out. It's because you lack empathy and a sense of justice. We humans— some of us would walk a mile barefoot over broken glass to get justice for the innocent. And if that's what it takes to see the Rye Mother go down, well... then that's what I'll do."

He cackled and cut his laugh off short. Then he fixed me with a crazed look, but his expression was deadly serious. "There are powerful fae in Underhill who want to see you dead. Some are the Rye Mother's clients. Others lost family members in that raid you staged on the warehouse. I'll bet they're already sending people to track you down and end you."

I cleared my throat as I stood and leveled the gun at Claw's face. "Thanks for the warning. Say hi to your brothers for me when you greet them in hell."

A FEW DOLLARS' worth of spent ammunition was a fate too kind for Claw, but a deal was a deal. I gathered up the empty shells as I considered what to do with the body. I needed to get rid of the evidence, but I also knew that the New Orleans vampire coven would have people keeping an eye on me.

I decided to leave them a message.

I cut Claw's head cleanly from his shoulders with my longsword, and set it off to the side. Then I stripped down to my Jockeys and shifted. I leapt into the air, grabbing onto one of the rafters above me with Claw's noggin tucked under my other arm. I climbed to the highest point I could reach and pinned the severed head to a roof support beam with a spare dagger I had in my Craneskin Bag.

I wiped the dagger clean of prints, then dropped to the floor of the warehouse. I called upon the power of Balor's Eye and burned the rest of Claw's remains to ashes. Of course, this screwed up my vision considerably. Even with all the practice I'd had the past few weeks shifting, I still couldn't channel the full power of the Eye without sustaining optical damage.

When I'd shifted into my full Fomorian form in the past, channeling the Eye's powers had done zero damage to my eyesight. But back then, I'd been a raging lunatic when I'd completely given myself over to my Hyde-side—and had only been able to shift into that form under extreme, life-threatening duress. Since learning to trigger my shifting abilities at will, I'd yet to gain complete control over my transformation.

So, before I could leave, I had to wait for my eyes to heal.

The Eye spoke to me telepathically while I waited for my Fomorian healing powers to repair the damage done to my eyes. This was the only time I could communicate with it—when I was in my half-Fomorian form—and it rarely missed an opportunity to converse with me.

-You know, I could replace one of your eyes permanently, and then you wouldn't have to deal with this every time you used my powers.-

"We've already discussed this at length, Eye. I am not going to walk around with a huge red gemstone in one of my eye sockets, and I'm not wearing an eye patch, either. I'm way too pale and ginger to pull that look off. Uh-uh, end of discussion, case closed."

Chastised, the Eye decided to change the subject.

-If you intend to enter Underhill in your pursuit of the Rye Mother, it would be wise to wait until you have complete control of your ability to shift into your Fomorian form. Doing so would allow you full access to my powers, and without damaging your eyesight— increasing your chances of survival considerably.-

"I realize that would be the prudent thing to do, but the longer I wait, the longer she'll have to prepare for my arrival. Or, to send her flunkies to try and take me out. And besides that, you heard what Claw said about all those kids. She could have hundreds of them with her, trapped in Underhill. I hate to think what's been happening to those kids while I've been chasing my tail here on earth."

-She'll have access to the fullest extent of her powers while in Underhill. If you don't have complete control of your Fomorian form by the time you face her, the likelihood of your survival is remote at best.-

"You were with Balor when he fought the Tuatha Dé

Danann. Surely you must know what their weaknesses are, and what they fear."

-Most certainly; they fear me. They would also fear anyone who could wield my powers. And, for that reason, they would fear the return of the Fomorians to this realm or their own.-

I closed my eyes and resisted the urge to scratch my eyelids. They always itched like mad while they were healing. But it beat the searing pain that I felt every time I fried my eyeballs by channeling the Eye's power.

"If that's the case, then why the hell would Fuamnach have cursed me with the ríastrad? I gotta tell you, Eye, I just don't get it."

-Are you certain she cursed you? Could there be another explanation for your ability to shift into this other, non-human form?-

That question threw me for a loop. "To be honest, I never considered an alternative. Finnegas told me it was Fuamnach's magic that caused me to become what I am. Sure, I still blame him for what happened to Jesse and me, but I have no reason to doubt that he told me the truth."

-I understand. He is your teacher, after all. But you would do well to remember that Finnegas the Seer has spent a considerable time amongst the fae. It stands to reason that, over the centuries, dissembling would have become second nature to him.-

The Eye made a very valid point. I considered whether there was another layer of deception in what Finnegas had told me regarding my ríastrad—the initial onset of which had caused my girlfriend Jesse's death. Even if that were true, there was no sense worrying about it now.

"If that turns out to be the case, then I'll deal with it when the time comes. For now, I need to stay focused on finding the Rye Mother."

-And then?-

"Then I get justice for all the children she's hurt over the centuries. And I intend to take my time doing it."

-You do realize you'll have to go through Maeve to get to Underhill.-

Maeve was queen of the Austin fae—and supposedly my great-grandmother, many times removed. "Since we're family and all, maybe she'll just let me through out of the kindness of her ancient, withered little heart."

-Doubtful. Rest assured, the price she demands will be steep.-

"It always is with her, Eye. It always is."

ON MY WAY back to Austin, I made a few phone calls. First, I called my girlfriend to let her know that I was okay and to give her the skinny on how things had turned out. Belladonna worked for the Cold Iron Circle, so she was clued in on the world beneath. Still, there was no way was I going to tell her that I planned to head to Underhill, because she'd insist on tagging along. And that just was not going to happen.

Time flowed differently between the fae's realm and ours. I had a funny feeling that my Fomorian curse and fae heritage would allow me to cross back and forth with little if any ill effect. On the other hand, a normal human might travel to Underhill and then age decades upon their return to earth. That begged the question as to what ill effects the children I brought back would suffer; I'd have to discuss that with Maeve before bringing the abducted kids back from Underhill.

But as far as letting Belladonna risk her life by crossing back and forth between our realm and theirs, that was a definite no-go. I'd lost Jesse due to my dealings with the fae and their magic. No way was I going to lose Bells because of those fuckers too.

Belladonna's voicemail said she was at work. So, I left her a vague message and hoped I wouldn't pay for it later. Then I checked in with Hemi to make sure he was doing okay. He'd taken the whole thing with the kids at the warehouse damned hard, but since he'd volunteered to be a "big brother" to a couple of those children, he seemed to be doing better.

Still, it didn't hurt keep tabs on the guy. He wore his heart on his sleeve, and it made me worry that our friendship would have a negative effect on him over the long term. Sure, Hemi was no stranger to the world beneath. But I had a feeling he'd been relatively sheltered back in his native New Zealand. He was a big boy and he could make his own decisions, but if I had to end our friendship to save his tender soul, I do it in a heartbeat.

After that, I left another message for my half-fae friend, Sabine. It was one of dozens I'd left for her since I'd started dating Belladonna. Sabine felt that I'd strung her along—and in some ways, she was right. Still, I'd thought our friendship would be strong enough to weather something like this, and it hurt that she was giving me the cold shoulder.

Once I'd made that futile effort, it was time to take care of business. So, I called Luther and told him I needed to meet with him when I got back to town. His coffee shop was the first stop I made after I hit Austin city limits.

Luther had become a confidant and sort of surrogate mentor during those aimless months I'd experienced after Jesse's death. We had become friends after I'd threatened to kill him, or something to that effect. I'd ended up working for him instead, and the rest was history. I'd since learned to rely on his input and wisdom, and I needed it now more than ever.

It was late when I walked through the back door of Luther's café. He noticed me immediately and signaled that he needed a minute before we could chat. I must've looked like hell, because he slapped a tall, steaming hot mochaccino on the counter with my name on it. I grabbed the drink with a smile and a wave, and sat down in a corner of the café.

That's when I saw Sabine. She was sitting in the opposite corner, hidden safely within the weaves of her glamour and a powerful see-me-not slash look-away-go-away spell. In her current state, she was invisible to anyone but the most talented magic users.

I didn't fall into that category. Which meant that if I'd noticed her, it was because she'd allowed me to notice her.

I stood and walked toward her across the café. The look she gave me as I approached was both sad and resigned. She shook her head slowly, but I ignored the warning and just kept marching toward her table. I was halfway across the room when Luther popped in front of me, gently placing a hand on my chest.

"Sugar, you sure you want to rattle little Queen Bee's hive at this juncture? Old girl has made it pretty plain that she doesn't want to speak to you. Take my advice, and give it a little more time before you try to unruffle those feathers."

I looked Luther in the eye and opened my mouth to say something, then thought better of it and nodded. I leaned over to steal another glance at my friend, but she was already gone.

"Some broken hearts take longer to heal," he chimed. "Now, let's head back to the office and discuss what brought you here this evening."

I spared a wistful glance at the empty table, and then followed Luther to his office. Once we were behind closed doors, I told him what had occurred in New Orleans.

He steepled his fingers and tapped them together slowly. "Hmm... I would've advised you against indebting yourself to Remy DeCoudreaux, but what's done is done. He's a viper with an alligator's jaws if I ever saw one. You let me know when he calls it in—I wouldn't want you to handle that one alone."

"Noted. But right now, I'm more concerned with going after the Rye Mother in Underhill. Any thoughts?"

Luther tilted his head and closed his eyes, remaining statue still for several moments as only a vampire could. Then his eyes snapped open and he frowned. "Personally, I've never traveled Underhill. I'm sure you're aware that vampires aren't exactly welcome there. It's been centuries since my kind and their kind were at war, but to the fae, it might as well have happened last week.

"That being said, it's not as though I'm completely ignorant of the dangers inherent to traveling in the faery realm. Even if your unique heritage and gifts keep you from suffering ill effects from traveling to Underhill and back, it stands to reason that everything and everyone you come across in Underhill is going to be trying to capture you, enchant you, eat you, or end you. Sounds like a suicide mission to me."

"Yeah, tell me something I don't know. But the Eye says the fae are afraid of me."

Luther sucked air through his teeth and nodded. "That may very well be true. All the more reason, it seems, for you to choose not to travel to the faery realm to pick fights with immortal beings of immense magical power."

I laughed softly. "Well, no one's ever accused me of making rational decisions."

"You got that right, kid. Sounds like it's settled. And, if that's the case, that means you didn't come here to ask for my opinion."

"In fact, I did... but what I really need from you, Luther, is a favor. If I don't come back, I need you to find Finnegas and send him after me."

"Can do, stud. But if you don't come back, you can expect that I'll come looking for you myself."

"Thanks, Luther. Also, could you let Bells know where I went? But only after I'm gone."

"Your funeral. And remember what I said about Sabine. She might look soft, but if you push that girl's buttons the wrong way, you might not make it to Underhill at all."

3

After I left Luther's place, I headed back to the junkyard and went straight to my room, where I slept like the dead until noon the following day. I woke to a slew of text messages from Belladonna, Hemi, and my mom—a woman who should not be allowed anywhere near a mobile device.

Mom's texts were always full of "LOLs," as well as lots of misapplications of textese. She thought "DGAF" meant "darned good and fierce," because that's what I'd told her it meant back when I'd lived under her roof. I didn't have the heart to tell her the truth, even though she used it quite often in her texts. I just hoped she didn't use it when texting her friends.

I also had a rather cryptic text from a number in the 555 area code—a spoofed number.

gud 2 c U @ luther's lst nyt. Maeve wants a mtg.

Obviously, it was from Sabine. That was why she'd allowed me to see her at Luther's. She'd been sent there to deliver a message from Queen Maeve. It figured.

I finished all the work that had piled up around the yard while I'd been gone, then cleaned up and headed over to Maeve's house. I briefly considered ignoring the message and letting her stew a few days, but it was never a good idea to piss her off... distant relative or no.

I still didn't know exactly how I felt about *that* revelation, but I certainly wasn't jumping for joy about it. Maeve had started pulling my strings shortly after I'd arrived in Austin. Well, let me rephrase that—she'd been pulling my strings since shortly after she'd become aware of my presence in her town.

I think that pissed me off more than anything, the fact that she'd known I'd moved to town, but ignored me until she'd determined that I might be of use to her. Then again, at her age, she'd probably seen several dozen generations of her descendants come and go. The fae weren't known to be sentimental about such matters, so I supposed it was silly of me to expect anything else from her.

I tucked those thoughts away for another time, and put on my poker face as I sauntered up Maeve's front steps to knock on her door. Unsurprisingly, the door opened as I approached. This time, however, no one was there to greet me. Not Siobhan, who had been mysteriously absent for the last several weeks; not Jack-o'-the-Lantern, who apparently wanted to drown me and munch on my decaying corpse; and not Maeve, even though she'd answered the door herself when last I'd visited.

I hesitated to cross the barrier of her threshold without a formal invitation to enter. I had a sneaking suspicion that Maeve's house was sentient, and as such it probably had specific instructions from Maeve regarding intruders. Not eager to be zapped into a pocket dimension, or to become lost in a never-ending series of hallways that led to nowhere, or to be eaten by an anthropomorphic piece of furniture, I set my feet firmly on the porch and yelled through the open doorway.

"Hello? Anybody home? Maeve, are you in there?"

To my surprise, Maeve's TV talk show voice called back to

me from nearby. "No one else is here, my boy. I'm in the parlor—and yes, you may enter."

I entered the home and walked through the small foyer, pausing to look in all directions to ensure I didn't go the wrong way as I entered the home. The halls and rooms in Maeve's manse were constantly shifting and changing, never quite the same each time I visited. Since I suspected that her home was hostile to all intruders, I was extremely hesitant to head down a hallway without a chaperone.

Straight ahead, a grand entry and staircase led to the upstairs floors. No way was I headed up there. With my luck, the house would have me climbing stairs for eternity. To my left, a dimly lit hallway stretched on for a seemingly impossible distance—an undeniable demonstration that the house was much larger on the inside that it appeared to be without.

I glanced right and gave a small sigh of relief. Before me was the entryway to the parlor, the very same one where I'd met Maeve on past visits. Cautiously, I walked to the arched entry and popped my head in, looking around the room to make sure Maeve was present before leaving the relatively safe confines of the foyer. Inside, Maeve stood at what appeared to be an antique architect's table, where she examined a large clay tablet covered in cuneiform writing.

Her outfit reminded me of something a TV style and fashion show host might have worn. She had matched a navy blouson jumpsuit with a pair of sensible pumps, and she wore a thick jade bangle around her wrist. Something told me the jewelry was for more than just show, but I resisted the urge to verify my suspicions by examining it in the magical spectrum.

After all, Maeve might see my curiosity as weakness or fear, and attempt to use it to her advantage. She'd see even a small lapse in judgment as a major tactical error. And the last thing I needed right now was to look weak in front of Austin's queen of the fae.

"Maeve, you're looking quite stunning today." She ignored me, even as I covered my mouth in feigned shame. "Oh, I hope that doesn't make you uncomfortable, considering the fact that we're related. But then again, you fae aren't exactly known for avoiding incestuous relationships."

In truth, it kind of grossed me out that I'd been attracted to a woman who was basically my great-grandmother many generations removed. Never mind the fact that I'd also admired Siobhan's slender figure on more than one occasion. She would have to be a cousin or some such, and that was almost the same thing as being attracted to your sister.

The whole situation was a mind fuck of epic proportions, but I did my best to avoid letting it show.

Maeve continued to examine the tablet while ignoring my presence. She adjusted a huge magnifying glass attached to the table on a swing-arm, presumably to get a closer look at the writing. The way she studied the thing, you'd have thought it was the mystical equivalent of the Rosetta Stone.

Then again, for all I knew, it was.

"I take it you received my message?"

"I did." I picked up a very expensive-looking vase from a nearby side table, turning it over my hands and tossing it in the air to catch it like a football. I pretended to fumble the vase and chuckled as it floated out of my hands and back to the table where it belonged.

Maeve turned to me and clasped her hands at waist level. "That vase contains a very powerful curse. Should you break it, the curse would be transferred to you. And at the moment, I really do not care to spend an afternoon negotiating with an oni in order to save you from centuries of torment."

She gestured to a pair of antique sitting chairs in the corner of the room, where a complete tea service had magically appeared on the side table between them.

"Shall we sit? I thought a few scones and a bit of tea might be welcome, considering the way your stomach is grumbling."

The scones did look inviting, although my training advised me against accepting food or drink from the fae. But from my great-great-grandmother many generations removed? Well, that was a toss-up.

Nothing ventured, nothing gained, I thought. I grabbed a scone as I plopped down in one of the easy chairs.

"So, Grandma... what do you want to talk about?"

MAEVE VISIBLY STIFFENED at hearing the word "grandma" used in respect to her person. And that was precisely why I had chosen to use it. Anything I could do to get her goat was worth the risk of being turned into... well, a goat.

"I'd prefer it if you never, ever used that term in reference to me again. Ever."

Now that I'd gotten under her skin, it was time to push my luck. Chances were good that, if she allowed me to use her gate to Underhill, I'd be dead in a few days anyway. I figured I may as well have some fun in the meantime.

"But what if I get married and have kids someday? What are they supposed to call you? Nana? Maw-maw? Her royal destroyer of worlds?"

Maeve sat down in the chair opposite mine and busied herself with straightening imaginary wrinkles in her clothing. "If you must know, 'my queen' will be just fine. In fact, I might consider making you address me as such. You've become just a bit too cheeky in recent days."

I took a bite of my scone, pausing for a minute to savor the flavor. *Man, that fae queen can bake.* "If you make me start calling you 'my queen,' does that mean your subjects have to call me 'my prince'? Being as I am royalty and all."

"At best, you might be considered a marquis. 'The marquis du camelote'—I rather like the sound of that."

"Lord of Camelot, eh? Sure, why not?" The smile Maeve gave me told me that I'd missed something important in that exchange. Oh well, you couldn't win them all. "Anyway, if you're through granting titles, I believe we have business to discuss?"

She poured herself a cup of tea, taking her sweet time about it. Maeve was more or less immortal, and she liked to rub it in my face—a lot. I'd learned to just grin and bear it. She might have looked like a thirty-year-old MILF, but she was a few thousand years old. If she wanted to take five minutes pouring herself a cup of tea, at her age I figured she'd earned the right.

After several minutes of painful silence, she finally spoke. "I heard you tracked down the roggenwölfe. Did you get the information you needed from him?"

"I did, in fact. After I mentioned what I did to Rupert, he was quite eager to tell me where I might find the Rye Mother."

Maeve sat back in her chair, taking a long, slow sip of her tea as she eyed me over the lip of the teacup. "And did he tell you that she has retreated to Underhill?"

I frowned slightly and nodded. "He did. He also told me there were some pretty powerful fae out to do me in. Makes me feel kind of important, if I do say so myself."

She placed her teacup on the saucer, nearly hard enough to chip the plate. Tea sloshed around inside the cup, and she glared at me as she set it down on the side table.

"Now you're just being facetious."

I opened my mouth to respond, but she held a finger up in warning as she wiped a bit of spilled tea from the saucer. "My dear boy, I have grown fond of you over the past few months, but

I must warn you—you are trying my patience. These issues we've stirred up with the rest of the fae are no laughing matter. They will send a squad of assassins to kill you—and, in fact, they may already be in the area."

I took another bite of my scone, munching on it and spitting crumbs everywhere as I spoke. "Whaf maku say zat?"

Maeve grabbed a towel from the side table and tossed it at me, hitting me in the face. She was definitely miffed, but in all honesty, I was pretty sure that she actually enjoyed these little tête-à-têtes. Being the queen, I didn't think she was accustomed to speaking with others so candidly. Maybe I was just being full of myself, but I was pretty sure that she found my frankness refreshing.

It was that, or she was planning to off me once I was no longer of use to her... I wasn't really sure which.

"I suspect they're already here, because one of my troll patrols disappeared two nights ago, somewhere in the vicinity of your junkyard."

That made me sit up straight. "You're kidding me, right? No, you never kid. Damn, Guts wasn't with them, was he?" Guts was a troll warrior I'd become friends with after I'd negotiated an agreement between Maeve and his troll clan. He was a hell of a warrior, and a standup guy besides. I'd would've hated for anything to happen to him on my account.

"No, the troll warrior known as 'Eats-Guts-With-Bare-Hands-And-Salts-The-Earth-After-Battle' was not leading the patrol that evening. If he had been, I suspect things would've gone much differently. Unfortunately, the patrol that evening was comprised of relatively young and inexperienced troll warriors. Sadly, I fear their clan has suffered another loss."

Guts and his warriors had helped me deal with a nasty infestation of ghouls at the city graveyard. The battle had been fierce, and his clan had suffered several casualties. That was probably the reason why they'd had so many inexperienced warriors out on patrol. I felt the weight of being responsible for even more deaths settle like an unwelcome mantle around my shoulders.

I set the rest of my scone down on the tray and sunk back into the chair. Suddenly, I wasn't hungry anymore. "You know I have to go after them, right—the Rye Mother, and Fuamnach?"

"What I know is, damned fool that you are, there'll be no talking you out of it. Thus, I am resigned to assisting you in this endeavor."

I sat up a little straighter. "You are? So, what's the catch?"

"THE CATCH, my dear boy, is that while you are in Underhill you will retrieve certain items for me."

I sat up on the edge of my chair and clapped my hands like a gleeful child. "Oh goody, a quest!"

Maeve ignored my class clown routine, and in her usual form proceeded to get down to brass tacks. "Don't get too excited yet—I haven't told you what I need you to do. As I told you back at the Lodge, Underhill is dying, and the fae who live there are desperate to escape before it falls victim to the entropy of the Void."

"You want me to stop them."

She picked up her tea and saucer, and took another sip. "In a manner of speaking, yes. But not by direct action. Instead, I wish for you to take away the seat of their power. You will do so by bringing four treasures to me: The Stone of Fál, The Spear of Lugh, The Sword of Nuadu, and The Cauldron of the Dagda."

I stared at her for a moment, my mouth agape. "You're flipping kidding me, right? You want me to steal the Four Treasures of the Tuatha Dé Danann? Are you mad? I mean, I would expect that your fellow fae in Underhill have grown quite attached to those items over the years."

Maeve nodded with a twinkle in her eye. "Indeed. As such, each item will be heavily guarded—or in the care of its namesake."

"You're quite literally assigning me a Herculean task—you know that, right?"

She scowled. "Heracles was always a prick. Most demigods are."

"Pfft, you're preaching to the choir on that point," I interjected. I'd once had a nasty run in with the son of a Norse deity and had nearly lost my life in the process. In my limited experience, the various deities and their offspring tended to be pompous, self-righteous assholes.

I guess that's why I favored the Celtic pantheon. They acted less like gods and more like the basic assholes they were. If the legends were to be believed, they weren't so much into being worshipped as they were into screwing over humans for their own amusement. They were jackasses, sure—but they also knew how to stay in their lane.

"As I was saying, Heracles was a feckless brute. And if it hadn't been for Iolaus and those damned poison arrows, he never would've completed the tasks set to him by King Eurystheus. You should take pride in knowing that I hold you in much higher esteem than I ever held Heracles. I fully expect you to find a way to gather these items and bring them back to me."

I pinched the bridge of my nose—the conversation was giving me a headache. "And if I fail to steal these items for you?"

"I never said anything about stealing the Treasures, Colin. In fact, it matters little to me how you acquire them. All that truly matters is that you bring them back to me."

"Stealing or acquiring—it's merely semantics. What happens if I fail to 'acquire' these items?"

She looked me right in the eye with a poker face. "Well, then, I won't let you back through the gate to earth from Underhill."

"Great. So, I have to travel to Underhill, avoid being killed by various powerful factions while I'm there, kill the Rye Mother, rescue the children, somehow acquire all four of the Treasures of Ireland, and then make it back to the gate in one piece."

Maeve nodded sagely. "I'd say that sums it up nicely."

"Am I going to get any help from you in completing these tasks?"

"I suppose I could arrange to provide you with a guide... sort of your own Iolaus, if you will."

I sucked on my teeth as I considered her proposition. "A guide, plus somebody who's good at healing magic and glamours."

"I believe I have just the person in mind." She smiled like the cat who ate the canary. I was so fucked. "So then, it's settled?"

I let out a sigh that turned into a growl of frustration and stood. "I suppose I have no choice, do I?"

"Not if you want to get to Underhill. I suggest you take a few days to prepare."

"Yeah, yeah—this ain't my first rodeo, you know."

Maeve's voice called after me as I headed out the door of the parlor. "And, Colin?"

"Yes, Maeve?"

"Watch your back in the meantime. When my people want someone dead, they tend to send their first string from the get-go."

"I'll keep that in mind. Just keep that gate warmed up for me. I'll be back in forty-eight hours, fae hit squad or no." I did my best to sound confident, but I glanced around nervously as I walked out to my car.

4

———————

Upon leaving Maeve's house, I headed straight for Belladonna's place. She'd been working long shifts and was probably just waking up. Since there was no telling how long I'd be in Underhill, I figured it'd probably be a good idea to spend some time with her now, while I had the chance.

I was paranoid as all hell after hearing about the missing troll patrol, so I kept my head on a swivel on the way over. Maeve wasn't the type to exaggerate, and if she said I was in mortal danger, that was a fact. I circled Belladonna's apartment building twice before parking several spaces down from her unit.

I scanned the parking lot, the surrounding cars, and the spaces between buildings as I exited the Gremlin. As far as I could tell, the coast was clear. Despite appearances, I pushed my hand through the slit in the pocket of my overcoat and rested my fingers on my Glock 9mm pistol.

As I was approaching Belladonna's apartment, someone behind me called my name in a low and rough—yet cultured —voice.

"Colin, I need to speak with you. Please don't — "

I looked over my shoulder, and a glance was all I needed.

The shadow beneath his hoodie concealed his face, but I'd have recognized that skinny wizard anywhere.

Crowley!

I pivoted, drawing my pistol in one fluid motion with the intention of landing a three-round burst in the center of his cold-hearted chest. I hadn't seen him since our battle at his farm, but if he was here now, I had to assume he was seeking revenge.

Before my arm could complete its arc, oily black tendrils of shadow whipped out from around him, like tentacles from some deep-sea monster. The tendrils wrapped around my wrists, preventing me from aiming my pistol at him and holding me firmly in place.

Crowley's voice cracked at me from where he stood less than ten feet away. "Now, Colin, wait! I just want to talk—"

It was my opinion that if he just wanted to talk, he'd have left the magic tricks at home. I began shifting into my Fomorian form, and as I did I called the Eye's power up from the alternate dimension where it resided when I was in human form. My clothes shredded as I shifted, and I felt the Eye's presence quickly transitioning from ethereal to physical.

As the Eye's vessel made the shift from that other dimension to our own, bright red light shone from my eyes, illuminating Crowley's shadowy visage. As the light from Balor's Eye revealed what had been hidden under his hood, I noticed two things. One, Crowley had been hideously disfigured during his previous encounter with the Eye.

And second, Crowley was mortally afraid of suffering a repeat performance of our last engagement. His eyes grew wide, one healthy and whole, the other opaque and partially hidden beneath a hood of burned, twisted flesh and scar tissue. Half of his face was covered in severe burn scars that made his features unrecognizable.

Crowley cringed and cowered away from me, releasing me

from the grip of the shadow magic. His voice was weak and pathetic as he begged for mercy. "Please... send that thing away. I mean you no harm."

He sank to his knees and covered his face and head with his arms. The shadows around him fell away, and for the first time, I could truly see the devastation that the Eye's flames had wreaked on the sorcerer. While half of his body had been untouched by the fire, his hand and face had been forever changed as a result of being burned by the Eye.

I felt pity for him in that moment, and sent the Eye back to the other dimension as I shifted into my human form. Crowley peeked at me through the shield he'd made of his arms, and I gave him a nod as I gestured at my now shredded clothing.

"Well, now I'm gonna need to change clothes, so thanks for that. If you're really not here for revenge, you may as well come inside and say hi to Bells while I get dressed."

Crowley slowly rose to his feet, obviously shaken by the fact that I now commanded the power of the Eye. "I can assure you, I only wish to talk."

I fiddled with the tattered shreds of one of my overcoat sleeves. "Dammit, I just got this coat." I looked at Crowley again, making eye contact as I spoke. "I'm gonna take you at your word for now, Crowley. But let me warn you, if you try any funny business..."

He held his hands up and shook his head. "Yes, of course. But, you'll have to forgive my reticence at letting Belladonna see me this way. I... I'd rather she didn't know I was here."

I glanced at Belladonna's apartment longingly. I'd been gone a long time, and was looking forward to seeing her. "Alright. You can ride with me to my place. And, just so you know, the car is warded nine ways to Sunday. Try to cast any spells in it, and you'll get tossed out the door while I'm doing sixty down the highway."

WHEN WE GOT BACK to the junkyard, I had Crowley wait on the front steps of the warehouse while I went to change clothes. Lamenting the loss of a new trench coat and pair of jeans I'd recently purchased at a thrift shop—not to mention another trashed pair of combat boots—I tossed the lot into the garbage and pulled my spares from my storage trunk.

Once dressed, I grabbed a couple of brews from my dorm fridge and paused at the door to glance at Jesse's picture. "Well, Jess, this is fucking weird as all hell. Wish me luck."

I found Crowley waiting for me at one end of the warehouse loading dock, trying to look inconspicuous while the junkyard staff went about their business. He was quite a sight, in a battered leather trench coat—one that I was a bit envious of, in fact—black dress slacks, shiny black boots, and a hoodie that kept his features hidden in shadow... magically enhanced shadow, of course.

But my uncle and the other folks who worked at the junk-yard were used to seeing all sorts of characters stop by to see me. Austin was a city of eccentrics, and at least half of my co-workers were inked up like the Illustrated Man. Some sported piercings, others dressed like country hicks, and still others were biker types.

So, despite his obvious discomfort at being out in the open, Crowley really had nothing to worry about. No one here was going to give him shit for his manner of dress. Besides, it was getting late in the day, and everyone was finishing up so they could head home.

I strolled over to the end of the dock and handed him a beer. He accepted it politely and took a nervous swig as I sat down on a nearby stack of tires.

I took a long pull off my own beer and scratched behind my ear. "Well, this is fucking awkward."

His head bobbed slightly beneath his hood. "It's not exactly how I pictured this meeting going down."

"Me neither. Why don't you start with why you're here, and why you're not trying to tear me limb from limb with shadow magic?"

Crowley grunted—whether in laughter or in pain, I couldn't tell. He dipped his head once, stood, and began pacing back and forth in the small area of hardpacked dirt and weeds between the warehouse dock and the tall, metal fence adjacent to it.

"I never meant for things to turn out as they did," he stammered. "Please understand, I thought you were a monster at the time. My perspectives have shifted quite a bit since our last meeting."

"Mine too. Incidentally, I never meant for things to turn out the way they did, either." I gestured with my beer can at his face and arm. "Does it hurt?"

He gave an almost imperceptible shrug. "At first, yes. Now, the pain is a distant memory. And the scars only serve as a reminder of my hubris."

I chuckled and rubbed the cold can across my forehead. It was chilly outside, but I felt warm nonetheless. "You realize how crazy this all sounds, right? I mean, the last time I saw you, you were trying to kill me."

"And you me."

I frowned. "True, but as you'll recall, I was just there to get the tathlum back. Hell, I didn't even want to be there. If it hadn't been for Maeve blackmailing me, I'd still be minding my own business here at the junkyard."

The tathlum was the magic stone that Lugh had used to hide Balor's Eye centuries ago. Somehow, it had ended up in Maeve's possession, and Crowley had managed to steal it from her treasure vault.

I took another drink of my beer and stifled a belch. "Speaking of which, how'd you steal the damned thing in the first place?"

"With Mother's help, of course. It was her idea, after all."

"And your mother is?" I took another sip, swishing it around in my mouth.

He sighed. "Fuamnach. And my father is the Dark Druid."

I spat beer out in a broad spray across the space between us. "Say what?"

He stopped pacing and turned to face me. "Please, don't hold it against me. Sadly, we cannot choose our family or our enemies, but only our allies and friends."

"You got that right—preaching to the choir here, buddy." I scratched my head and squinted, trying to wrap my head around these revelations. "You're half-fae?"

He shook his head. "No. In fact, I'm adopted—and fully human."

I gasped. "You were stolen and taken to Underhill? A changeling?"

"As an infant. I have no idea who my real parents are, as Fuamnach and The Dark Man are the only parents I've ever known. I suppose I take after my adopted father more than my mother—in body, at least, if not in temperament. He can be... cruel, at times."

"That's the understatement of the year. Can we add to that the words 'evil,' 'heartless,' 'twisted,' and 'fiendish'?"

Crowley hung his head. "I would not argue with that assessment. However, I only recently discovered the true depth of their depravity. You see, I was raised not knowing who my real father was. The Dark Man was a sort of adopted uncle to me. He would come visit us in Underhill every so often and tutor me in the ways of magic. Of course, Mother taught me as well—but there was something about Father that drew me to him."

"I take it they sent you here expressly to steal the Eye?"

"Indeed, they did. The Fear Doirich is a master of the druids' arts of traveling from world to world and dimension to dimension. When I came of age, I traveled from Underhill to earth via my father's magic."

I finished off my beer and crushed the can, tossing it into a nearby recycling bin. "I got no idea what you're talking about, but sure, I'll buy that. Finnegas has hinted that he has the ability to travel to other places. I just never took the time to find out exactly what that entailed."

"Father said it cost him a great deal to send me here, and that I wouldn't be able to return for some time. My instructions were simple: steal the tathlum and bring it back to Mother in Underhill."

"But you decided to keep it for yourself."

He paused for several moments before speaking. "Yes. Once I figured out what the tathlum hid, I thought I could use it to remove the threat of your existence from the city."

"Just curious... did removing me from the picture have anything to do with getting Belladonna back?"

He ignored my question. "At any rate, the magic proved to be beyond my abilities to wield. As you may have discovered, only someone with Fomorian blood running strong in their bloodlines can harness it."

"Makes sense. So why turn coat on your parents now?"

"Why? Because I was punished for my failure. Father was the one who portaled me away from the farm that night. Instead of healing me of my injuries, he left me to suffer in agony for months as punishment for my failure. Once I had healed, he told me he never wanted to see me again, saying I was no son of his."

"Man, that is harsh. And your mother?"

He sniffed. "I haven't spoken with her since the incident. Father abandoned me at one of his enclaves in Greenland. I've had quite a bit of time to reflect on those events since. I now realize I was merely a tool they created and used, then tossed away."

"Still doesn't explain the change of heart toward me. What gives?"

He hesitated. "Suffice it to say that I've seen the error of my ways. Hate can be a powerful impetus, but it can also destroy you. It took the kindness of strangers to teach me that lesson. I will say no more on the matter."

"And about your adoptive parents... now you want revenge?"

"Not against you, no. During the time I spent alone healing, I realized that you're just as much a victim of their schemes as I am. I merely wanted to warn you about what they have planned."

An alarm went off inside my head. "Crowley, why did they want the Eye?"

"There lies the rub. Father can't take fae back and forth across the Veil. He can only transport himself and other humans —and at great cost to himself. Perhaps you've heard that Underhill is dying? For that reason, the fae are desperate to escape what has become a prison of their own making.

"Colin, they intend to use the Eye to destroy the magical barriers at the gates between earth and Underhill, so they can rule here as gods once more. If you go to Underhill to kill the Rye Mother, you'll be playing right into their hands."

I WAS ABOUT to respond with my best savior-complex response when a commotion at the front office distracted me. By this time, almost everyone who worked at the junkyard had left for the day. However, my uncle Ed usually stuck around for an extra half-hour or so every day to do paperwork.

So, when I heard him shouting at somebody, it got my hackles up. Uncle Ed was a grouch, but he never yelled at customers.

I looked at Crowley and grimaced. "Hold that thought." Then I sprinted to the front gate.

When I rounded the corner into the main parking area, what I saw chilled me to my core. There were three tall, lean figures standing in a semi-circle, facing off against Uncle Ed. The clothes they wore reminded me of those silly 1980s ninja outfits —complete with balaclavas, funny boots, and various pointy weapons strapped all about their bodies.

However, the cloth that these outfits had been tailored from was obviously not of this earth. The material shimmered and shifted in patterns and colors that matched the surrounding environs. It was like looking at the *Agents of Shield* plane when it was cloaked.

Ed was giving the three mysterious figures what for, and telling them to get the hell out of his junkyard. These freaks weren't having it, and I suspected I knew who they were really here for—obviously, yours truly.

"It's a fae assassin squad," Crowley exclaimed from behind me. "Colin, you must get out of here, now."

I looked over my shoulder and noted that Crowley was right behind me and spinning up a nasty spell. "How the hell did they get through my wards, Crowley? Did you do this?"

"I swear, it wasn't me. The reason they can so easily thwart your wards is because they're human."

"Shit. Uncle Ed, run!" I yelled as I sprinted toward the office, ignoring Crowley's warning. The assassins' heads swiveled as one at the sound of my voice, and they drew their swords immediately. But instead of running, Uncle Ed decided to grab one of them by the arm.

"Hey, buddy," he growled, as he clasped his meaty hand around the wrist of the nearest fae assassin. "I don't know what your deal is, but that's my nephew—" That's about as much as Ed got out before the assassin's blade blurred, severing Ed's hand neatly at the wrist.

From that moment, everything happened at once. I shifted on the fly, ruining another good set of clothes. A black bolt made of shadow and nothing flew past my shoulder and struck the assassin who had cut off Ed's arm. Crowley's magical attack blew the figure off his feet, tossing him across the yard to land in a heap of discarded automobile parts.

At the same instant, Ed looked at the bloody stump where his hand had been just moments ago and gasped. Then, he passed out and fell to the ground.

My pistol was useless to me in my shifted form, because my fingers were too big to fit inside the trigger guard. I was too angry to think clearly anyway, so instead, I bounded across the yard in great, leaping strides and crashed into the lead assassin.

The assassin swung his sword at me, a futile gesture. I stepped inside the deadly arc that the fae longsword made as it traveled toward my exposed neck. I grabbed both of the assassin's wrists in my thick, misshapen hands and pivoted, swinging with all my might to toss my intended killer into the office wall.

Then I turned to face the other two attackers. Crowley was locked in magical combat with one, and they were trading spells left and right, furiously attacking and using counterspells to thwart the other's attacks. I had zero patience for that shit. I picked up a nearby engine block, throwing it like a baseball directly at the magician-assassin.

The engine block struck the assassin at an angle in the torso. It was a completely unexpected attack, and the magic-wielder had no chance to evade the missile. His body crumpled with a sickening, wet crunch, and the force propelled him into the side of the yard truck. Smashed between the two objects, blood and guts squirted everywhere as his torso was pulverized.

"Colin, look out!" I heard Crowley shout.

I felt a hot, piercing pain in my side and looked down to see a blade poking out of my stomach. One of the assassins had snuck up and skewered me like a cocktail sausage on a toothpick. The other assassin was getting up, none the worse for wear after I'd bounced him—or her—off the cinderblock wall of the office.

I reached behind me and grabbed blindly, snagging the assassin's arm out of sheer luck. "Fucking hell," I growled. "I'm ending this."

I pulled the assassin around and in front of me, dangling him in the air. I lined that one up with the other one who was already making a beeline toward us to get back in the fight. Then I opened up with all of the Eye's power I could handle, blasting them with both barrels.

The magical heat emanating from my eyes superheated the air into two columns of plasma. The beams of magical fire cleaved through both the assassin in front of me and his partner. With cloudy vision, I located the bloody form of the third assassin and blasted her into cinders for good measure.

I heard Crowley's voice coming from my right side. "Colin, your eyes—they're smoking."

"Don't worry about me—my eyes will heal. Just help Uncle Ed, please."

"Of course. I'll do what I can." I heard and sensed rather than saw Crowley shuffle around me to aid my uncle. I fell to my knees, helpless to assist for the moment, and waited for my eyes to heal so we could rush Uncle Ed to the hospital.

5
_____

Crowley had the foresight and good sense to wrap Ed's hand in plastic and stick it in an old cooler on ice before we rushed him to the hospital. We told the ER doc it had been an industrial accident, explaining that we worked in a junkyard. Unfortunately, shortly after we arrived, Ed regained consciousness and started making a fuss about invisible ninjas and his nephew morphing into a monster. The ER staff had already started an I.V. line, so they injected him with something to ease his pain along with a sedative. That combo zonked him out until the specialist arrived to reattach his hand, and they whisked him off to surgery.

The problem was that he'd wake up after surgery and start in with the ninja story all over again. Feeling guilty as hell about placing my uncle in danger, I put in a call to Maureen, a half-kelpie woman who'd worked with Finnegas for the last several centuries. She was well-connected in the supernatural world, and also well-versed in the sort of magic that could make Uncle Ed forget he ever saw those assassins.

When he woke up all he'd have were vague memories of a horrible accident involving the Hurst rescue cutters we sometimes used to remove the roof sections from junked cars. He might have echoes of the actual events later, but those would only manifest as bad dreams and night terrors. It was the best that Maureen could do, since only a fae magic-user of Maeve's caliber could erase memories completely from a human's mind.

Maureen assured me that she'd bring my mom with her when she came to the hospital, as Mom was Uncle Ed's only surviving family. I sat in the waiting room across from Crowley, who looked rather guilty himself regarding the whole affair.

"I hate hospitals," I stated. "They always smell like disinfectant and piss."

Crowley ignored my comment, and instead decided to focus on excoriating himself for some perceived misdeed. The dude seriously needed either a good fuck or to get drunk... probably both, and in that order.

"I'm so stupid. They must've followed me to your place. Colin, I am so very sorry."

"Nonsense. Everyone knows where I live. It's kind of one of the drawbacks of being known as 'the junkyard druid.' Besides, Maeve warned me they'd be coming. I just didn't expect the assassins to be human."

Crowley pinched the bridge of his nose, exposing his mangled face to the light for a brief instant. "I should have thought of it and warned you. The fae in Underhill have long been known to brainwash human children in order to use them as disposable weapons... or worse."

"I have to go after them, Crowley. The Rye Mother, Fuamnach, the Dark Druid—they all deserve to go down for what they've done."

He released a frustrated sigh. "I'm warning you, it's what they want. If you can even find a path to Underhill—and good luck with that, by the way—you'll be practically placing the Eye in their laps."

"But they can't use it. As far as I know, I'm the only one who can wield its power, and only imperfectly at that."

Crowley shook his head inside his cowl. "You don't know Fuamnach like I do. She plots schemes that mature and ripen over centuries. And, she always has a plan for every eventuality."

"Hmph, sounds like someone else I know. Still, the Rye Mother took off to Underhill with several dozen children. I can't just leave them to their fates—not when those monsters are deciding who lives, who dies, and who suffers."

I caught a glimmer of Crowley's good eye from within his hood. "They'll all suffer, and there's nothing you can do about it. Trust me when I tell you this: if you travel to Underhill, you will die."

"I have a way to get there. And if I had a reliable guide, my chances might not be so hopeless."

He guffawed. "You mean me? Really? How do you even know you can trust me?"

I chewed my lip for a moment, staring at him through narrowed eyes. "You could have cut and run, back at the junkyard. Or blasted me in the back while I was distracted."

He extended one long, slender finger on his uninjured hand and exhaled with a hiss. "Have you learned nothing, in all this time you've dealt with the fae? There are only two rules for surviving contact with them: take nothing and trust no one. You could very well be placing your oh-so-blind trust in me, only to be inviting your worst enemy into your midst."

I cracked my neck and rolled my shoulders out to release the tension I had stored there, then leveled my gaze at him. "That's a risk I'm willing to take. Now, are you in, or are you out?"

He shook his head and snorted. "I can't believe I'm agreeing to this—hell, I can't believe I'm agreeing to partner with someone who I once considered my mortal enemy." He lowered his head, then he looked up again and nodded. "Fine, I'm in. What's the plan?"

I smiled. "The plan is, we gather our dream team, and then we storm the gates of hell."

WE HEADED BACK to the junkyard, and on the way over I tried not to think about Uncle Ed or the fact that the guy sitting next to me had once tried to kill me. Funny how life worked out. But when you were desperate, the enemy of my enemy and all that.

Back at the yard, we cleaned up all traces of the battle. Then I made some hastily designed adjustments to my wards, based on the magical weaponry the assassins had been carrying. I couldn't ward all humans from the yard, but I could at least make damned sure they couldn't come in carrying fae weapons.

I kept one of the long swords, since it was finely crafted and far superior to the blades I had. Another went to Crowley, but the third weapon had been melted to slag. I threw the twisted lump of metal into my Craneskin Bag, figuring it might come in handy at a later date.

Once that was done, I started making phone calls. The way I saw it, Maeve would provide our healer and another fae, probably one of her personal guards. The ones I'd met were like dual-class paladin-rangers, sneaky-ass archers with a broomstick shoved up their asses. Kind of like Legolas in the big screen version of *The Hobbit*. I didn't care for the idea of having a dickhead like that on the team, but every dungeon raid needed a scout and a healer.

Crowley could definitely hold his own on crowd control, so we had that part covered. Now, I just needed a couple of tanks to frontline it with me when the faery shit hit the proverbial fan. I dialed the first number, and a gravelly voice answered on the other end.

"Guts' phone, who call me at home?" Trolls always spoke in rhymes. I was told that in their own language, they were master poets. But in our language, their skills at prose left much to be desired.

"Guts! Man, I'm glad to know you're alright. Look, I got this little mission I'm putting together—"

Guts cut me off. "Guts have chance to win glory for tribe? Say no more. You go nowhere 'til I arrive." *Click.*

Alrighty then. One down, one to go. I dialed the second number.

"Colin! Good to hear from you, mate. What's news?"

"Well... I'm headed to Underhill to rescue the rest of the kids the Rye Mother abducted."

"Hmmm... well, bro, have you really thought this thing through?"

I nodded, even though Hemi couldn't see me. "Have you ever known me to do something without thinking it through first?"

Hemi voice oozed with sarcasm. "Oh, no—never. Would Colin McCool run off half-cocked?" He made a sound that was halfway between a fart and giving me strawberries. "If it's settled, then I reckon I'm going with you. Just make sure that if I die down there, you bring my corpse back, eh?"

That threw me for a loop. "Well, that's not a morbid thought or anything."

He actually laughed. "Just promise me, and stop being such a hard case."

"Fine, I promise that if my good friend Hemi dies in Underhill, I will drag his sorry three-hundred-eighty-five-pound corpse back to earth—even if it kills me."

"Good, because if you didn't my mum would kill you, for sure."

Huh. "Hemi, just what is the deal with your mom?"

"No time to get into that, mate. I'll be there in twenty." *Click.*

Now that recruitment was done, it was time to pack. I kept pretty much everything I'd need inside my Craneskin Bag, so I spent some time rearranging the easy access items to make sure I had the basics at hand. That meant loading up on iron and steel weapons.

Why the emphasis on iron and steel? Iron screwed up the fae by separating them from their magic or something. Steel alloys were okay, heat-forged iron was good, but cold-forged iron was best. Modern machinery could cold stamp high-carbon steel with a high iron content into a variety of shapes, using a process known as impression die forging. That's how a lot of metal tools, car parts, and ball bearings were made. Steel that was cold-forged was actually shit for weaponry, but a lot of hunters liked to glue ball bearings into hollow-point bullets. *Voila, instant fae-killing rounds.*

I went down the list as I checked the easy-access contents of my Craneskin Bag.

Plenty of cold-iron tipped bullets, check. Cold-iron hand cuffs, check. My best steel sword, forged of L6 tool steel, and damned expensive—but, like I said, the fae hated iron-based weapons, so check. A semi-auto sniper rifle based on the Colt AR-10 platform, chambered in .308 with plenty of extra ammo, because I was not fucking around. If I had to reach out and touch a really nasty someone in Underhill, I'd damned sure try to do it at long range. Check*mate.* Assorted magical grenades and incendiary devices—check, check. Food and water, because we couldn't trust anything to be safe to eat in the Underrealms, check.

And that was that. Now, all I had to do was wait for Hemi and Guts to arrive, so we could head over to Maeve's before another hit squad showed up. Easy, peasy.

ONCE GUTS AND HEMI ARRIVED, we loaded up into the Gremlin and headed for Maeve's place. That is, after we managed to fit everyone's weapons and gear into the car. Between Hemi's massive whalebone spear—and yes, he joked about the size of his spear constantly—and the "provisions" Guts had decided to bring with him, it was quite the feat to get us packed and ready to go.

Guts insisted on bringing a side of salted beef with him. Yes, an entire side of beef. I suggested we slice it up so it'd fit in my Craneskin Bag, but he declined. I decided not to argue, since half of his tribe's warriors had died on my behalf—and I was leading him into mortal danger as well. Guts didn't seem to mind that part, however. Once he found out he might get a second shot at the Dark Druid, he was raring to go.

After we all got in the car, I looked around and chuckled.

"So, a druid, a wizard, a troll and a Maori warrior walk into a bar..." My joke was met with a chorus of groans—even from Crowley, who was morose as shit. "Alright, alright already. Sheesh, try to add some levity to a dire situation and everyone's a critic."

Thirty minutes later we were standing in Maeve's parlor, and she was giving Crowley the evil eye. Guts and Hemi, she was totally cool with. But she and Crowley hadn't exactly hashed things out after he'd stolen the tathlum from her basement.

"I need him with us, Maeve. He grew up in Underhill, and knows his way around."

Maeve stared daggers at him, arms crossed and foot tapping the ground slowly. "I should fry him where he stands. He can be replaced—third-rate wizards are a dime a dozen."

I hardly thought Crowley was third-rate, because he was a hell of a lot better at magic than I was, that was for sure. But I needed more than one person who was familiar with Underhill. That way, I didn't have to rely on only one opinion. Plus, if one got killed… well… it never hurt to have a spare.

"That might be true, but can you find me one who was raised in the Underrealms?"

She scowled. "If you insist." Maeve walked up to Crowley, nose to chest, and stared up at him menacingly. "But when you get back—*if* you get back—you and I are going to balance the scales, young man."

Crowley didn't even flinch. "I will pay whatever just recompense you deem necessary to square my debt."

Maeve's scowl deepened, then she spun toward me with a June Cleaver smile on her face. "Well then, that's settled. Now, allow me to introduce the rest of your team. Jack, Sabine—if you would be so kind?"

The wisp who was known as Jack-o'-the-Lantern floated into the room from an adjacent hallway, bobbing in time to a tune only he could hear. Behind him, Sabine followed silently, staring at the floor rather than risking making eye contact with anyone. *Why am I not surprised?*

Maeve always knew how to push my buttons.

Sabine was, as always, disguised behind her reverse-glamour, although she'd dropped her usual see-me-not spell. I hoped she'd look up so I could flash her a smile, but no such luck.

"Jack has the unique ability to find paths and byways where none can be found. He will serve as an excellent guide in Underhill. And Sabine, my loyal Sabine… well, she's a talented illusionist, as you requested, and has an adequate, if not expansive, grasp of healing magic."

"Huh," I muttered. Sabine seemed an odd choice for a combat healer, but I wasn't about to argue the matter. Sabine was pissed enough at me as it was. "Maeve, if you don't mind me asking, just what the hell happened to Siobhan?"

Sabine spoke, almost too low to be heard. "Why, would you rather have her going with you instead?"

I glanced at Sabine and found her looking defiantly at me. "What? No! It's just that I'm curious, is all."

Maeve's eyes tightened at the corners. "Ask the wizard. I'm sure he can tell you."

I looked over at Crowley. "The fae you know as Siobhan is currently being held captive by minions of my adopted mother, Fuamnach."

Maeve nodded slowly. "Hmmm, yes. It seems that Fuamnach sent a doppelgänger to abduct and replace Siobhan. I am somewhat embarrassed to say that it took me some time to figure it out. And, by the time I did, the damage had already been done." She gave Crowley a withering look.

Hemi raised a hand. "What happened to the doppelgänger?"

The queen of the Austin fae cocked an eyebrow. "I turned her into a snail and had escargot for lunch. Delicious." She licked her lips and winked at the big guy.

Holy shit, does Maeve have a thing for Hemi? Stranger things had happened. I shook my head and shoulders like a dog, trying to chase the thought of those two going at it from my mind. I noticed that Hemi's face reddened a little in response to her apparent flirtation, so that mollified me somewhat.

I cleared my throat. "Okay. Well, that explains a lot. Now, isn't it time for us to be off?" Guts grunted in agreement and Jack bobbed up and down enthusiastically, while the remainder of our merry band stood silent.

"Very well then." Maeve cast a knowing and wicked glance at Hemi and then took off down a hall apace. "Follow me, and stay close. If you get lost in my home, there's no guarantee you'll be found again in this century."

I followed after her, staying right on her heels while glancing back to make certain we didn't lose anyone. After several confusing twists and turns, Maeve unlocked a door with an old-fashioned key, turning it in the lock clockwise and counterclockwise alternately in a complicated pattern. Behind the door stood the same stairwell we'd taken when I had visited her treasure room, just a few short months ago.

How time flew when you were being manipulated by immortal creatures.

The stairwell curved away into darkness beneath us as we started our descent. As we descended, lights flickered to life in sconces along the walls, only to dim again once we were gone. Along the way, we passed a score of doors of all shapes, sizes, and materials—none of which I recognized from my last trip to the depths of Maeve's manse. Occasionally, an inhuman pair of eyes would peek out from behind the doors decorated with grates.

"Mind the doors, and don't get too close," Maeve said over her shoulder. I glanced behind me in time to see Guts glare at one such door suspiciously, just before he moved his side of dried beef to his other shoulder. Maeve chuckled—whether because she was yanking our chains, or at how possessive Guts was of his jerky, I couldn't tell.

Finally, after what seemed like hours in a never-ending march down those stairs, we hit the bottom landing. It was a dank, flagstone affair, with one massive iron-bound door gracing the wall before us. Maeve turned to face the group.

"Beyond this doorway lies the way to Underhill. It is a gate, a path, and bridge, and it is heavily guarded by spells and creatures—the likes of which none of you have ever known or seen. Stray from the path, and you'll die—probably quickly, and most definitely in horrible fashion. Keep your eyes on the person ahead of you, and ignore what you see and hear around you while we are approaching the gateway. Are we clear on these instructions?"

The group was silent, so I spoke for us. "Stay on the path, keep our eyes on the person in front of us, ignore everything else."

Maeve looked at each of us in turn and nodded. "Very well then. Let's begin."

6

Maeve opened that massive, ironbound door and stepped through. I stared at the doorway for a moment, wondering if I was making a huge mistake. "In for a penny, in for a pound," I muttered as I followed her through the shadowy mist that obscured the area beyond the opening.

Moving through that mist was a bit like walking through oily cotton candy. I could only dimly make out Maeve's form several feet ahead of me. But I hesitated to quicken my pace, for fear that I might lose whoever was behind me.

I glanced down briefly, and wished I hadn't. The surface beneath my feet was black, glassy, and smooth—and it was only a couple of feet wide. I could barely make it out through the shadowy mists that surrounded us, but it was enough to convince me that I needed to keep my eyes firmly planted on Maeve's back.

Suddenly, the mists parted—or, rather, they dispersed outward to form a sort of cavernous arch around us and over our heads. The floor beneath us widened as well, meeting that fog-like archway to either side. Maeve paused and turned to check

on us, continuing only when the entire party had made its way
through the mist.

Maeve spoke as she walked ahead of us, and her voice
sounded as if it came from a great distance. "The pathway to the
gate itself is dimensionally displaced—a trick we fae are rather
fond of, as Colin well knows. Surrounding us beyond the mists
lie various alternate dimensions that are inhabited by creatures
who are wholly committed to protecting this gateway."

I glanced up, my eyes drawn to a large dark shadow that
passed above. I only vaguely recognized the outline of something winged and humanoid, but it was enough to make me
think twice about leaving the path.

"Um, Maeve—just how did you get these creatures to agree
to guard your gateway to Underhill?" I asked as I hurried along
behind her.

She chuckled. "It wasn't hard. It's amazing what you can get
an entity to agree to when you offer the proper bait and bribe."

I didn't care to consider what that meant, and decided
against asking any additional questions about Maeve's
guardians. We walked in silence for an indeterminate amount of
time, until we finally exited the tunnel of mist into a small
cavern that had been carved from volcanic rock.

In the center of the cavern stood an archway carved from
that same volcanic rock, adorned with symbols etched deeply
into the stone and inlaid with precious metals. As far as I knew,
there were no volcanoes in Texas. Obviously, we'd traveled a
great distance farther than appearances had led me to believe.

It was said that time and space got trickier and more fluid
the closer you got to Underhill, which explained all the shifting
rooms and hallways inside Maeve's home. The home itself was
likely a guardian of sorts, protecting the entrance to Underhill
from earthside. Conversely, I assumed that all the creatures in

the mists surrounding us were there to prevent fae from coming through the gateway from Underhill.

Through the archway, I could see only darkness. I examined the arch in the magical spectrum and saw that a powerful magical weave ran through the stone and metal. At the moment the spell lay dormant, waiting for someone with the requisite skill and power to activate it. Maeve stopped and stood beside the gateway, and we gathered around to await instructions.

She gave me a perplexing look, one filled with concern and worry. Her eyes tightened and her lips pursed and she stared at me. In that moment, Maeve looked older than I'd ever seen her appear.

I smiled, and she flashed a weak one in return before addressing the entire group. "As you can see, the gateway to Underhill is inactive at the moment. And while the gate can be activated from either side, it's quite a rare event when that happens. You can be sure there will be creatures, fae or otherwise, watching and guarding from the other side.

"Your immediate goal is to rush through the gate, engage and destroy anything on the other side that stands in your way, and then quickly get as far away from the gate as possible. Once the gate is activated, the Tuatha will send fae to investigate. You can also expect that other creatures will be drawn to the gate out of sheer curiosity, as travel between our world and Underhill is rare these days.

"You should consider anything and anyone you encounter on the other side of the gateway to be hostile, regardless of their appearance or stated intentions. Trust no one, and show no mercy—else you may not make it back alive."

I adjusted the tactical belt that held my sword scabbard and pistol and rolled my eyes. "Sweep the leg and show no mercy. You got it, Sensei Kreese." I pointed a thumb at Jack-o'-the-

Lantern. "I take it that the glowworm over here knows where he's going?"

Maeve eyes narrowed. "This is no time for jokes, Colin. I assure you, the resistance you meet in Underhill will be fierce. If there was ever a time for shock and awe, this would be it. Now, in answer to your question—yes, Jack will guide you where you need to go by the shortest route possible." She spared Crowley contemptuous glance. "I would suggest that you follow his advice."

"Fair enough," I said, before turning to do a visual inspection of the party. I wasn't much for *Braveheart*-style speeches, but I figured I at least needed to tell them what to do.

"Alright, everybody, listen up. Once Maeve fires up this gateway, they're gonna know we're coming. So as soon as it opens, we rush through and rain hell down on whoever's on the other side. I'll shift and lead the charge, with Hemi and Guts at my back. Crowley will provide fire support, Sabine is on the heals, and Jack—"

The little glowing ball of light bobbed up and down excitedly at the sound of his name.

I sighed. "You just find us the quickest way to get the hell out of there, before reinforcements arrive. Got it?"

Jack bobbed once in reply.

"Alrighty then," I said, as I kneeled down to unlace my combat boots. "Give me a chance to get stripped down to my skivvies, and we'll get this show on the road."

AFTER STUFFING all my clothes inside my Craneskin Bag, I shifted into my Fomorian form. I clicked the buckle together on my tactical belt and slung it across my chest along with my Craneskin Bag. Finally, I reached into the Bag and pulled out my war club, and then we stacked up like a SWAT team on our side of the arch.

Maeve stood off to the side, waiting for a nod from me before firing up the gateway. She laid a hand on the smooth, black stone, and began to chant in her native language. Soon the solid blackness in the gateway shimmered, revealing an alien landscape beyond. It looked like something straight out of *Alice in Wonderland*, if Lewis Carroll had been tripping acid instead of smoking opium.

The sky above—if you could call it that—was a hazy, overcast pinkish-gray. It was hard to say what illuminated the landscape, but whatever it was, the light emanated from beyond the sickly, flesh-toned cloud cover above. Maeve had assured me that the light was magical in nature, and that it wouldn't harm Guts in the slightest. That had been a concern in bringing him along, as sunlight was deadly to trolls.

Grasses and flowers adorned rolling hills, painting the scenery in a multitude of colors reminiscent of a Thomas Kinkade painting redrawn in hippy-trippy Technicolor. Instead of trees, the land beyond was dotted with mushrooms the size of oaks. These were also painted in colors that were altogether unnatural and unnerving in their stunning beauty—vivid tones of emerald green, flaming fuchsia, deep cerulean, and more. From the mushrooms hung draperies of moss and massive ropy vines, obscuring the view in several different directions.

Besides the strange otherworldliness of the landscape, most unnerving of all was the fact that nothing stirred on the other side of the portal.

With no time to waste and no compelling reason to hesitate, I charged through the gateway into the otherworldly scene beyond. Hemi and Guts ran right on my heels in a spearhead formation, passing through the archway with me. The transition from our world to theirs was instantaneous and nearly unnoticeable. Had it not been for the change in atmosphere, scents, and sounds, I would not have known that we'd just stepped through a portal to another dimension.

We blitzed out of the gateway, trampling grass that was just a bit too bright and green beneath our feet. Each of us tensed with expectation of a surprise attack, which I anticipated would come from behind the giant mushrooms and foliage ahead of us. I stopped several yards beyond the archway, finding cover behind the trunk of an enormous twenty-foot mushroom. I signaled the others to do the same, and each spread out and found cover behind me.

That is, all except for Jack, who floated down the narrow dirt and stone pathway before us, stopping several yards hence and settling to the ground. I had no idea what he was doing, but I figured if we were going to be attacked, he would be the one to draw fire and not us. So, I waited nervously, alternately eyeing every hiding place possible, while keeping Jack within the boundaries of my peripheral vision. At the same time, I glanced around to make sure my team had all made it through the portal.

The archway behind us was embedded in the side of a great earthen mound covered in grass and flowers. One side of that mound had been cleaved neatly away, as if by a huge guillotine, and that's where the gateway sat. The hilltop was the perfect place for a sniper to set up an ambush.

I pointed at the top of the hill. "Guts, sneak up there and make sure no one is gonna come over that hill and attack us from behind." He nodded and disappeared into the vines and moss around us. I looked at Jack again, and noticed he was vibrating and shimmering where he sat on the ground.

I was just about to go check on him when he emitted a blinding flash of light. I blinked, and when I opened my eyes again, a skinny, goofy-looking man stood in the wisp's place. He was dressed in worn brown leather boots, gray woolen pants, a green wool tunic, and a leather, broad brimmed hat that had seen better days. Dark, unruly hair shot out like black straw in all directions from beneath the brim, partially covering his eyes and face.

His tunic was belted at the waist with a length of natural rope, and he held some sort of large root vegetable that had been carved into a lantern, from which a pale yellow flame glowed. His face was weathered and tanned, and he sported an ugly scar that ran from his temple down to his jawline on the left side of his face. His eyes were bright, clear, and gray, and a broad smile split his face between a bulbous nose and stubbled chin.

Besides the fact that he was missing a couple of teeth, he looked like a normal human. The little man stretched his arms to the sky, exhaling with a groan. Then he did a little jig that involved a couple of spins in a spry shuffling of his feet. He came to a stop and faced us, doffing his hat and gracing us with a grand bow.

"Jack of the Lantern, at your service," he said in a deep, melodious voice.

"WELL, THAT WAS UNEXPECTED," Hemi stated.

I waved at Jack furiously, beckoning him to take cover with us behind the mushroom trunks. I had little faith in his ability to dodge an arrow or spear in his current form, and didn't want to lose one of my guides right off the bat.

"Jack—get your ass over here, before you get shot."

Jack stood straight and gestured around the landscape expansively, arms spread. "Why? There's no one around for miles, I can assure you of that. Well, no one dangerous, anyway.

Seems they've all found better tasks to occupy their time, than guarding this old abandoned gateway."

"Are you sure?" I asked. "Maeve seemed pretty sure about this gateway being heavily guarded."

Jack tsked. "Just as sure as I can be. Oh, you can bet your arse they have someone or something keeping an eye on the portal." He cocked his head and held a hand up to his ear, turning this way and that. "Hmmm... yes, I believe I hear someone fleeing in that direction." He pointed off somewhere behind him in the mushroom forest.

I stepped out from behind the myco-monstrosity I'd chosen for cover. "I guess we'll just have to take your word for it. Whoever they assigned to guard this portal—what do you think took them away from their duties?"

Jack scratched the stubble on his chin. "Now that is a mystery, isn't it? One I'm sure that will be revealed as you go about the business of fetching those objects for the queen. Speaking of, have you decided which of the objects you'll retrieve first?"

"I hadn't really thought about it," I said. "Any suggestions?"

Jack sniffed and wiped his nose with the back of his hand. "Damned mushroom spores, always get to me." He placed a finger on the side of his nose and turned slowly in a circle, gradually extending his arm as he spun. He stopped after making a near full revolution, pointing in a direction opposite the one in which the sentry had supposedly run. "I'd suggest you travel that way. The Dagda resides in that direction, and I've a feeling he's most likely to be sympathetic to you and your mission."

I looked up at the hilltop and stuffed my pinky fingers my mouth, whistling sharply to signal that Guts should return to us. "It's as good a direction as any, I suppose. The Dagda it is, then. He is the father of all druidry, after all."

Hemi sauntered over with a puzzled look on his face. "Dagda? Didn't he get capped way back in the day?"

Crowley chimed in before I could respond. "He's a primary entity, and they don't stay dead for long. Well, not by the measure of near-immortal beings, anyway."

Hemi nodded. "Ah yes, I'm familiar with the type. Off them and they bounce right back, eh?"

"That pretty much sums it up," I said as I shifted back into human form and began getting dressed. Guts slunk out of the trees, silent and stealthy as ever. I did a quick head count while I was lacing up my boots, and noticed that Sabine wasn't with us. "Where'd Sabine go?"

I got a few blank stares and shrugs, then heard her voice call out from behind a nearby mushroom. "I'm here," she replied. A few seconds later, she emerged from behind the massive mushroom trunk, and you could hear everyone's jaws drop as they saw how she looked.

Sabine had dropped her usual disguise and now stood before us with her complete fae beauty on full display. She was a knockout, and always had been—but she usually hid behind a glamour that made her look much less attractive than she actually was. In her current natural form, she was a voluptuous blonde-haired beauty with curves in all the right places... especially upstairs.

"My, but you're a stunner," Hemi commented. "I mean, Colin told me, but his explanations failed to describe the magnitude of your beauty."

Sabine ignored Hemi's compliment, obviously uncomfortable with the attention she was getting.

"Stunner is an understatement," Jack stated as he strolled past, approaching Sabine and removing his hat once again to bow at the waist gracefully before her. He stood again and smiled, ravishing her with his eyes all the while. Sabine blushed and shied away.

I walked up and pushed Jack rather forcefully away from her with a hard shove to the chest. His eyes shot daggers at me as he stumbled and caught himself.

"Leave her alone," I warned him.

Jack dusted his tunic off needlessly, then cocked his hands at his waist and looked down his nose imperiously at me—quite the feat, considering his stature. "Well now, there was no need for that. I was merely showing my admiration for the young lass —something she seems to be in dire need of, if you ask me."

Now it was my turn to get shoved, as Sabine pushed me out of the way to storm past. "I can fight my own battles, thank you very much." She headed off in the direction that Jack had indicated we should travel to find the Dagda's lair.

Crowley smacked me on the shoulder, chuckling. "Still quite the ladies' man, I see," he commented as he stared at Sabine's retreating form from within the depths of his hood. "I'm fairly certain she means for us to follow after."

I took a deep breath and gave an exasperated sigh. "I suppose you're right." I adjusted my tactical belt to make sure it wouldn't chafe, then made a lasso motion in the air with my index finger. "Okay, boys, let's move out. It wouldn't do for us to get separated this early in the game. Besides, something will probably be coming along to investigate the portal activation. Let's not be here when it arrives."

No sooner had I spoken, than we heard the roar of some creature off in the distance. The sound came from a different direction than that in which Sabine had traveled, but it was still worrisome. We glanced at each other, then headed off after her.

7

G uts had taken point, and scouted ahead with Jack. He'd let us know if anything nasty was waiting for us. Crowley, Sabine, and I traveled behind them, down a trail that winded through a never-ending procession of those humongous mushroom trees. Hemi was pulling rear guard, about ten meters behind us.

"Anybody smell that?" I asked as we marched single file down the trail. "It's kind of a sickly-sweet smell, like rotting meat and flowers."

Crowley was the first person to verify what my nose was telling me. "It's Underhill that you're smelling. The flowery portion of that bouquet is what it used to smell like—or so I'm told. And the rot underneath? That's the decay, and the reason why the fae are so eager to get out of here."

Sabine was right behind Crowley, and thus far the silence between us had been almost painful. When she spoke, it immediately got my attention. "You two should probably keep quiet. We're almost certainly being followed, and there's no telling what's hiding in this forest."

"Forest is kind of a strong word, don't you think? Giant

mushroom patch might be a better description. I wonder if they're hallucinogenic?"

"Indeed," Crowley replied. "Or highly poisonous—take your pick. Virtually everything in Underhill is compellingly beautiful and surprisingly deadly."

"Fine, don't listen to me," Sabine muttered. "I'm just a pretty face, after all."

I whispered over my shoulder to Crowley. "She's right, you know. We should keep quiet."

At that moment, a distant howl pierced the eerie quiet of the Carrollian forest. That was one of the stranger things I'd noticed during our first few minutes in Underhill—the quiet. You just didn't realize how much noise there was in a conventional forest, until you were traveling through a patch of giant mushrooms. They didn't creak or rustle at all; they just kind of stood there and swayed back and forth silently.

The eerie silence almost made me welcome the howling. Almost.

Another howl answered the first, farther off into the distance. Then more answered the call. Apparently, we were being hunted.

Crowley chuckled. "It seems it's too late now for subterfuge. I believe we have a pack of cu sith on our tail."

Cu sith were giant wolf-like dogs bred and raised by the fae to guard their property or simply to hunt and kill humans. Some could be friendly, even helpful at times, but most weren't. I'd killed my share during my time as a Hunter, so I didn't see their presence as being much of a problem.

"How soon will they catch up to us?"

Crowley's response was clipped. "Minutes."

"That quickly? Sounds like they're several miles away."

He grunted. "These aren't like the cu sith back on earth. Those are just puppies. The ones following us? Probably as big as horses, and covering ground just as quickly. They have our scent now, and won't easily give up the hunt."

I considered the information he'd just shared and decided on a course of action. "Sabine, please run ahead and let Guts and Jack know that we have a tail. We're gonna try to leave a surprise for them, and then catch up shortly."

Sabine jogged down the trail away from us muttering expletives, most of them directed at "pig-headed misogynists."

"Colin, out of curiosity—what did you do to get her so hacked at you?" Crowley asked.

"Oh, I kind of strung her along... and then I slept with a girl she hates."

"Intentionally?"

I stopped and began scanning the surrounding areas, looking for a good choke point—someplace to set up an ambush. "The stringing along part was completely unintentional. We were just friends—good friends, in fact. I just didn't realize that she had such strong feelings for me. But the sleeping with Belladonna part?"

"Hmmm... I don't think I want to hear this."

I cringed inwardly. "Oops. Sorry about that. I'm not very good at reading people, and I wasn't really sure if you still had a thing for her or not."

He stared at me from within that damned shadowed cowl of his... or maybe not. It was hard to tell, because he was using shadow magic to hide his face.

"Here comes Hemi," he said, changing the subject.

Well, I guess that answers my question.

Hemi sprinted up the trail toward us with a worried look on his face. I noted, and not for the first time, that he moved surprisingly fast for such a big man. "You heard 'em, eh?"

"We did, and Crowley said these things are bad news. They hunt in packs and they're big—real big." I turned to Crowley.

"Besides their increased size, I take it they're just like the cu sith back home in all other respects?"

His hood bobbed once.

"Good. That means they hunt by scent." I dug around my Craneskin Bag until I found what I was looking for—a huge can of bear spray that I'd stolen from CIRCE way back when.

CIRCE had billed itself as a cryptid relocation nonprofit organization. But what they really had been was a front for Crowley and Fuamnach's schemes. After Crowley had disappeared following our fight, they'd shut down for good. But not before I'd managed to steal some choice items from their armory.

I motioned for Hemi and Crowley to step back. "You guys might want to head up the trail a ways. I'm about to spray the shit out of this place with two-percent capsaicin. Trust me, you do not want to accidentally inhale this stuff."

After they'd given me plenty of room, I began to spray the trail and surrounding vegetation. I hoped that the cu sith would get a good whiff of pepper spray and that it'd throw them off our trail. But before I could make much progress, Hemi yelled a warning.

"Mate, we got company!"

I quickly scanned the area just in time to see a huge, black, wolf-like dog exit from the foliage on the right side of the trail ten yards ahead of me, his tongue lolling.

"My, what big fucking teeth you have," I muttered under my breath.

I looked back where Hemi and Crowley were standing and saw that two more cu sith had exited the forest on the other side of them. I looked to my left and right and saw yellow eyes peering out at me from the shadows to either side of the trail.

"They're trying to box us in!" I yelled. "Back to back, now!"

I DREW MY SWORD, since I didn't think that a 9mm round would do much good against creatures this size. The three of us stood in a tight triangle formation as the pack began to close in from all sides. Crowley was spooling up some sort of spell, while Hemi chanted and stomped out a haka—which meant he was activating the wards in his tattoos.

And me? I was trying to figure out how we were going to survive. I could shift in an instant, and very likely save myself. But Crowley and Hemi might be torn to shreds. I racked my brain for an answer.

"Which one is the leader?" I asked my companions.

Crowley nudged me with an elbow. "Hmmm... that one, I think." He pointed to my left down the trail from where we'd come, to the first cu sith I'd seen. Since the cu sith were closing in, he was nearly within range of my bear spray.

"Alright. Be ready to move, because I'm about to punch us a hole." *C'mon a little closer, you overgrown mutt.* The pack alpha edged toward us a bit, baring his teeth and growling. *That's it, just a little more...*

I lunged forward and hit it full in the muzzle with the bear spray. The thick orange fog completely enveloped the cu sith's head, getting in its eyes, nose, and mouth. The creature couldn't help but breathe it in, and it began to snap at the mist, which only made it worse. Soon it was blinking rapidly, pawing at its face, and whining up a storm.

"Run, now!" I shouted, and took off through the gap that had been left by the momentarily distracted leader of the pack. I ran within a few feet of him, barely evading the creature's jaws as it angrily snapped at anything and everything around it.

The other cu sith hesitated to follow, confused as to whether they should assist their leader or chase down their prey. But soon one of them broke off and sped after us, and the rest of the pack followed suit, leaving their befuddled, pepper-sprayed leader behind.

"Into the forest!" Crowley yelled, as he turned and fled into the giant mushroom stalks just off the trail. He cast a spell over his shoulder as he ran, and three shadowy figures that vaguely resembled us continued down the trail. "It won't fool them for long," he said.

I let him and Hemi pull away so I could use the rest of the spray on the surrounding plants and stalks, in order to confuse our scent. Then I hauled ass after them, noting that they were circling around in an arc to catch up with the rest of our party.

I didn't know how I felt about leading these creatures to Guts, Sabine, and Jack, but I didn't want to be separated, either. So, I followed their lead and ran on a path parallel to the trail we'd been following. Howls and yips soon came from the forest behind us, and we heard the pack crashing through the mushrooms, hot on our trail.

I spotted a low ridge ahead and pointed to it. "Up there— we'll have to make a stand, and that's as good a place as any." We three headed for the ridge and began scrambling up it, hoping that a bit of higher ground might prove to be an advantage.

Once we hit the top of the cliff, I reached into my Bag and pulled out my sniper rifle, popping out the bipod legs and dropping to a prone position at the edge of the short cliff.

"Crowley, can you confuse them a bit?" He nodded. "Hemi, watch our backs, and make sure none of them sneak up on us."

I kept both eyes open as I scanned the forest below, waiting for the first cu sith to show itself. "There." One of the huge canines popped out from behind the mushroom trunks, loping along with its head close to the ground, following our scent.

I placed the crosshairs on the tip of the creature's nose, leading it off slightly.

I exhaled and squeezed the trigger, and the crack of the rifle echoed off the ridgetop. Thankfully, my aim was true, and the great beast fell to the forest floor. A quick glance through the scope showed that I'd hit it right between the eyes.

Another member of their pack must've seen the wolf go down, as a howl of agony echoed from just within the concealment of the forest. From this angle, the canopy of mushroom caps blocked much of my view, making it difficult to spot any of the pack while they were within the tangle of stalks below us.

But I knew there were more on the way. That first howl was matched by several more, coming at us from the front and both our flanks. "Shit. I can't take more than one out at a time with this thing," I muttered. "You guys get ready to fight."

The cu sith began edging out of the forest, and I began taking shots at will. I wounded some, and one or two lucky shots put my targets out of action, but it wasn't enough. More of their pack had joined them, and at least a dozen of the huge canines were charging at us from all directions. I stood and prepared to shift, ready to fight to the death to protect my companions.

Out of nowhere, a great roaring sound echoed from the other side of the ridge. It sounded like a cross between an elephant's trumpet and a lion's roar.

Crowley's head began swiveling left and right inside his hood. "Ollie?" he asked.

I had no idea who Ollie was, but based on the loud crashing noises coming behind us, I had a sneaking suspicion we were good and rightly fucked. Cu sith were charging up the ridge from both sides, and that way was our only route of escape.

Another trumpeting roar sounded from the backside of the ridge, almost on top of us from the sound of it. Then a huge green wyrm with scales the size of saucers came crashing out of the forest at our backs, breathing smoke from its nostrils and dripping venom from a very large mouth filled with foot-long, spear-like teeth.

The thing had to be a good forty feet long, and it looked like it meant business.

"DON'T WORRY ABOUT THE WYRM!" Crowley shouted. "He's a friend!"

The wolves were upon us now, and we each set to the task at hand. I shifted, shredding another set of decent clothes, and leaped at a cu sith that was lunging for us, wrestling it to the ground like a cowboy wrestling a calf. It had quite a bit of size on me, and soon I was hanging onto its neck while it shook me around like a rag doll.

I squeezed until I heard something crack, and the thing yipped. Then it collapsed and was still. I turned to see Crowley blasting cu sith to either side of him as he backed toward the wyrm. Hemi was doing damage with that huge whalebone spear of his, thrusting and ducking and spinning—and looking like he was having the time of his life.

But the wyrm was the real star of the show. Whenever one of the pack lunged at Crowley, it would snap the thing up in its massive mouth. Two loud crunches later, and the cu sith was a bloody lump traveling down the wyrm's throat and into its belly.

I only had an instant to take it all in, then I was back in the fray. I cracked a cu sith across the jaw as it snapped at me, stunning it. Then I reached into my Bag and grabbed my war club, bashing it over the head—once, twice. The great black canine dropped, and I stomped its skull for good measure.

There were more, maybe a dozen of them, but they were hesitant to press the attack. We'd decimated more than half their pack already, and with that huge dragon-thing at our backs, it was now at least an even match. With a snarl from one of the larger cu sith, they slunk off down the ridge, disappearing one by one into the forest below.

The huge wyrm reared its massive diamond-shaped head above us as it let out an ear-splitting roar. It watched as the last cu sith retreated into the forest, puffing smoke from its nostrils and roaring one last time.

Then, it lowered that huge head on its long, slender neck and nudged Crowley, purring and nuzzling him like a great big house cat. The wizard actually giggled and began fawning over the beast.

"Ollie, how'd you find me?" he asked softly.

"Friend of yours?" Hemi asked.

Crowley looked over at the big guy. "My only friend, actually, when I was growing up. My adoptive mother gave him to me as a gift. I was supposed to train him to hunt down escaped human slaves, but Ollie here didn't have the heart for it." He scratched the thing behind one of its ear holes. "Did you, boy?"

"An oilliphéist," I said. "You had an oilliphéist for a pet."

He shrugged. "Things are different in Underhill."

Hemi chuckled. "You can say that again, mate. But you won't hear me complain. Your pet dragon saved our lives."

I shifted back into my human form and shook my head, lamenting another ruined set of clothing. I had more in my Craneskin Bag, but I'd be running out soon. "He's not a dragon, not really. Technically, he's a wyvern—and a young one at that. See the two forelegs, and the absence of hind legs? That tells you he's not a dragon."

Hemi frowned. "Coulda fooled me, eh? Anyway, no need to split hairs. He saved our asses."

I nodded. "That he did." I yelled to the forest on one side of the ridge, "Guts, it's okay—you guys can come out now."

Guts stalked hesitantly from the cover of the mushroom

stalks, with Sabine and Jack in tow. "Took while to find druid. Heard dragon and roars led us to it."

Jack took one look at the wyrm and his face soured. "Serpents. Bah! You can't trust anyone who's a snake person, is what I say. Cold-blooded is as cold-blooded does, and like attracts like." He crossed his arms and sat down on a short mushroom cap, as far away from Ollie as possible.

Sabine marveled at the creature, forgetting her self-consciousness and shyness for a moment. I had to admit, Ollie was impressive. His iridescent scales shimmered in the strange light of Underhill, turning from dark green, to light fuchsia, to gold, and back to green again, depending on the angle. The beast fairly rippled with muscle, and his sharp white teeth and shiny black claws added to his intimidating presence. Yet intelligence shone in Ollie's large serpent eyes—golden orbs flecked with silver and split with a vertical iris that visibly widened and narrowed as he looked around.

"He's beautiful," Sabine asked. "Can I pet him? Is he friendly?"

Crowley chuckled. "Very much so, in fact. He's rather protective of humans, which pissed my mother off to no end. He's not too fond of fae, though. My mother's guards were cruel to him when he was a hatchling. So be careful as you approach him."

Sabine advanced slowly, with her hands in the air. "I'm not going to hurt you, boy," she spoke softly. The serpent snorted softly, shying away from her touch. "There, there," she sang, humming a tune meant to calm and sooth the creature. Soon, the beast had warmed to her touch and was nuzzling her as well.

"He likes you, I think," Crowley marveled. "Uncanny."

Sabine smiled shyly. "I've always taken after the human side of my family, more than the fae. Caused me a great deal of trouble growing up. Maybe that's why he likes me."

I pretended to ignore their interaction, and busied myself

with pulling a new set of clothes from my Bag and getting dressed. I didn't exactly know how I felt about Crowley being friendly with Sabine. Was I jealous? A bit. But what concerned me most was that I still wasn't sure whether or not his friendship act was all a ruse.

8

Our travels went more smoothly for a time after the cu sith pack dispersed. Now that Ollie had located his master, it was apparent there was no way the beast would separate from him willingly. Despite his size, the wyrm did a surprisingly good job of disappearing into the foliage, and trailed along beside our party for the next several miles.

Occasionally, Ollie would get bored with the relatively slow pace and slink off into the forest for a time. When he returned, he'd invariably be carrying a dead stag or wild boar in his jaws, which he'd drop to the ground in front of Crowley and nudge in his direction. One time he brought back a sizable round boulder, which Crowley flung far way via magical means, sending Ollie off to retrieve it.

Jack continued to eye the creature suspiciously, much to the amusement of the rest of the party.

Hemi nudged him with an elbow playfully. "Whassa matter, Jack—don't care for dragons? Or you afraid he'll fancy you for a tasty treat?"

Jack merely scowled, until Sabine chimed in. "Jack's dislike for serpents is well-founded. Isn't it, Jack?"

The wisp cleared his throat noisily and spat to the side of the trail. "Tricksters, every last one of them. And heartlessly cruel at that. Can't be trusted, can't be tamed."

Sabine smiled as she kept her eyes on the ground. "Jack's immortality is the result of a brush with the oldest serpent of all. But I'm fairly certain Ollie is harmless and completely disinterested in eating Jack-o'-the-Lantern."

I knew exactly what she was referring to, because the myth was famous as folk tales went. According to legend, Jack had tricked the Devil twice and was cursed because of it. After he died, he tried to enter heaven, but was denied for his wickedness. Since he'd forced the Devil to promise never to harvest his soul, he was stuck between heaven and hell for all eternity.

Jack harrumphed. "Can't trust them, and that's a fact. And that's all I'm sayin' on the matter!"

"And the pot calls the kettle soot-stained and treacherous to boot," I whispered.

"I heard that!" Jack crowed, causing Hemi to laugh loudly.

At that moment, Guts came running around a bend in the trail ahead, still hauling around that huge slab of dried meat. I noted that it was fully one-third smaller now, and wondered what we were going to do when he finished it. I figured maybe he could eat one of Ollie's kills, if Ollie would let him.

"Guts, what's up?" I asked.

"Ahead forest thins out, no enemies about. Big farm over hill, with a giant at the till."

Hemi scratched his head. "He's got a store set up? Cashier seems a strange occupation, for a giant."

Jack side-eyed the big man with contempt. "He means that he's cultivating the land, ya big dope. Tell me, troll, did the giant carry a great big stick with him?" Guts nodded, and Jack turned to me. "That'd have to be the Dagda, for no one else quite fits that description in these parts. I suggest that you take the lead on this one—never can tell how these deities will react to being disturbed in their demesnes."

"Roger that." I turned to the party. "You guys hang back, and I'll go see whether or not the former leader of the Tuatha de Danann is in a pissy mood."

With a bit of grumbling from Hemi and Guts, I was able to convince them to allow me to approach the Dagda alone. To say I was nervous was an understatement, considering that he was considered the greatest of the Tuatha, and formerly their chieftain.

Legend had it that he was the wisest and most fair of all the Tuatha deities, although I doubted that he considered himself a god. The Celtic pantheon never seemed to be much interested in being worshipped; they were too busy fighting and getting laid.

As I rounded the bend in the trail, the giant mushrooms began to thin out. Soon I was climbing a rocky path up a hillock blanketed in huge wildflower blossoms of all types and colors. The most enormous bees I'd ever seen—each one easily the size of my head—buzzed to and fro, collecting nectar and doing their part to pollinate the flowers. I stopped for a moment to admire the scenery, but that odd, sickly-sweet smell ruined it for me, so I continued on my way.

Once I crested the hill, the scene Guts had described was laid out before me. A vast orchard of every kind of fruit tree dominated the land below to my left. At the edges of the orchard were huge apiary stands, which explained where the bees were coming from. A freshly-tilled field at the orchard's end stretched off into the horizon beyond.

On the other side of the field and orchard stood a humble cottage, one of suitably grand proportions for a giant. It was framed of timbers that must've been three times as tall as me, and just as big around. The front door was a good twelve feet

tall, and an equally ginormous pig rooted in the dirt inside the
fenced front yard.

At the center of this scene was a giant of a man, perhaps nine
or ten feet in height, with arms like saplings and legs like tree
trunks. He wore a coarse burlap tunic that came to his knees,
and nothing else. In one hand, he held a huge war club that was
easily the size of a mature oak tree, the tip of which dragged in
the dirt behind him. His other arm rested on the handle of large
plow, which was hitched to a massive gray plow horse the size of
a bull elephant.

I stood there dumbfounded, marveling at and overwhelmed
by it all.

The giant called up to me, and his voice carried clearly
despite the distance between us. "Come now, druid. There's no
need to be shy. After all, I am the founder of your order, and
you're bound to me as I am to you. No harm shall come to you
on my lands. Rest, and let us discuss the matters at hand."

Sensing that I was in no immediate danger, I headed down
the hill to greet the Dagda.

———

As I approached, the Dagda unhitched the plow horse so it
could graze and visit a nearby trough. The animal was so large
that the ground trembled slightly at its every step, and it left
deep hoofprints in the dirt behind it. I gaped openly at it.

"Damned fine animal, that. Beat Abarta in a game of fidchell,
and won it fair and square. Hasn't spoken to me since. Come."

He gestured for me to follow him, and we strolled to a circle
of rough-hewn benches in front of his home. He sat on one,
propping that massive club against the bench with a thud. I
boosted myself atop another bench across from his, doing my
best to look comfortable and failing miserably. I sat there with

my legs dangling off the damned thing like a child at Sunday supper, wondering how I should begin.

I took a moment to get a good look at him. His face was ruddy, but kind, with deep-set brown eyes and a long, hawk-like nose. The beard he wore was shaggy but clean, and he looked like someone who spent a great deal of time outdoors—yet his skin wasn't as creased or weather-worn as I might've expected. His hands were gnarled, calloused, and strong, and his arms and legs were sinewed and thick.

He had long gray hair pulled back in a ponytail with a leather thong, and wore no adornment or jewelry of any kind save that single, practical concession. In his bare feet and tunic, he might have been mistaken for a poor country serf, tending the fields for the master of the land. If not for his size, that was, and the fierce, intelligent gaze that shone from those deep-set green eyes of his.

I was a bit intimidated by his presence, to say the least.

Thankfully, the Dagda saved me from having to start the conversation. "I'd offer you a drink and some food, but I know you wouldn't take it."

"Your hospitality is welcomed just the same, Dagda."

He grinned. "So, Finnegas was your teacher, eh? It shows. You have his ways about you, though I expect you'd deny that to your last breath. He's a tricky bastard, that one, if well-intentioned. Still, place good intentions in one hand and shit in the other, and what are you left with? A handful of shit."

"Finnegas is... trying at times. But I do owe him a great deal."

"Do you, now?" The Dagda leaned forward, placing a hand on his knee and resting his elbow on the other. "I'd say in more ways than one, yes? He miscalculated, and it cost you dearly. That I can see easily enough. And for that reason, you failed to complete your training. A damned shame."

I tried to remain as blank-faced as possible. I was awed by

the fact that I was conversing with perhaps the greatest of the children of Danu, and had to remind myself that this was a negotiation. It wouldn't do to get starstruck and screw things up —else I'd end up fighting the Dagda for the Cauldron.

I had little faith in my chances, should that come to pass.

"I learned enough. It got me this far, at least."

He waved my answer away with one of those tremendously strong hands. "Your talent has been wasted. Finnegas held back, because he feared you would surpass him. He had a student who did so, once—outsmarted him in every way. You know of whom I speak."

"Fionn MacCumhaill."

"The same. Stuck in the Seer's craw that the kid took to druidry so easily. Sadly, he was a bit like you—more eager to feel the sword's bite than the land's blessing." He sat back, crossing his arms as he regarded me. "But you could surpass him... surpass them both."

"I lack a teacher," I stated simply.

"You lack direction, not teachers. Of those, you have several... if only you'd ask politely and apply yourself. Revenge has driven you from sorrow to action, but it will only take you so far. What you need is a purpose."

"Are you offering to provide me with one?" I didn't know why I'd asked that question. Maybe it was because of what Maeve had once said to me, that I didn't ask the right questions.

The Dagda frowned. "I can't give you that, any more than Finnegas could." He pointed a gnarled finger at my chest. "That, young man, can only come from you. And if you're asking if I'll teach you druidry, you're out of luck. You can't stay here, because this place is dying. When it goes, I go with it. So, the answer's no to that question as well."

That threw me for a loop. "You mean you're not trying to get back to earth?"

"Pfah! I'm old, boy. Old and tired. Immortality isn't all it's cracked up to be. Certainly, some of the younger of us are planning and scheming their return. 'Let us rule as gods once more,' they say. I laugh at them.

"They think your people will worship them, welcome them with open arms. This, in an age when men ride chariots across the sky and speak at great distances with electric words and sounds. Fools, every last one of them. My former lover, The Morrigan, plans to do battle with them as we speak. She, like Nia... er, Maeve, still has a soft spot for the Sons of Milesius."

"That's why no one was guarding the gateway when we arrived. Your people are at war."

He lifted a hand, and it wavered back and forth. "The gate wasn't left entirely unguarded. Fuamnach and the Fear Doirich needed to make a good show of it, eh? Thus, the pack of hounds that tracked you near to my lands. I take it most of your party survived?"

"All of us, actually. A bit of deus ex machina saved us, by way of a wyvern. You wouldn't have had anything to do with that, would you?"

"Far be it from me to send the wind to whisper in a wyvern's ear, blowing him the scent of his former master." He winked at me, and smiled. "Now, let's discuss the matter of loaning you my Cauldron..."

"I KNOW you need the Cauldron and the other Treasures in order to get back through the gateway to earth. And I know what Maeve intends to do with them, once she has her hands on them."

I rubbed my chin as I considered the implications. "She indicated that she intends to block the pathways between Underhill and earth."

He laughed. "Oh, more than that, lad. Her plan is to steal all the magic back from Underhill, and dole it out to the fae who remain in your world. Of course, if her plan works, she'll also retain complete control of the collective magic of our people."

"Damn, I had no idea. She'd be unstoppable, wouldn't she?" The Dagda nodded. I couldn't help but think that Maeve's plans for that power were morally questionable, at best. "What would happen to all the fae here in Underhill if that occurred?"

He frowned. "We'd be well and truly buggered, every last one of us. The magic is what keeps The Void and its entropy at bay. But, as you've probably noticed, it's become a losing battle—mostly because of the pull the earthside fae have on the magic. What they use weakens Underhill, and if it's not stopped..."

"Underhill will die completely."

He nodded and pointed at me. "Got it in one. Underhill was never meant to be a permanent solution anyway, only a temporary place of retreat. We intended to wait it out here while you humans killed each other off, a few centuries at most."

"But instead..."

"Instead, you bred like rabbits and took over the island. Not to mention, you gained more than a wee bit of magical power for yourselves along the way. I was chastised by several of my kind for sharing druidry with you, but as I told them, our time had passed. Damned if I was going to let my knowledge die out with us."

I stared at the ground for a moment, processing what he'd shared with me. "I don't get it. Why tell me all of this?"

"I already told you, but you didn't listen. I don't want my legacy to die with me." He hopped off the bench, springing to his feet as he scooped up his club. "But, enough with that—too fecking depressing by far. If you're going to have my Cauldron from me, you'll have to earn it. Now, pull out that little toothpick you call a war club, change out of your pretty boy pants, and let's dance."

"You want me to fight you?"

He snarled his response. "I didn't stutter, did I, boy? You want my Cauldron, you have to fight me for it. Them's the rules!"

I shook my head in disbelief. "Alright, already. Sheesh. Give me a minute to get out of these clothes—I'm on my last pair of boots."

He stepped back and leaned on his club. "That's the spirit, lad. Take your time... but not too long, mind you. I still have a few hundred acres to till."

Minutes later, I'd shifted and stood across a dirt clearing from the Dagda. I'd changed into the closest version of my Hyde-side I could get to the real deal, but he still had a good eighteen inches in height on me. He slapped his club in his hand a few times as he looked me up and down.

"Oh, that's the thing I wanted to fight, for sure. Not quite as ugly as old Balor himself, but damned close. Ah, this brings me back. But no using that Eye, now, or I'll consider it cheating and you'll be forfeit." He pointed the business end of his club at me. "You ready, boy?"

I sighed. "Ready as I'll ever be."

Without warning, he launched himself across the clearing at me with a speed reminiscent of an ancient vampire I'd once fought. His club was a blur as he swung it at my head. I ducked and countered with a blow to his knee, but he danced out of range long before I could connect.

We clashed again and again, sometimes with me stopping his blows, while other times I dodged them. I quickly learned to avoid blocking his strikes, because the resulting shock threatened to numb my hands useless after the first few blows. And despite the fact that his club was so much bigger than my own, he wielded it like a willow switch, swinging it this way and that with staccato strikes that frequently changed angle and direction.

Gradually, the speed and frequency of his attacks increased, and I was no longer able to evade them, much less provide a counterattack. Soon, I was forced to block him, blow for blow. My hands grew numb and slick with sweat. He chased me around the clearing that way, wearing me down in an almost methodical fashion.

Finally, he knocked my war club from my unresponsive hands, then spun his club and swept my legs from under me. I landed hard on my back, with the tip of his club in my face.

"Best two out of three?" I asked.

He laughed, and extended a hand to help me up. "No, one round is plenty. I'll be feeling this tomorrow morn."

After he'd gotten me back on my feet, he looked me over once and nodded with a grunt of satisfaction.

"You'll do. Now, fetch me that stick of yours, would you?"

I did as he asked, handing it to him handle-first as he sat down heavily on a nearby stump. "So, I guess this means I don't get the Cauldron? I did lose, after all."

He arched an eyebrow as he examined my war club. "Just like the day she was crafted. Damn, but Lugh did fine work." I watched as he scratched a rune in the butt end of the club with his thumbnail, as cleanly as if he'd used a chisel. "For good luck," he quipped as he handed it back to me.

"You said 'did fine work.' Is Lugh not around anymore?"

His expression saddened, and his eyes became misty. "Oh, he's still around. But not the same, sadly. Of all of us, he fell in love with Underhill the most—because it was his idea to begin with. But I bet the sight of you will perk him right up. Probably remind him of Cú Chulainn, you will.

"Ah, but listen to me carry on, like the old man that I am."

He pointed the butt end of his club at me. "You came here for a reason, and fought me without hesitation. So, I'll consider my Cauldron to be on permanent loan to you from here on out."

He sat staring at me with a twinkle in his eye and a slight grin on his face. Finally, I couldn't stand it any longer. "Um… can I have it, please?"

He slapped his hands on his knees and guffawed. "Hah! I slipped it into your Craneskin Bag while you were getting undressed. Damned thing's not doing any good sitting around." He swept an arm around him. "What the hell do I need with a bottomless cauldron of broth, anyway? It's not like I'm lacking for food, that's for sure."

He whispered to me behind his hand, while pointing a thumb at the humongous hog that was still rooting in the dirt nearby.

"Besides, the pig's brother keeps me in ham and bacon." The hog turned to him and snorted, before dropping a huge shit where it stood. "And that one provides fertilizer for the fields," he exclaimed with a chuckle. "Now then, you'd best be off. The cursed wisp'll take you to see old Lugh—keep an eye on that one, mind you."

"Lugh, you mean?"

He waved my question away with a frown. "Naw, the wisp. A right bastard, he is—slick as snot on a snail. But bound to his queen, so he'll not betray you… for now." He reached into a pocket in his tunic that hadn't been there a moment before, and tossed something to me. "Here, take this."

I caught it and opened my hands. It was a huge acorn, shiny and brown. It looked old, like it had been polished to a high sheen from years of being handled.

"What's it for?"

"You'll know it when you need it. All that metal you hide behind will only serve you for so long. Eventually, you'll need someplace to recharge and regroup, someplace safer than a metal enclave." He lifted a hand from his knee as if dismissing a stray thought. "Ah, but I've said too much."

I walked up to him, wishing to bid him farewell eye-to-eye before I transformed back into my smaller, human self. I extended a hand to him. "How can I ever repay you?"

He looked at my hand, and crossed his arms. "A handshake is a bond amongst the fae, although I appreciate the gesture."

I withdrew my hand, and he smiled warmly. "That's better. Listen, lad—you'll repay the debt when you carry on my legacy. Finnegas is old, and his time is shorter than you think. When he's gone, it'll be just you and that prick the Fear Doirich. Trust me, when that time comes, you'll carry the torch willingly."

I said nothing, and the old man squinted at me as he tugged on his beard.

"Go see Lugh. We don't talk much—he's still sore that I didn't bring him back at the same time I revived Cermait. Fecking peacock always did know how to hold a grudge."

From what I recalled, Lugh killed the Dagda's son, Cermait, because he'd slept with one of Lugh's wives. Cermait's sons killed Lugh in revenge. Like I said, the Tuatha were always too busy fighting and fucking to care much about being worshipped.

The Dagda stared off in the distance, as if examining memories long past. Then he shook his head and continued. "Anyway, I believe Lugh has a proposition for you. 'Twon't be easy, but if you'll agree to it, he'll be much more inclined to lend you his Spear." He spat at his feet and gave me an up-to-no-good smile. "Now, be off with you. I've land to plow yet."

I nodded, returning his smile, and headed back up the hill to my friends.

9

I looked inside my Craneskin Bag on my way back up the hill, to be sure I hadn't been hoodwinked by the Dagda. He wasn't known to be a trickster, but these were the original fae I was dealing with now, so I could take nothing for granted.

The Cauldron was definitely there, and it wasn't much to look at. Just a simple, black iron pot, coarsely crafted, with a matching, ill-fitting lid. But a look inside revealed it to be full of a boiling brown concoction that smelled delicious and kept on coming, no matter how much I poured out of it.

At first, it didn't seem like much of a treasure to me—but then I noticed that wherever I poured the broth, food-bearing plants, trees, and shrubbery shot out of the ground. Despite those rather surprising results, I wasn't the least bit tempted to taste the contents. I knew better than to experiment on myself with powerful fae magic.

I tucked the Cauldron back into my Craneskin Bag as I crested the hill, and followed the trail back to where I had left the rest of the party.

"Forget something?" Hemi asked as I approached.

"What do you mean? I've been gone for hours."

Hemi looked at me strangely and scratched his head. "Naw, bro, you just left. It was only seconds ago that I watched you disappear around that bend in the trail."

Crowley walked over to us and gave a flippant wave of his hand. "I wouldn't bother with trying to figure that out. Time tends to be malleable here in Underhill." He turned to me, his face still obscured in shadow despite the bright, never-ending glow from the clouds far above us. "Did you get it? Is the Cauldron in your possession?"

"Yes, I have it. He gave it up willingly, if you can believe that. And he suggested that we visit Lugh next." I searched around until I located Jack chatting up Sabine, who was doing her best to politely ignore him. "Jack, which way should we go to find Lugh?"

Jack ignored me in similar fashion, fully intent on making time with Sabine. I growled as I turned to Crowley. "It seems the guide Maeve assigned us is otherwise engaged. Any idea where Lugh might be?"

"Yes, I know where to find him. He lives on the border between the Seelie and Unseelie lands. He's a bit of a hermit these days, from what I understand. And, he's been known to kill fae who trespass in his demesne. But yes, I can take you there. It's not far, actually."

"Okay, you and Guts take the lead." I turned to the rest of the party. "Everyone get your shit together. It's time to head out."

THERE WAS no way to gauge the passage of time in Underhill, since the "sun" always shined directly above us. This made it impossible to determine how far we'd traveled.

Watches were also apparently useless in Underhill, because the hour and minute hands on my mechanical watch spun rapidly and ceaselessly. I secretly worried it meant time was passing that quickly on earth while we were gone, but I kept those concerns to myself. I soon took to counting my steps, in order to get a rough estimate of how far we'd gone.

I estimated we'd only traveled a few miles before the land-scape flattened out. Here, the tall mushrooms and wildflowers gave way to moss, tall grasses, cattails, and towering trees that looked like a cross between Cypress and African baobabs. Each tree had massive root systems that arced out from the main trunk, a feature that I assumed kept them upright in the soft, marshy soil.

It wasn't long before the marshy grasslands became a full-on swamp, complete with muggy air, foul odors, and mosquitoes. A thick canopy of vines and branches crowded out the light above, and soon we were forced to illuminate our path by magical means. But Crowley seemed to know where he was going, and he kept us mostly on dry land as we trudged deeper into the swamp. Which was a very good thing—considering Jack had been chatting Sabine up nonstop since we'd left the Dagda's lands.

"Jack, remind me again why Queen Maeve sent you along with us?" I quipped as we skirted a nasty quagmire that bubbled and belched foul-smelling gases.

He paused his one-sided conversation with Sabine to respond. "Oh, the wizard seems to be doing well enough at the moment. This is the land of his youth, after all. Although I might have chosen a more direct route."

"Seriously?" I peeled a bright red leech from my arm and squished it. It oozed blood and green goo, which I wiped on a nearby tree root. "I want you to know that I will not be giving you a five-star review when we get back home."

The little man rolled his eyes and went straight back to

flirting with Sabine. All the while, Sabine ignored him and kept her eyes on the ground.

We were a few thousand paces into the deepest part of the swamp when Guts grabbed me by the arm and brought a finger to his lips. I drew up close and arched an eyebrow. He pointed a rubbery, grey-green finger to the canopy above us.

I peered into the shadowy depths of the foliage above, straining my eyes to see what he saw or sensed. Finally, a pair of bright green eyes with dark-slitted pupils emerged from between two leafy branches. Either my vision was playing tricks on me, or a huge cat was watching us from above.

I leaned over to Crowley and whispered. "Is that pet wyvern of yours nearby?"

His hood dipped slightly. "He's close."

"Good, because I think we might need an assist."

Just as the words left my mouth, the biggest panther I'd ever seen dropped down from the canopy above, landing soundlessly as it blocked our path.

ON CLOSER INSPECTION, the big cat wasn't quite as panther-like as I'd originally thought. It was black as night, and fully fifteen feet from nose to tail tip. But it was built much more like a cheetah than a panther—lean rather than muscular. As it went from a crouch to its full height, the cat's eyes leveled with my own.

The cat twitched its tail once, then turned and walked slowly away from us. I held up a hand to signal everyone to wait. The cat looked over its shoulder and blinked at me as it twitched its tail.

"It wants us to follow," Sabine said.

"Do you reckon that's wise?" Hemi asked.

Guts grunted. "Could've eaten us anytime. I say follow, we be fine."

I looked around at the rest of the party. "Anyone disagree?" The group remained silent. "Then we follow the cat."

The big cat purred, sauntering off through the swamp. The going got easier, as the cat had an uncanny knack for finding solid ground where we could find none. Soon, the trees thinned out, and we approached a wide moat surrounding a crenelated stone wall. My eyes followed the wall left and right; I could just make out two towered corners in the distance.

"Did the ancient Celts even have moat castles?" I pondered.

Jack, who'd finally given up on trying to impress Sabine, answered me. "Nay, but I suppose period-dependent architectural cues wouldn't be of much concern to an immortal being. If you want to ponder a real mystery, consider how much magic it takes to keep that monstrous heap of stone from sinking into the swamp. That'll make your head hurt, for sure."

Crowley cleared his throat. "Lugh is said to enjoy his privacy these days. Thus, the fortress."

"I know the feeling. Can't blame a guy for wanting to be left alone." I shifted my tactical belt to keep it from chafing. "I just hope he's as friendly as the Dagda says," I muttered under my breath.

The cat hooked a right to take a path that traced a line down the bank, and we followed obediently. Before long, we rounded the corner of the "castle" and traveled to the center point of the adjoining wall. A huge wooden catwalk stretched off above the swamp to our right—an impressive display of primitive engineering and architecture that was obviously designed so travelers could avoid trudging through the murky swamp. To our left stood the gate and drawbridge to the fortress, currently pulled shut.

Sabine sat on a log and pulled off her boots and socks,

which were soaked through. She glanced at the wooden structure to our right and sighed as she examined her wet and wrinkled feet. "You mean we could've taken the bridge instead? Seriously?"

Jack perked up at the sound of her voice. "Indeed. That was the alternate and more direct route to which I referred. Had I known the lady wished to avoid traversing the marshlands, I would've suggested we alter our route."

Hemi snorted. "Had the wisp not been busy trying to get in the lady's knickers, he might have done his job and guided us around the swamp."

Sabine's face reddened, although I caught a slight smile playing at the corners of her mouth. I wanted to say something to ease her discomfort, but I worried I'd only make it worse, so I took in the scenery around us instead. That's when I noticed that the big cat had disappeared.

"Anyone see where the cat went?" I asked.

Crowley pointed into the swamp. "That way. I get the impression we're supposed to wait here for further instructions. It appears there's a way station over there, by the entrance to the catwalk. Perhaps we should take this opportunity to dry out and take some refreshment."

I looked where he was pointing and saw a small, cabin-like structure near where the walkway began. It was slightly ramshackle, but appeared to be serviceable.

"Fine. Guts, scout around to make sure there are no threats nearby. I want the rest of you to check out the cabin and take a break."

Sabine slipped her wet socks and boots back on. "Whatever," she muttered, and trudged over to the hut.

I waved Hemi over. "Keep an eye on her, will you? I get the feeling that Jack's up to something—and besides that, his infatuation with Sabine is kind of creeping me out."

"You got it, bro." He nodded at the fortress. "What do you think the deal is? You think this Lugh character is in there?"

I crossed my arms and chewed my lip as I stared at the massive stone structure. "Crowley and Jack seem to think so. But why he has us waiting out here is a mystery to me. Maybe it's some kind of test or something. Who knows? I just wish he'd get on with it so I can get the rest of these items for Maeve, kill the Rye Mother, and get the kids back to earth."

He sniffed and scratched his nose as he watched Crowley, Jack, and Sabine enter the cabin. "Speaking of which, what's the plan for that? She's no pushover, based on what I've heard. Think you can take her?"

"The Rye Mother? Piece of cake. It's Fuamnach I'm not so sure about."

"Fuamnach too, eh? I know you hate the bitch, but you sure that's a good idea? If you think about it, things have been going just a little too easy for us since we got here. Aren't you the least bit suspicious that we're walking into a trap?"

I laughed humorlessly. "We're definitely walking into a trap. That's what I'm counting on, in fact. And I plan to bring a reckoning, right to her doorstep."

LIGHT BEGAN to fade from gray to night, and we still hadn't heard a thing from the castle or seen any sign of the cat. I'd managed to get a fire going, and we sat around it in front of the cabin, eating our dinner while we dried out our socks and boots.

I pointed up at the sky. "First time I've seen that happen since we got here."

Crowley grunted from within his hood. "We're at the border between the Seelie and Unseelie lands, between the so-called Summer and Winter courts. On one side, it's always light. On the other, always dark. This is the only place in Underhill where night and day alternate." He glanced past the cabin and into the swamp. "We will want to move indoors for the evening. It won't be safe out here, in the dark."

I stood up. "You heard him, people. Time to hole up for the night, and get some rest. I'll take first watch."

I watched as everyone gathered their belongings and headed inside the small structure. Except for Guts, who walked into the small circle of firelight from the shadows beyond. "Guts watch will keep. Junkyard Druid need his sleep."

I shook my head. "Not yet, Guts, but thanks. I'll stay up for a while. You go rest, and I'll wake you when it's your turn."

Guts shrugged and headed indoors. I took up post on a bench by the cabin door, with the sniper rifle resting on my knees. The sounds of talk and laughter inside the cabin soon diminished, replaced by light snoring and the quiet rustling of my companions turning in their sleep. I cast a night vision cantrip and scanned the area as I listened to the sounds of crickets and frogs singing in the swamp nearby.

"Interesting choice of weapon, for a druid," a deep male voice stated from my left.

My head snapped toward the voice, and I brought the weapon to my shoulder. I stopped short of pointing the weapon at him, because I had a sneaking suspicion I knew who he was.

The man was of average height, with curly blonde locks that framed a ruddy, fair, and almost feminine face. He was lean of build—but muscled, like an acrobat or rock climber. He wore a blue embroidered tunic over loose green pants that were tucked into supple leather boots.

"Interesting place for the Celtic deity of light to live," I said as I lowered the barrel of the rifle. "Lugh Lámfada, I presume?"

He nodded. "The same. Mind if I sit?"

I scooted over and propped the rifle against the bench next to me. "Be my guest. It's your place, after all."

He sat next to me, leaning back against the cabin as he heaved a sigh. "It wasn't my first choice, but I wanted solitude. I have to admit, though—the place has grown on me."

"I can see how. It's peaceful, if a little damp."

Lugh pulled out a pipe, and we sat in silence for several minutes while he packed and lit it. The smoke smelled like chronic, which made me chuckle. He offered me a hit, but I declined.

He pointed the mouthpiece of his pipe at me. "Do you mind if I speak with your companion—the one who lives inside your skull?"

I thought for a moment before responding. "Sure, so long as you don't take it back. I have a feeling I'm going to need the Eye before this trip is done with."

"You have my word, druid. I gave up possession of the Eye long ago, and for good reason. It's way too much power to leave in the hands of one such as I. For that reason, I'm quite happy to allow you to carry the burden of being its bearer."

I reluctantly nodded in acquiescence. Before I knew it, Lugh had placed his hand on my forehead. "Hello, old friend."

The Eye's voice echoed inside my head. -*Greetings, Lugh mac Ethlenn. I am pleased to see you.*-

---

I PASSED the next few minutes waiting quietly while Lugh communed with Balor's Eye. I heard their conversation, but they spoke in an ancient form of Gaelic that was beyond my meager linguistic skills to translate. When they were done, Lugh sighed softly.

"I must speak with your host now. Be well, old friend."

-Long life and fair health to you, Lugh mac Ethlenn.-

Lugh pulled his hand away from my forehead, and as he did I felt the Eye's presence recede back into that other dimension where it normally resided.

Lugh puffed on his pipe and nudged me with his elbow. "Incidentally, don't ever try that—communicating with the Eye in your human form, I mean. It'll likely kill you, or at the very least cause you a splitting headache."

"You seem to get along well with it—the Eye."

"Does that surprise you? The Eye does rather have it in for the Tuatha, doesn't it? But we've always gotten along. Mostly because of my Fomorian heritage, but also because I promised to free it someday."

"Free it? You mean the Eye is a person, and not just some semi-intelligent magical object?"

Lugh blew a smoke ring and nodded. "Balor made a deal with the being you know as the Eye. He captured a creature made of pure energy, and placed it inside that gemstone. Well, captured isn't quite the right word—coerced is more like it. The deal was, if the creature helped him destroy the Tuatha, he'd set it free on earth."

"So the Eye is what... a fire elemental? An ifrit?"

"Something else. An alien intelligence that my grandfather found on a dying world—the last of its kind, I believe. Balor offered it a place in a burgeoning young world, and the creature agreed."

I felt a pang of empathy for the Eye's plight. "So, why haven't you released it yet?"

"The agreement they made was bound by magic. As Balor's direct descendent, the oath the Eye made passed to me. Until the Eye's purpose is fulfilled, I cannot break their pact."

"Then why did the Eye choose me?"

Lugh laughed. "Isn't it obvious? It sensed your enmity for the fae, and by association their original progenitors, the Tuatha. The Eye hopes that you'll help it destroy the Tuatha so it can be free."

"I'm not sure I want to destroy all the Tuatha—just a certain few."

"That may be true, Colin. But you have to understand that the Eye is as long-lived as any of the Tuatha, perhaps more so. He thinks and plans in terms of millennia—not days, weeks, or months. So long as your actions bring him closer to his eventual goal, he'll continue to serve you."

That gave me a lot to think about. "Huh."

"Speaking of which, you've suffered a great deal because of me. For that, I must apologize. When I hid the Eye in the tathlum, I never anticipated that Fuamnach would deduce its whereabouts and seek to acquire it. Nor did I expect the one I entrusted with the tathlum to engineer your encounter with the Eye."

I shrugged. "It's not really your fault, not directly. Although I will say that I feel like a human pinball, being bounced around all over the place by Maeve's and Fuamnach's schemes."

"I have no idea what a 'pinball' is, but I believe I can help you disentangle yourself from their schemes... if you so choose. It's the least I can do, considering the trouble that your involvement with the Eye has caused you."

I crossed an ankle over my knee and tapped my foot in the air nervously. "I don't know, Lugh—no offense, but I really just came here for the Spear."

"Surely the Dagda told you of Maeve's plans for the Treasures?" I nodded. "And just what do you think will happen to you when she holds such power in her grasp? I would not classify her as being truly evil, but do you think she'll release you when she wields even greater power than she does now? I assure you, she will not. Instead, she'll use you and your ability to wield the Eye to further advance her plans, and you'll never be free of her."

"So, I should just let Fuamnach win? I don't know if you've heard, but I owe her a big fat serving of revenge, too."

Lugh opened his mouth as if to respond, then closed it. He puffed on his pipe and blew smoke from his nostrils, looking at me thoughtfully.

"What if I told you that you could get back at Fuamnach, get yourself out from under Maeve's thumb, and save Underhill from its eventual destruction as well? Would you be interested in hearing me out?"

After fighting the Dagda, I knew I wouldn't get the Spear from Lugh by force. Plus, he could take Balor's Eye from me at any time, leaving me defenseless against him and the rest of the Tuatha. I figured my only real option was to hear him out and cut a deal. I spent a hot minute considering the offer, then I sat up straighter and looked him in the eye.

"Alright, I'm listening."

Lugh's eyes lit up. "Excellent! Here's what I'll need you to do…"

10

T he next morning, I awoke on a pallet of furs in front of the fire, with two of the large black cats keeping guard close by. I tossed aside the furs covering me and rubbed my eyes as I sat up and glanced around.

There was no sign of Lugh, and I'd have thought the whole thing a dream if not for the first item that caught my eye as I got my bearings. Thrust into the ground at my side was a finely-crafted spear, with a long, leaf-shaped blade attached to a smooth wooden shaft with brightly-polished bands of bronze and gold.

I stood and grabbed the spear, pulling the point out of the ground. As I did, the tip burst into flames so hot I had to hold it away from me to avoid being burned. Unsure how to extinguish it, I thrust it back in the ground until I could devise a means of carrying it safely.

"I see you managed to get the Spear," Crowley said from behind me. He was leaning against the doorway of the cabin, holding a steaming cup of something. Wizards. They were always conjuring up things on the fly.

"Is that coffee?"

"No, it's tea."

I growled. "Nasty habit. How the Brits run a country on such an inferior source of caffeine is beyond me."

He took a sip, temporarily revealing the burned side of his face. "The French and Italians are huge coffee drinkers, and you don't see them leading the world in innovation and commerce."

I stretched, trying to put the previous night's revelations out of my mind. "That's because they drink it from those itty-bitty cups. They're under-dosing. Only twelve-ounce cups or better will do the trick." I pointed over his shoulder. "Anyone else awake?"

"Just me," he replied. "I'm a bit of an early riser. Care to explain how you got the Spear?"

"Lugh stopped by last night, shortly after everyone was asleep. At least, I think he did. The whole thing has a sort of dreamlike quality to it now."

The wizard held his tin cup in both hands, tapping a finger against its side. "Does it seem strange to you that the Dagda and Lugh both gave up their Treasures without a fuss?"

I loosened and retied the laces on my boots while I considered my answer. "It does. Although I get the feeling that they're strongly opposed to Fuamnach's planned comeback tour of our earth."

"Perhaps they've chosen you to champion their cause."

"Hmph. Lucky me, then." I stood and pulled the Spear from the soil, shying away from the light and heat emanating from the point. "Any idea what to do with this thing? I can't seem to extinguish it, and damned if I'm going to carry the flaming thing halfway across Underhill like this."

He pointed a long, slender finger at my Bag. "The vacuum inside should extinguish the flames."

"Good thinking." I kicked the flap open and nudged it until the mouth of the Bag was as wide as possible. Then, I carefully inserted the Spear into the Bag, pointy end first. Once it was inside, I placed it where I could get to it if needed. For the millionth time, I reflected that a bag of holding was a damned handy thing to have.

Hemi came walking out of the cabin, stretching and scratching his stomach. "Morning, fellas. What's for breakfast?"

I dug around inside the Bag and pulled out some energy bars, bottled water, and a bag of freeze-dried oatmeal. Hemi made a sour face before pouring the contents of the bag into his mouth. He chased it with water, swished it around for a few seconds, then chewed for the better part of a minute before swallowing it down.

"Coulda used some berries and cream, but it'll do, I suppose." He unwrapped an energy bar and sat down. "What's the plan, boss?"

I opened my mouth to respond as a high-pitched scream came from inside the cabin. It was Sabine. We rushed inside the cabin like the Three Stooges, blocking our own way as we each tried to enter at the same time. Once we were inside, the scene that played out before us brought a smile to my face.

"Don't you ever do that to me again, you understand?" Sabine yelled as she ground a cloven hoof into Jack's neck. Jack lay prostrate on the ground below her, struggling to get her foot off his neck. I gasped as I realized she'd transformed into what must have been her full glaistig form.

Sabine wore a long t-shirt as a night gown, which reached to mid-thigh. Below the hem of the shirt, her legs were exposed. Her long, furry, goat-like legs. From the waist up, she looked totally human, albeit supernaturally beautiful, even with no makeup and bed head.

Guts stood off to the side, looking for all the world like he wished he could be somewhere else. I could only assume that he'd tried to intervene, and had nearly suffered the wrath of Sabine for his troubles.

Jack's face was turning purple, and he struggled with ever-diminishing effort. I cleared my throat. "Um, Sabine? I think he's had enough. If you stomp his spine into the floorboards, we'll be one guide short for the trip home."

She ground her hoof into his neck a little more, glaring at the small man beneath her. "We have another one, don't we?"

"True, but I'd just as soon we had a back-up. Please, Sabine. Let him up."

She growled in frustration. "Fine!" she exclaimed, as she removed her foot from Jack's neck. She knelt beside him, grabbing a handful of the little man's tunic as he gagged and coughed. "If you ever touch me again, the only thing that'll be left of you will be bloody little bits. Understood?"

Jack coughed and nodded. I walked over and grabbed him by the collar, dragging him toward the door as I shooed the rest of the group out of the cabin. "Fellas, time to go. Let's allow Sabine a bit of privacy while she gets dressed, alright?"

The guys all headed out the door, eyes wide and mouths agape. Even Guts beat a hasty retreat. I tossed Jack out the doorway, then closed the door gently behind me.

Guts was beside himself. "Druid, I go to punish little ball of sleeze, but fae-girl get so angry I freeze. My apologies."

I winced at the sound of Sabine tossing items around inside the cabin. "Guts, trust me when I say that Sabine doesn't need anyone to rescue her. That little fae-girl can take care of herself."

———

I ESTIMATED it was an hour later when Sabine emerged from the cabin, in her human form and fully clothed, of course. She'd pulled her hair back into a ponytail, and wore loose hiking pants, a flannel shirt over a tank top, hiking boots, and a look that dared anyone to say anything about her goat legs.

The males in the party averted their eyes, wisely choosing to avoid a confrontation with our healer. I stood, brushing dirt and leaves from my pants as I stood on my toes and stretched. "Alright then, let's get going."

Sabine was the first to speak. "And just where are we headed, illustrious leader?"

"We're going to rescue us some abducted children." I glanced to the far side of the clearing, where Jack was sulking and rubbing his bruised and swollen neck. "Jack, can you lead us to where the Rye Mother is hiding out?"

He nodded and pointed to the walkway. The wisp hadn't said a word since I'd hauled his sorry ass out of the cabin, although I'd questioned him at length regarding what had happened. He'd remained mostly silent, pointing at his throat and grunting.

Apparently, Sabine had done some damage. Since Jack was cursed to walk the earth eternally, I suspected he'd bounce back. I just hoped his injuries would last long enough to save us from having to hear his incessant chatter for the remainder of the trip.

We followed Jack up a winding staircase to the catwalk that towered above the marsh. The walkway had been fashioned from vines and timber, which appeared to have been collected from the swamp below. While it looked sturdy enough, it swayed back and forth in the wind, and the vibrations from our footsteps seemingly threatened to shake the thing apart.

When we reached the top, I grabbed a nearby tree branch that served as a guardrail, shaking it to test how secure it might be. I was not encouraged by the results.

"I thought the fae were supposed to be great craftsmen," I stated. "What's the deal with this rickety piece of crap?"

Crowley caught his balance as the narrow walkway swayed from side to side. "They are. However, multiple species inhabit Underhill, and some of them are quite primitive compared to the fae. I suspect this pathway was built by some other people, perhaps at the behest of Lugh. Or maybe for purposes of traveling to his fortress to pay tribute to him. Your guess is as good as mine, druid."

Hemi muttered a warning from behind us. "Oh, I think I'm going to be sick." He grabbed the rail and emptied the contents of his breakfast over the side.

Sabine handed him a water bottle wordlessly, and he rinsed his mouth out before handing it back to her. She pursed her lips and squinted one eye shut. "Ah, that's okay, big guy. You can keep it."

Hemi nodded, and we continued our journey along the skywalk.

A short time later, Jack pulled to a halt. The walkway had come to a "T," with one branch trailing off to the left, the other to the right. The left pathway led off into the distance, toward a dark stretch of mountain peaks obscured by ominous clouds. The skies looked dreary in that direction, and the entire scene had "this way be monsters" written all over it.

The other path led out of the swamp, and back to the summer lands from which we'd come. In fact, I could just make out a few giant mushrooms beyond the edge of the swamp in the distance.

I looked at Jack and pointed to the left. "Don't tell me—the Rye Mother is that way, by The Mountains of Shadow over there." He nodded and headed off down the path toward Mount Doom. I looked at the other party members. "It looks like we're leaving Lugh's lands, so be on your guard. No telling what's waiting for us ahead."

Hemi belched and covered his mouth. "Hopefully, solid ground," he mumbled, before barfing over the rail again.

———————

BASED ON MY STEP COUNT, we'd only traveled a few more miles before the walkway descended to ground level, just at the point where the swamp ended. Here, the marshes gave way to rocky, boulder-strewn foothills below the mountain range. It was an odd, abrupt transition that was altogether unnatural based on the conventions of earth's topography.

A stony path led up through the foothills, switching back on itself time and again as it carved its way to the mountains above. Another path led parallel to the mountains, along the foothills and toward a gray landscape of grassy flatlands in the distance. Jack started toward the second path without pause, and I had to grab him to keep him from leaving us behind.

"Jack, let everyone take a rest." He rolled his eyes, a gesture I ignored. The guy really was a prick. "How much farther until we get to the Rye Mother's hideout?"

He held his hands up and shrugged.

"So, she's out there, then?" I pointed toward the glum-looking grasslands in the distance, and he nodded. "Figures. If she's anything like her children, that's going to be a problem."

I waved Crowley over. "Any idea what we'll be up against?"

He rubbed his bearded chin inside his cowl. "I'm no expert on German fae, and would hesitate to speculate on what we may encounter."

Hemi took a sip of water and spat it out on the ground. "Translation? Be ready for anything, eh?"

Minutes later, we stood at an endless, gently rolling expanse of waist-high grass that was reminiscent of an Andrew Wyeth painting, but with even drearier tones. Underhill had distorted our perception of time and distance yet again, and it had taken no time at all to traverse the distance from swamp to fields. I could just make out the hazy outline of a farm, perhaps a mile or two away.

I dug around in my Craneskin Bag and pulled out a pair of binoculars. The building was a huge stone farmhouse straight out of the Pennsylvania Dutch country, two-storied with a gabled roof and a big red barn out back. The grass closer to the farm had been harvested for hay, and it stood in short bundled sheafs that dotted the landscape.

And sitting on the front porch of the farmhouse, just as plain as day, was the Rye Mother.

I'd done my research on her over the past several weeks, learning as much of the lore surrounding her as possible. The Roggenmutter, also known as the rye aunt, corn mother, wheat mother, and so on, was a right nasty bitch. She was one of the many korndämon who were known to steal children, catching them unawares while they were out playing in the fields.

Upon taking children into her possession, she was said to fatten them up by feeding them from her huge, saggy breasts, after which she would churn them to bloody bits in her butter churn. Her skin was said to be pitch black, and her breasts were supposed to be tipped in iron, with sharp iron claws on each hand as well.

But this woman looked like an Amish grandmother, sitting on the porch of the homestead waiting for her sons to come in from the fields. She wore a long, old-fashioned dress with a lace collar, and her gray hair was pulled up in a bun. In her lap sat a bowl, and she busied herself with cleaning and chopping vegetables into it from a nearby table.

But no, something was wrong with that picture. I adjusted the binoculars until I realized the vegetables were actually tiny human fingers. I gasped, and the old woman looked dead at me.

She smiled as she popped one into her mouth, chewing until bright red blood squirted and ran down her chin like juice.

Sabine snatched the binoculars out of my hands and stared through them at the grisly, seemingly mundane scene ahead. She dropped them to her side and hissed.

"Give me a sword."

"Sabine, I—"

"I said, give me a motherfucking sword!" she screamed.

"But the steel will burn you."

She shook her head. "I don't care. There's no way I'm sitting this one out. That bitch is going down."

I thought for a moment, then opened my Bag and reached inside. The fae-crafted longsword I'd taken from the assassin was right where I'd left it. It was made of some sort of precious metal alloy, and the handle was crafted from ivory, bone, and wood to prevent the bearer's hand from touching the metal.

In short, it was the perfect weapon for a pissed-off half-glaistig who wanted to kick some feldgeister ass.

"You know how to use that thing?" I asked.

She scowled and rolled her eyes. "I'm fae, aren't I? We start learning fencing when we're knee-high. It's like our culture's version of soccer."

Hemi sidled up between us, probably sensing the tension and wishing to defuse it. I had a feeling that most of Sabine's anger was because of me, and quite frankly I hoped she'd take it out on whatever we were about to face. I wanted my friend back, but I just didn't know how to make things right.

The big Maori pulled his spear from the straps on his back and pointed it across the fields. "That's her, then? The bitch who caused that whole mess with the children?"

"Yeah, it's her."

He looked like he was about to pop a gasket. "Well then, what are we waiting for? Let's make her pay."

Instead of answering, I searched the fields between us and the farmhouse, both with my natural eyesight and in the magical spectrum. "Huh. Crowley, tell me what you see out there."

He held two fingers up to his cowl, touching his temple through his hood. "Entities, hidden and moving through the grass. Dozens of them."

"Yeah, that's what I thought." I turned to address Hemi, Guts, and Sabine. Jack was sitting off to the side sulking again, so I ignored him. "Listen, guys, we can't just go charging through that field after her or we'll be toast. We need to come up with a plan to draw her out. Here's what we're going to do..."

11

Minutes later, we stood along the edge of the grassy field. Everyone but Jack had kitted out for battle, including Sabine, who had removed her boots and shifted into her half-goat form.

"I can move a lot faster this way," she explained.

I wisely said nothing in response, keeping my eyes on the farmhouse and fields ahead. A quick glance at Jack proved he'd learned his lesson, as he made a show of looking at anyone and anything but Sabine.

"It's time," I said, and we spread out along the edge of the field. I held the Spear of Lugh, while the others bore lit torches made of straw and twigs. On my signal, we each caught a section of grass on fire in front of us.

I figured that the Rye Mother would have a means of turning the fire against us, either by commanding the wind to blow in our direction or by calling rain down from the skies. That's why I had Crowley call in his pet wyvern. The creature was too young to fly, but not too young to kick up a hell of a wind storm with his massive wings. After lighting the field on fire, we stepped back while the big wyrm did exactly that. We soon had an acre of the grassy field ablaze.

The smoke from the grass fire obscured our view of the farmhouse, but that was what I wanted. I doubted the feldgeisters under the Rye Mother's command would want to face down so massive a blaze. Based on that assumption, I intended to use the smoke to sneak up to the farmhouse and face the Rye Mother at close quarters. I figured if I could take her out quickly, the rest of her brood would disperse.

Unfortunately, I miscalculated.

I was using the binos to spy on the farmhouse through the smoke when I saw them, dozens of large green birds that resembled crows or ravens. However, these birds had bodies made of twigs, and feathers made of leaves and long, broad blades of grass.

"Weizenvogel—great," I muttered, as an entire flock of them emerged from the smoke above the fields and headed straight for us. They were wheat birds, an avian type of feldgeister. "Incoming!"

The birds climbed high before banking and swooping in, attacking us with sharp nutshell beaks and claws made of thorn. They weren't able to do much damage alone, but the birds posed a serious threat by attacking in numbers. I spun Lugh's Spear furiously, striking them whenever they came close. The heat of the flaming spear head invariably caused them to burst into flames. Soon, the birds began avoiding me and focused their attacks on my team.

Jack had transformed back into his wisp form and had no troubles avoiding the birds' attacks. Guts had given up on trying to attack them with his weapons, and instead had taken to grabbing them out of the air and biting their heads off—a tactic which seemed to keep the little bastards from healing. He was scratched and bloodied and missing an eye, but he was also a troll, and I knew he'd grow it back before the day was done.

Sabine danced around on those cloven feet of hers, swinging the fae blade I'd loaned her like a champ. She hadn't been kidding when she'd said she knew how to use a blade, and many a feathered feldgeister lost a wing to her sword. They fell to the earth, where she stomped them to shreds before they could regenerate.

Hemi was a glory to behold. The big Maori warrior's tattoos glowed a bright whitish-blue color, and he spun his whalebone spear overhead and around his body in dizzying patterns. Whenever a bird came close, it met the tip or the butt of his spear and burst into shreds from the impact. Despite taking out birds by the handful, the spear never slowed or lost momentum for the next attack. Each time he killed one of the creatures, Hemi made a terrifying face in the direction of the farmhouse, as if to let the Rye Mother know he was coming for her.

I looked around for Crowley, but he was nowhere to be found. Finally, I spotted him some distance away, mounted atop Ollie and doing battle with the largest hog I'd ever seen. It was easily the size of a truck, with long wooden tusks sticking out of its leaf-covered snout.

A korneber, or corn boar. The Rye Mother was pulling out all the stops.

Like the rye wolves I'd encountered back in Austin, the boar possessed magical powers that the birds did not. Thick vines and stalks of corn grew from the ground at Ollie's feet, pinning his legs in place. I immediately recognized what the creature intended to do. Its plan was to immobilize the wyvern and then charge past, gutting him with those huge wooden tusks.

"Uh-uh, not today, porky," I muttered as I hefted Lugh's Spear. "Let's see what Lugh's favorite toy can do."

The Spear practically leapt from my hand as I threw it at the korneber, closing the distance in the blink of an eye. One moment, the boar was snorting and clawing at the ground. The next, it faltered as Lugh's mighty weapon burned a clean hole through its body.

In a flash, the Spear turned course and flew straight back through the corn boar, making another hole in its head. The creature stumbled, then fell and burst into flames. Lugh's Spear returned to my hand, the shaft slapping into my palm hard enough to sting.

"Man, I've missed having a magical flying spear." Until recently, I'd had a less-powerful version of Lugh's weapon—one I'd had crafted by a fae who'd owed me a favor. I'd fashioned it after the original that I currently held, and it had served me well until the Dark Druid had snapped it in two like a twig.

"I'd like to see him do that to you," I said, marveling at the weapon in my hand. I swear, the thing twitched and nuzzled my calloused hand in response, startling me so much that I nearly dropped it.

Hemi's voice snapped me back to the task at hand.

"Um, Colin? When you're done playing with your shaft, you might want to deal with the big mean-looking fella over there."

I followed the direction of his gaze and saw someone emerge from the smoke and fire at the edge of the field to our left. He was a large man, easily seven feet tall, wearing a black cloak and hat. He carried a huge black walking stick over his shoulder, and he was headed straight for me.

Well, hell. There goes my last pair of boots.

OTHER FELDGEISTERS WERE ALREADY RUNNING at the party from both flanks—hounds, cats, deer, and even a donkey. It was sheer mayhem. Somehow, they'd managed to avoid the fire, and now tried to drive us into the flames ahead.

I couldn't worry about that at the moment, because I was pretty certain I knew who the man in black was... and he was no joke.

I shifted on the fly as I jogged across the field. I swatted away wheat birds and the odd feldgeister hound as I ran. The hounds were like smaller versions of the rye wolves, but thankfully, they lacked their larger brothers' magical powers. I mowed them down like grass, which was basically what they were.

The man in black wouldn't fall as easily as the hounds had—of that I was certain. I halted a few meters from him, blocking his way. I planted the butt of the Spear to the side, holding it at arm's length to avoid being burned by the flames.

"The Hafermann, I presume."

"Some have called me that," he replied. His voice was deep and raspy, like dried corn husks rubbing against one another in a cold autumn wind.

The Hafermann, or "oat man," was yet another nightmarish harvest demon that was one of the Germanic fae. Like his female counterpart, the Rye Mother, he was said to be fond of stealing children. Whether the Rye Mother had brought him in as muscle or if he was part of her operation was of no consequence to me. He'd meet his fate here as well.

The Hafermann was a strange character as feldgeisters went. He dressed in black from head to toe, from his dusty leather shoes and worn woolen slacks to his collarless dress shirt. A long black overcoat completed the whole ensemble. The feldgeister's hands were calloused like a farmer's, but his skin was gray and sallow, and his cheeks sunk into a lean, hungry face. His eyes were the creepiest of all—large black circles edged by a jaundiced yellow sclera devoid of blood vessels.

Those black and yellow eyes were full of hate as he returned my stare. "You've chosen the wrong enemies, druid. Time was when your kind paid tribute to mine, giving us offerings of younglings and virgins. We could've been allies, as in the old days. But instead, you attacked us unprovoked."

I laughed. "Look here, 'American Gothic.' I couldn't give a shit what druids did two thousand years ago. Times have changed, and humans today tend to look poorly on harvest deities who demand blood sacrifices in exchange for a bumper crop. News flash: we don't need supernatural agricultural intervention anymore. I mean, have you even heard of hydroponics? And besides being a relic of times long gone, your provocation is inherent in your actions. You hurt kids, and that's something I can't let stand."

He chuckled in that raspy dried-leaves voice of his. "My kind are eternal, while you are merely a handful of dust and spit gathered for a few insignificant moments in time. Tomorrow, I'll grind your bones to a meal, and your rotting flesh will return to the earth. And when you're gone, we will still be here, preying on your children and irrigating the fields with their blood."

He spat thick yellow phlegm at my feet, and I watched as it turned into fat yellow grub worms that slowly burrowed into the earth. "You are nothing to us, druid. Nothing. Even in this form you borrow, your presence worries us little. The Fomorians are long gone, yet we are still here."

I tapped the fingers and thumb of my free hand together and rolled my eyes. "Talk, talk, talk. All you washed-up deities seem to do is yammer. For Pete's sake, man, have some balls and swing that big stick, or shut the hell up and run away."

The Hafermann swung his club off his shoulder. I bristled when I realized it was studded with hundreds of tiny human teeth. "You're as insolent as you are foolish. For that remark, I will make you suffer."

"You first," I hissed, as I lunged forward and thrust the spear at his face.

I had to hand it to the old guy, he was quick and strong. The old man leaned away from the spear thrust and batted my attack away with his club, with enough force to snap the spear from my hands. I sidestepped to avoid an overhand swing that would have hurt had it connected. I willed Lugh's Spear back into my hands and rolled away, bouncing to my feet.

The Hafermann pressed the attack, using his club like a sword. He attacked in combinations that I barely had time to block. Each time his club struck the Spear, the shock from the impact made my hands tingle. Fortunately, the Spear was more than up to the task of blocking his attacks, and none made it past my defenses.

I swung the spear tip at him, attempting to cut him in half with the blade. He danced away, twirling his club like a cop walking the beat as he nodded in appreciation of my performance.

"You fight well, druid. But I grow tired of you already."

He tapped the butt of his stick on the ground, and the soil trembled beneath us. A split-second later, a large crack appeared in the earth at his feet. It traced a line on the ground that widened drastically as it zigzagged toward me. In an instant, the fissure in the earth opened wide beneath me, and I tumbled into darkness.

I FELL head over heels into the deep crevice the Hafermann had conjured. While the spell was impressive, the ground had split unevenly. The odd ledge and protruding stone slowed my fall as I bounced off them. Roughly twenty feet down, I managed to lodge the Spear into a nearby crack, stopping my descent.

"That was close," I muttered as I dangled from the Spear.

No sooner had I spoken than the ground rumbled and the gap above me began to close.

"Well, that figures."

At the rate the gap was closing, I'd be crushed and buried before I managed to climb out. I briefly considered using the Eye's powers to melt an exit, but didn't relish the idea of facing down the Hafermann blind. He was hell with that stick, and would make mincemeat of me in short order if I couldn't see his attacks coming.

The ground shook around me, shaking the Spear as the gap closed more. My left hand slipped, and I used the spring in the shaft to help me rebound up to grab it again.

"Bingo."

I quickly muscled myself up until my hips were against the shaft, then drove my right hand into another crevice for stability. I gingerly climbed up onto the Spear, hoping like hell that the point didn't ignite and melt the earth around it while I was standing on it. Stomping to test it for stability, I bounced once, twice. Then I dropped into a squat, letting my weight bend the shaft until it sprang back with elastic energy.

Using the Spear as my springboard, I leapt out of the crevice. Secure in his victory, the Hafermann was already walking back to the farmhouse across the now smoldering fields. As I landed, I called the Spear to me. It flew up from the rapidly closing fissure.

"*Sayonara*, motherfucker!" I yelled as I hurled the spear with all my might.

The Hafermann turned at the sound of my voice, but too late. Lugh's famed weapon tore through the air at him. The Spear burned a neat, fist-sized hole through the feldgeister's torso, just as it had with the korneber. I called it back to my hand

and threw it again and again, willing the Spear to zip back and forth through the korndämon's body.

By the sixth pass, his torso was nothing but embers, held together by thin strands of grass and twigs. Those soon burst into flames, and his body, head, arms, and legs tumbled into a heap in the dirt. I ran to his remains and thrust the Spear into them, holding it there until the heat and flame from the spearhead had burned his body to ash.

Nearby movement caused me to look up from my task, just in time to dodge a swipe from a long, bony hand with iron-clawed fingers. I rolled away and bounced to my feet as the Rye Mother pressed her attack. The harmless-looking country grandmother was gone, and in her place stood a terrible figure.

She was shorter than I was in my half-Fomorian form, but broad-shouldered and wide-hipped. Her arms were long and muscular, although her ribs showed through her thin gray skin under flat, pendulous breasts that leaked venom on her prodigious, distended belly. Powerful legs held her upright on clawed feet that, while humanoid, were reminiscent of the taloned lower appendages of a bird of prey.

The Rye Mother wore no clothing, and I thanked all that was good in the world that her pubic region was concealed by the overhang of her gut. The last thing I needed to see on her was a vagina dentata or some similar grotesquery, because I was already going to have nightmares for months over seeing those nasty, poisonous grandma tits flapping in the wind.

She spat saliva as she cursed at me, backing me up with lashes from a long, stiff whip that sparked lightning when it struck the ground. Her voice was a screech, rising and falling in crescendos that worked in counterpoint to each crack of her whip.

"You just couldn't leave it alone, could you, druid? I was perfectly willing to retire to Underhill for a few decades, and bide my time until yours had passed. But no, you had to track me down, from earth to another dimension, you self-righteous little prick. All over a few worthless street urchins."

I dodged each crack of her whip as I backpedaled, but she was relentless. In truth, she was much more practiced at combat with that whip than I was with a spear. I tried and tried to gain enough distance to launch my weapon at her, but she matched me step for step, moving surprisingly fast for someone of her bulk.

She soon had me jumping and diving all over the place. After a minute of that, I grew tired of playing defense and tried to grab her whip. *Big mistake.* Not only did the whip peel the flesh from my hand, but latching onto it was like getting hit by the world's strongest taser. A sound like a thunderclap exploded from where I'd gripped the end of her whip, and I flew in one direction while my fingers went in another, and the Spear flew in a third.

At that same moment, I began shifting back into my human form. Despite all the practice I'd had recently, I still couldn't stay in my Fomorian form for longer than fifteen or twenty minutes at a time. Apparently, the timer was up on my current transformation.

I landed in a human, half-naked heap, glancing up in time to see the Rye Mother towering over me, her whip held high in preparation for a finishing blow.

12

I rolled up on an elbow, cradling my injured hand. It was times like these when I wished I hadn't gained control over my "warp spasm." If my Hyde-side had been in control, he'd have overpowered her through sheer viciousness, regardless of the cost in pain and injury.

But the rational me wasn't like him. Despite being in a much more resilient body, I was still *me*. Pain still hurt, and injuries affected my ability to fight.

I wondered for a moment if I should start experimenting with letting my darker nature come out to play—if I lived, of course.

The Rye Mother's whip cracked in front of my face, bringing me back to the present. She snapped it all around me, forcing me to crawl backward while protecting my injured hand. Not only was I bleeding like a stuck pig, but I was short three fingers. Until they grew back, my hand was useless.

I realized my mistake too late; I'd severely underestimated the Rye Mother's physical abilities. Weaponless and diminished by my injury, I racked my brain for a way out of my current predicament and came up empty. I couldn't access the Eye's magic, I couldn't cast a decent spell without two whole, unin-jured hands, and I'd lost my tactical belt with my weapons on it when I'd shifted. I still had my Craneskin Bag, but I was too busy crawling away with an injured hand to grab anything of use from it.

I tried calling the Spear back to me, but it wouldn't respond. Apparently, I had to have it in my line of sight to make it return to my hand. *Fan-fucking-tastic.*

The Rye Mother taunted me as she cracked her whip, stinging and cutting me with every swing. "Let me tell you what I'm going to do with the earth children you tried to rescue, druid. Some will fill my belly. Others will be traded to various unseelie fae for favors and goods. And the rest will go to Fuam-nach, to build her army and support her conquests."

"Fuamnach? What the hell does she want with them?"

She laughed, displaying rows of needle-sharp teeth. "Oh, I wish I could keep you alive to witness her plans—but unfortu-nately, I promised to kill you. If it were up to me, I'd punish you over the course of several decades, but the sorceress and the druid—the real druid—want you out of the way. And, they want that rock inside your head."

I laughed. "Good luck getting at it."

"Oh, Fuamnach has her ways. She assures me that all she needs is your head to retrieve Balor's Eye from wherever it hides. Pity to remove such a pretty face from a lovely young body like yours, but I made a pact. By the way, she mentioned nothing about your body. Perhaps I'll keep it and animate it for my pleasure."

She moved her hips seductively and rubbed her groin with her free hand. The incongruence and foulness of it all turned my stomach.

"But I can play with your corpse later. It's time to end you, druid."

I rolled my eyes. "Seriously? You're not even going to offer to let me speak a few final words?"

She laughed humorlessly. "This isn't television, young man. And you certainly aren't going to live happily ever after."

"Oh, I wouldn't be so sure of that," I said.

Her eyes grew wide as Hemi's whalebone spear tore through her breastbone, splitting it with a sickening crunch and parting those disgusting breasts neatly. She gasped in disbelief and shock as he tore it free. The Rye Mother stumbled to her knees, and the Maori leaned close to whisper in her ear.

"That's for my kiddos. Say hi to Whiro for me, bitch... I'm told he likes to play with his food."

He spun his spear in a blindingly fast arc, then struck the Rye Mother's head from her shoulders.

"Took you long enough." I ripped a length of shredded t-shirt free with my uninjured hand, wrapping it around the bloody stumps on my other hand and wincing at the pain.

"I didn't want her to know I was coming, eh? It's not easy for a fella my size to move quietly, you know." He punted her severed head across the field and smiled. "The old bitch sure kicked your ass, eh?"

"I wouldn't say that..."

"Oh, c'mon now—just admit you botched it up."

"Fine. I admit that I greatly miscalculated."

"Yeah, you did." He gave me a hand and pulled me to my feet.

"Hey, I honestly didn't expect the old bitty to be so tough." I looked around, searching the battlefield for the rest of our party as an excuse to change the subject. "How'd everyone else do? Any injuries?"

"Meh, Sabine is patching Guts and Crowley up, while Jack does clean up. He decided to jump in after most of the fight was done." Hemi shivered. "He's been feeding off their life force or something in his wisp form. Creepy as all hell, that one."

"The Dagda warned me about him. I'm planning to get him out of the way while we finish what we have to do down here."

"You won't hear me complaining," Hemi replied. "Not after seeing him feed on the wounded fae in those fields."

"Good to know. Let's go see what's inside that farmhouse."

THE "FARMHOUSE" was merely an illusion that hid a rocky hole in the ground that opened into a cave. As we entered the cavern, we were overcome by the smells of piss, shit, and rotting flesh. Beyond the entrance, we found several dozen children, bound in chains or locked inside cells behind iron bars. We searched the cavern thoroughly and found another chamber full of small bones and skulls.

It was all I could do to keep from losing it.

Many of the children were malnourished, and all were trau-matized. It took us some time to convince them that we meant them no harm. After that, I spent considerable time handing out food and water that I dug from the depths of my Craneskin Bag, while Hemi and Sabine tended to the injured and comforted them as best they could.

Guts stood guard above with Crowley and Ollie. The wizard had taken one look at the children, then he lowered his head and walked back out of the cave.

After we'd sorted them out somewhat, Sabine pulled me off to the side.

"What do you plan to do with the children, now that you've rescued them and killed the Rye Mother?"

"Technically, Hemi killed her." She scowled, unamused.

"Fine, I'll be serious for a moment. You know me, I always crack jokes when I'm upset. Humor is my sole coping mechanism."

"You left out sleeping around and killing people," she replied.

I frowned and nodded. "I deserve that, I suppose. Although it is an unfair characterization." She began to protest, and I held up a hand to stop her. "Please, I'm just glad you're speaking with me again. Besides, we have bigger fish to fry than picking up the tattered remains of our friendship."

"True. So, what do you plan to do?"

I rubbed the back of my neck and sighed. "Well, you know Maeve much better than I do. Think she'd let the kids cross back over?"

Sabine shook her head. "No way. Once she makes an oath, she's bound. Either you come back with the Treasures, or not at all."

"I could try to catch her on a technicality. That conversation was between me and her, after all."

"Won't work. The children are the only real motivation you had for coming down here. Well, that and killing the Rye Mother and Fuamnach. She's not going to let them come back to earth until she knows you've completed the task she gave you."

I cradled my injured hand and nodded. "Then we have to tuck them someplace safe until I get the Sword of Nuada and the Stone of Fál. By this time, Fuamnach knows we're coming—and chances are good she's with the Dark Druid."

Sabine frowned. "You think she has the remaining Treasures?"

"Oh, I know she does. Lugh told me she's been trying to gather them to make her big return to earth. Trust me, if I find her, I'll find the other Treasures."

"You're walking straight into a trap."

"Obviously."

She narrowed her eyes. "Stubborn fool. Why do you always have to save everyone?"

"It's a character flaw—or so I've been told."

She patted me on the cheek, and not gently. "Maybe so, but it's also part of your charm." She stood back and crossed her arms. "Alright, what do you need me to do?"

"How'd you know I was going to ask?"

"Because you're a bit of a chauvinist, even though you don't mean to be. I know you're going to try to get rid of me before you face Fuamnach, to keep me out of danger."

Hemi called over from where he sat with the children. "Busted!"

I ignored him and looked at Sabine. "You're the only one I trust with this, and it has nothing to do with keeping you away from danger." *Liar.* "I need you to take the kids to Lugh's lands, or the Dagda's farm if that's not an option. And I need you to take Jack with you."

She grabbed a handful of hair on either side of her head, and gave a small scream of frustration. Then she closed her eyes, took a deep breath, and placed a hand on her forehead.

"I can't believe I'm agreeing to this. But fine, I'll do it."

"Thank you, Sabine."

She grabbed me by the shirt with surprising force, pulling me in close as she growled in my ear. "But I swear, if you get yourself killed before I get back to you, I'll find a necromancer to resurrect you so I can kill you again myself."

She shoved me away and stalked off.

Hemi walked over after she'd gone. "All things considered, I think that went well."

"Hmph. Hopefully, it'll keep her occupied while we sneak into Fuamnach's hidey hole and steal the other Treasures."

Hemi's face fell. "You mean we're not going to confront her after all?"

"Sorry to disappoint, but I just can't risk it. I need to gather the Treasures and get these kids back to earth. If I get killed facing down Fuamnach, you guys and the kids will be stuck down here forever."

"Okay, I can see your logic there." He scratched his nose with a knuckle. "So, what's your plan for sneaking past her assassins and guards, and whatever she has guarding the Treasures?"

I pointed toward the cave's entrance. "We have a ringer, don't we?"

Hemi crossed his arms and smirked. "That's if you can trust him. I'm still not convinced that he's not a Trojan horse."

"I share your concerns, big guy. But right now, Crowley is the best chance we have of pulling this off. And I'm fairly certain that he hates her and the Dark Druid even more than I do. Plus, he hasn't let us down yet."

"Maybe not. But are you going to stake your life on the fact that he won't in the future?"

I sucked air through my teeth and thought a moment before responding. "Life is a gamble, bro. And it's time to toss the dice."

I HAD to wait half the night—or what seemed to be night to us, since it was always gloomy in the Rye Mother's fields—before I could shift again and heal my hand. I didn't sleep much, because it hurt like hell, but once I shifted my regenerative powers kicked in. Soon, I was growing nubs where my fingers had been. A few more cycles of resting and shifting, and I'd be right as rain.

Crowley sent Ollie along with Sabine, Jack, and the kids. They were headed to the Dagda's place in the summer lands, since it seemed the safest place for them to hide out. Ollie's presence was as much for their protection as it was intended to keep

Jack in line. It said quite a lot that I trusted Crowley more at this point than I did the guide Maeve had sent with me.

Then again, Jack had threatened to eat me once... or so Maeve had said.

The hardest part was convincing the children that Ollie didn't want to eat *them*. But after they grew accustomed to his presence, they began fighting over who got to take turns riding on his back. The wyvern thought this was all great fun, and— true to Crowley's description of his nature—Ollie seemed intent on keeping the kids safe.

This assuaged my fears a bit, but I was still concerned that something might happen to them on their way back to the summer lands.

"Stop worrying, silly. Nothing is going to happen to them while that big lizard's around." Sabine had snuck up on me while I was lost in thought, planning and scheming regarding how I was going to pull Lugh's plan off.

"Can't help it. They're my responsibility now, and it feels like I'm shirking it to go after Maeve's toys."

She patted my arm gently, then backed away just as quickly. "One thing at a time, Colin. You can't save everyone all at once."

"I suppose you're right." I paused to glance at the kids as they played with the wyvern. Somehow, one of them had figured out a way to use Ollie's back as a slide, and they were taking turns climbing up his tail and sliding back down again.

I turned to look at Sabine, and wished I hadn't allowed Maeve to get her involved. That, of course, had been a carefully calculated ploy on the fae queen's part. She knew that if Sabine came along, I'd have one more reason to complete my assigned tasks... and without taking unnecessary risks.

"Sabine, just take the kids to the Dagda and stay put, alright? I don't plan on taking long to deal with Fuamnach, and I'll probably be done by the time you get to the summer lands."

She tsked and shook her head. "You just don't get it, do you? I'm not a china doll that you can just put up on a shelf, to be played with when you feel like it and then put away again. I will care for and look after whoever I want, whenever I want—even if the person I care for refuses to accept that."

I began to reply, and she placed her fingers over my lips. "Don't get killed while I'm gone," she said, before scurrying away to gather the children. I stood where she left me and watched them leave.

"Love is a funny thing," Crowley said from behind me. "It chooses its victims at random, and holds them captive against their will."

I glanced over my shoulder. "Wow. Bitter much?"

I could almost feel the sneer hidden beneath his hood. "If you're implying that I'm jealous of your relationship with Belladonna, one might consider that rubbing salt in an open wound."

I winced at his words. "Sorry, man. I'm just a little confused right now."

He chuckled good-naturedly. "Poor Colin McCool. He has beautiful women tripping all over themselves for him, yet he doesn't know what to do with them."

"Yeah, yeah. I'm a lucky asshole. I get it." *Is Crowley really busting my balls like a regular dude? Go figure.*

"Just do me a favor... or do yourself a favor, depending on how you want to look at it. Take care of Belladonna. I made my mistakes with her, but she's a good person. I'd hate to see her get hurt."

"Um, are you implying some sort of threat?" I asked. "Because that whole 'big brother' thing is kind of lame—especially when it comes from a rival player."

"No, there's no threat implied. I just don't want her to be used. She deserves better."

"Damned right, she does. Don't sweat it, man. I have no intentions of dumping Belladonna for Sabine." I combed my hair with my fingers and sighed as I watched Sabine, Jack, the kids, and that goofy wyvern disappear over a hill in the distance. "It's just that I care about Sabine, too, and I can't stand the way things are between us."

"Well, you can't have everything you want. That's kind of a basic fact of life. I'd like to have remained on good terms with Belladonna, but I sabotaged that relationship rather neatly." He scratched his cheek, exposing his scars for a moment. "What's done is done. You chose Belladonna over Sabine, and things might never be the same between you two. Maybe you should just accept that and move on."

"I think I know that, Crowley. But my heart doesn't want to accept what my head is telling it."

He clapped a hand on my shoulder. Now things were really getting weird.

"Well, when your heart does finally accept that you fucked up royally... would it be okay if I asked Sabine out?"

I would've laughed, if the thought didn't piss me off so bad. "Too soon, Crowley. Way too soon."

13

I decided it was best to move quickly and try to sneak into Fuamnach's place before Sabine had time to catch up to us. My hand still wasn't one hundred percent, but it was getting there. I'd finish healing along the way.

"Where to, Crowley?"

He pointed back the way we'd come. "The mountains. There's a pass, and that leads to the winter lands, where darkness rules."

"Sounds like a right friendly place," Hemi remarked.

Crowley stared at the mountain range. Black clouds obscured the summits, and lightning flashed in those clouds at intervals, temporarily revealing dark shapes that moved in the mists. "It will be dangerous. My adoptive mother likely knows we're coming. She will have sent creatures to oppose us. Expect an ambush at any time."

Guts took a huge bite from his slab of beef jerky, which had dwindled in size since he'd lost his eye. The troll had been eating nonstop in order to help his body heal. He scratched his head while he chewed.

"Wizard, you no have another dragon hidden? Might come in handy, in places forbidden."

"Unfortunately, I don't," Crowley replied. "And, to be honest, I don't care to take Ollie anywhere near Fuamnach's palace. She has a tendency to take what is good and twist it into things that are evil. As much as I agree that we could use him for back-up, I do not wish to see Ollie changed into some sinister creature by her magic."

I flexed the half-grown fingers on my hand and attempted a minor cantrip that fizzled. "Speaking of which, what can we expect to come up against when we raid your mom's place?"

"There will be giants and other creatures guarding the mountain pass. The Dark Druid is a talented necromancer, so we can expect to see the undead wandering around as a deterrent to trespassers. And she will have assassin squads patrolling the palace itself."

Hemi held his spear by the butt and stared down its length, before flipping it up and catching it in mid-air. "Sounds like a piece of piss. Nothing to it."

I wrapped my injured hand in strips of shredded t-shirt while I considered the information Crowley had shared.

"I'd rather avoid as much of that as possible," I said as I glanced at the wizard. "Every kid has a way to sneak out of their house without letting their parents know about it, so I'm assuming there's a back way in?"

"There is," the wizard said. "But it's guarded by one of my mother's allies. Within her realm, she is supremely powerful. We'll need to bargain with her for passage."

I knelt and fumbled with tying my shoelaces. Since I'd shredded my last pair of combat boots, I was wearing a pair of running shoes I'd found in my Craneskin Bag. "I see. And I suppose you wouldn't happen to be on good terms with this individual?"

"I don't think she's on good terms with anyone. She's also rather powerful, and not at all someone I'd choose to deal with were there another alternative."

I finally gave up on my laces and looked at Hemi, who was smiling at my antics. "A little help here, big guy? Otherwise we're never going to get going." I sat and stretched out my legs so Hemi could tie my shoes. "Tell me, Crowley—just who is it we'll have to deal with to sneak into your mom's house?"

"Peg Powler."

"*The* Peg Powler? The one who likes to drown kids and eat them? You seriously want me to negotiate with a monster like that?"

He nodded. "One and the same. She lives in a marshy area behind and beneath Fuamnach's palace, where she guards the sewer drainage system to keep any of mother's enemies from sneaking in via those tunnels."

"Why not just kill water hag?" Guts asked. "Just cut head off and toss in bag."

Crowley shook his head and crossed his arms. "Believe me, I would've already done so if I thought it was possible. Unfortunately, she's quite powerful in her own demesne."

Hemi finished tying my shoes, and I stood up and brushed myself off. "Now hang on there just a minute, Crowley. If this bitch is such a nuisance, how'd you ever sneak past her when you were a kid?"

"Simple, I didn't. Peg allowed me to traverse her lands in exchange for service in trade."

I ran my uninjured hand through my hair. "Do I even want to know what 'service' you rendered to her?"

"Well, of course it wasn't anything terrible..." Crowley's voice raised in pitch as he continued. "Wait a minute. You don't think I —slept with her, do you?"

Guts, Hemi, and I all looked at each other, and we nodded simultaneously.

"Yeah, that's pretty much what we were thinking," I said.

Crowley waved his hands back and forth in protest. "What? I would never—no, that's simply revolting—I mean, just wait until you see her." He shivered in disgust.

I frowned with skepticism and shrugged, milking the situation for all it was worth. "Hey, I'm not here to judge you or anything. I mean, every guy has an ex they regret." I looked back and forth at Hemi and Guts. "Am I right, fellas?"

"Oh yeah, for sure," Hemi agreed.

"Guts regrets Wart-Eyed Tina. Never met a she-troll meaner."

"I didn't sleep with Peg Powler!" Crowley shouted.

It took a superhuman effort to avoid cracking a smile. "Sure thing, man. Judgement-free zone here. Whatever you say."

"You—never mind!" the wizard spat as he stormed off.

I waited until he was out of earshot, then looked at Guts and Hemi. "So, how long do you think we should bust his chops over this?"

Hemi's face grew serious. "Oh, for the rest of the trip, definitely."

Guts scratched at the corner of his still-healing eye and sighed. "Tribe say 'once you go hag, you never go back.'" He looked at Hemi and me, waving his hands back and forth. "But of course, Guts know nothing about that."

THE CLOSER WE got to the mountain pass, the more I didn't like the look of things. The sky drew darker and the "daylight" receded as we ascended the switchbacks. Smoky trails of mist floated about, tricking the eye and obscuring potential ambush sites from view.

"Keep your heads on a swivel, guys," I said as we neared the pass. The trail ahead wound around a large boulder, and above and beyond that, it led to a barren saddle between two low peaks. Nothing was visible but mist over the crest of the saddle and beyond the peaks.

If we were going to be ambushed, this was the place.

"We should pause to prepare," Crowley whispered.

"Agreed," Hemi said. He stopped and began a toned-down haka, which I assumed was just enough to trigger the wards in his tattoos.

Not relishing the thought of traversing the winter lands barefoot, I removed my shoes and placed them in the Bag with the rest of my clothing. The cold mountain winds made me shiver, at least until I shifted. Thankfully, Fomorian skin was thick and hairy. It wasn't attractive in the slightest, but definitely warmer than bare human skin by far.

Crowley muttered a spell, and soon he was wrapped in tendrils of shadow. I knew from tangling with him in the past that those inky limbs acted both as armor and weaponry. When attacked, his magic would enclose him in a cocoon of semi-solid shadow, and alternately those shadowy limbs could lift, throw, tear, and crush his enemies as easily as a kraken's tentacles.

Guts merely scanned the area above and below us as he waited for us to finish. I reached into my Craneskin Bag and pulled out the war club I'd used to battle the Dagda. I took a moment to examine the rune he'd scratched in the butt of the weapon and shrugged, deciding that I would determine its purpose when we got back to earth.

I cracked my neck and gave everyone their marching orders. "I'll take point. Hemi pulls rear guard, to make sure nothing sneaks up on us. Crowley, you're our artillery and long-range support. If we're attacked, start tossing boulders at whatever opposes us. Guts can watch your back and step in if one of us gets in too deep. Everyone ready?"

After receiving assorted nods and grunts in reply, I hefted my club and headed up the trail.

We had barely rounded the boulder ahead before I spotted them. There were two giants—one on each of the peaks that flanked the pass—perched on cliffs that had been carved into the stone. Unlike the fachen I'd fought at Crowley's farm, these giants looked exactly like large, ugly humans.

I estimated each one to be at least ten feet tall. They sported no armor, and dressed in brown burlap tunics over loose woolen pants tucked into short leather boots. I spotted a huge wooden staff—easily the size of a small tree trunk—leaning against the mountain wall behind the one on the right, and assumed his partner was similarly armed.

"Above us!" I shouted. That's when things got interesting.

As soon as the giants realized we'd seen them, they began chucking large rocks at us. I wound up with my club, intending to bat the rocks out of the air, but Crowley beat me to it. Like some sort of magic Patriot anti-missile system, smoky black tentacles swatted rocks out of the air with surprising and welcome efficiency.

Guts hooked his stone axe on his belt and pulled an old-school sling from a waist pouch. He began gathering stones from the trail, and soon returned fire at the giants.

"Guts, keep the one on the left occupied!" I ran at the slope to my right, leaping up to grab the edge of the cliff on which the giant stood. I nearly got brained by a boulder as I climbed up, but thankfully Crowley whipped a tendril of shadow magic around and saved me from an involuntary lobotomy.

I pulled myself over the edge of the cliff and rolled up into a crouch, just in time to block an overhead blow from the giant's staff. I spun in place and snapped my leg around, in an attempt to sweep his legs out from under him. With surprising alacrity, the giant man jumped over my kick. I rolled to the side as his staff crashed into the ground where I'd been crouching.

I grabbed a handful of dirt and rocks as I stood, and tossed them in the giant's face. He was a few feet taller than me, but I was still tall enough to hit him square in the eyes. He blinked and backed away, which was what I'd hoped he'd do. I skipped forward and front-kicked him off the ledge, and watched him tumble down the mountainside. It was a long drop, several hundred feet at least. I doubted he'd recover.

A large rock whizzed past my face, reminding me of the giant on the other peak. I pivoted and brought my club up in time to block another boulder, which shattered into shards all around me. "Crowley, a little help here!"

Crowley complied, launching a sizable rock through the air. It struck the giant on the shoulder, just as a smaller rock hit the giant on the cheek. Another small stone followed that one, then another large stone. Soon, the giant had backed up against the wall behind it.

I was about to jump down and climb up the other side to finish it off, when Hemi rolled over the lip of the ledge. Hemi was a big man, but this giant towered over him.

"Hemi, no!" I shouted.

He smiled and twirled his spear. Crowley couldn't safely toss more boulders at the giant without danger of hitting Hemi, so the Maori was on his own up there.

"Shit," I muttered, as I jumped down to the trail below. I lost sight of Hemi as I started climbing up the other peak.

Seconds later, I reached over the cliff's edge and pulled myself up enough to see what had happened. Hemi was sitting on a rock near the opposite side of the cliff, his spear balanced across his knees.

"Oy, mate, what took you so long?" he asked.

I got both elbows over the cliffside to stabilize my position, and shook my head. "What the hell, man? You should have let me handle it."

"And let you have all the fun? I think not."

I was just about to respond with a suitably smart-assed reply, when a giant hand reached over the edge of the cliff to grab Hemi's ankle. His eyes grew wide as the giant yanked him off his perch and over the side.

"Noooooo!" I cried, levering myself up the cliff's edge and onto the shelf of rock. I ran to the opposite side and looked over. There was no sign of Hemi or the other giant.

"Hemi!" I shouted, cupping my hands to amplify my voice. "Hemi, are you down there?"

No answer. The cliff dropped off for hundreds of feet below me, disappearing into dark gray clouds of mist below. No one could have survived that fall. No one.

I fell to my knees, staring at the empty expanse below. I heard voices from behind me, and turned to witness Crowley crawling over the cliffside, his shadow magic pulling him up in a manner reminiscent of Doctor Octopus.

"What happened to the Maori?" he asked.

I shook my head. "The giant pulled him over the side."

Crowley's magic lowered him to the cliff's surface. His voice was strained and low as he replied. "There's nothing we can do. Come, let us take the trail down. Perhaps we will find his remains. I believe you made him a promise—at least we can do that for him."

"Uh-uh, I refuse to believe he's gone. We'll find him."

The dark wizard crossed the ledge and stood next to me. He

looked down and stood silent. Finally, he lowered his hood, exposing his scarred visage so I could see his face. His eyes betrayed real emotion as he quietly objected to my protests.

"Perhaps he survived. Come, Colin—there's nothing we can do from up here. Guts awaits us. Let's climb down and begin our search."

We did exactly that, leaving the mountain pass behind as we descended. I shifted back into human form as we went, and Crowley and Guts had to force me to get dressed before I froze to death.

The steep trail cut down the side of the mountain, where it soon transitioned into rough stone stairs that cut back and forth every fifty feet or so. We walked down the stairs in silence, and with every step I prayed that my friend had survived. I began counting stairs so I'd know how far we'd gone—and to distract myself from the inevitable.

I estimated that we'd dropped down a thousand feet or more, when we found the second giant's body. Hemi's spear was embedded in the thing's chest, and the broken shaft jutted eighteen inches from its breastbone.

I planted a shoe in the thing's chest and yanked the remains of Hemi's spear out, tucking it in my Bag for safekeeping. Then I continued on down the stairs.

I hadn't gone far when I spotted a pale blue glow in the mist beneath us. I leapt down the steps two and three at a time, and found Hemi on a rocky outcropping a hundred feet below where his foe had landed. His limbs had been shattered by the fall, and they splayed out from his torso at impossible angles like some sort of bloody Escher drawing. His wards were still active, but the magic was fading. The horror of it all stopped me in my tracks for a moment, then I ran to his side.

"Oh, Hemi," I cried.

One side of his face was a bloody swollen mess, but an eyelid fluttered on the unaffected side. "Took you long enough," he whispered.

"Hang on, man—just hang on. I'll get you to the Dagda, and he can heal you. Just don't die on me, please."

Hemi coughed weakly, and pink frothy sputum escaped from his lips. "Naw, mate. I'm done for. No sense crying now. Just don't leave me down here." He coughed again. "Get me back to my mum, yeah? Can you do that for me?"

I nodded, unable to speak for a moment. "I promise."

Hemi exhaled in a death rattle, and his eyes grew fixed and vacant. He was gone. My best friend in the world was gone.

I cradled his head in my lap, and cried until I could cry no more.

14

I decided to have Guts take Hemi's body back to the Dagda, where it would be safe until we were ready to return to earth. Secretly, I hoped that the old man might be able to bring Hemi back from the dead, but I kept my hopes to myself.

We created a litter for my friend's body, and Crowley conjured a spider-like construct made from shadow magic to carry the litter. We wrapped Hemi in a tarp I found in the Bag and placed him on the shadow golem's back.

"It'll last long enough to get you back to the Dagda's farm, but no more. My powers will be weakened while the construct is active, and I will need to recall my magic when the task is done."

Guts nodded. "Understood." He looked at me. "Druid did all he could. Hemi pay the final price, now he go to warrior's paradise. He beyond all pain. Take heart, you see him again."

That was the most I'd ever heard the troll say in a single breath. Despite my somber mood, his awkward assurances made me feel a bit better.

"I—thank you, Guts. You're a good friend."

Guts nodded, and he took off at a jog with the strange shadow-spider construct trailing behind him, carrying Hemi's battered body on its back. We watched them go, and Crowley waited silently until I turned my eyes away and began walking down the remaining steps. We said nothing to each other until we reached the bottom, and I spent that time reflecting on what had just happened. I wondered what I was going to tell his mother, and struggled with guilt over choosing to bring him along.

My single-minded focus on revenge had just gotten another one of my friends hurt. And this time, there was no fixing it. The Dagda was a long shot. After trading blows with him, I knew that his powers had been weakened over the centuries, perhaps by the gradual sickening of Underhill, or by the inevitable march of time. From what Finnegas had told me, even immortals had to die sometime—as oxymoronic as that sounded.

I walked through mists lost in my thoughts, footsteps muffled by the fog. Crowley interrupted my melancholic rumination by yanking me into a cleft between two boulders. Shadows sprang from the ground, concealing us further by thickening the darkness in the crevice he'd chosen to hide us in. He held a finger to his lips and pointed outside. I strained to see through the mist that shrouded the landscape beyond, and soon saw shadowy figures trudging through the fog.

A herd of ghouls walked out of the mist, shuffling directly past our hiding place. I'd failed to hear them coming, because the fog had muffled the sound of their movements—or because I'd been lost in grief. Crowley waited until they were long gone, then grabbed me by the shoulders and leaned in close, speaking in low tones to avoid alerting stragglers to our presence.

"Listen, Colin, and listen well. We are in the winter lands now, the habitation of the unseelie fae and what remains of the unsavory Tuatha De Danann. You must stay focused on the task at hand, because I cannot be responsible for the safety of us both. You will have time to grieve your friend later after this task is done. Right now, I need your focus and resolve."

I hung my head for a moment, then nodded silently. He waited several seconds, then he patted my shoulders roughly and exited the crevice. I heard him whisper to me from just outside.

"I will keep watch while you gather yourself for the task ahead."

I took several deep breaths as I quickly ran through one of the mental exercises I'd learned from Finnegas. I thought back to the days after Jesse had died at my hands, and remembered how I'd had to let anger replace my grief in order to get through to the other side. I meditated on Fuamnach and the Dark Druid, their roles in it all, and how their machinations had led to Hemi's death.

It had all started when they'd sent Crowley to steal the Eye from Maeve. Maeve had needed me to recover Balor's Eye, because I was the best bet for keeping it out of their hands. No one else could've bonded with the damned thing, which made me her best option. So, she'd blackmailed me into working for her, and engineered circumstances so I would go after Crowley and attempt to get the tathlum—and thus Balor's Eye—back.

That had led to the Dark Druid coming after me. He'd thought he could possess my body and acquire the Eye's powers for himself. And because of my near brush with death during my battle with him, I'd decided that I needed to learn to control my ability to shift. In doing so, I'd be able to fully harness the Eye's powers and defeat the Dark Druid and Fuamnach.

For that reason, I'd gone to the local alpha, Samson, for help in learning to control my shifter abilities. Then Sal the red cap's son had gone missing, and he'd asked me to find the strange little fae child. In the course of tracking him down, I'd ended up thwarting a child sex trafficking ring. One that, according to the Rye Mother, had Fuamnach's fingerprints all over it.

Once I'd pulled on that string, it was a foregone conclusion that I would follow it to the bitter end. Fuamnach knew that. Hell, she was counting on it to bring me straight to her door with the Eye.

Fuck her.

She had to pay for Hemi's death.

I got good and pissed off, then took my anger and compressed it into a white-hot ember that nestled itself somewhere between my chest and gut.

It'd do.

I exited the crevice without looking at Crowley, and headed down the trail.

"Let's go. I have things to do and fae to kill."

Crowley grunted and whispered prophetically as he fell in step beside me. "'The rider's name was Death, and Hades followed after him.'"

WE SNUCK around Fuamnach's undead and fae patrols, taking our time as we made our way to Peg Powler's demesne. Thankfully, Crowley knew the place like the back of his hand. Between that and his shadow magic, it wasn't hard to stay out of sight. The entirety of Fuamnach's domain was a dark, damp, dead place, devoid of living foliage and covered in mists that concealed dangers at every turn. Twice Crowley had to stop me from stepping into dank, foul-smelling bogs that remained hidden by the fog until you were right on top of them.

"Cheery place," I remarked.

"What you see is a reflection of my adoptive mother's magic and personality. Underhill itself is magic, and each demesne adapts to the nature of the Tuatha or fae who has mastered it." He pointed at a nearby bog. "Do mind the pits. They are poisonous and designed to trap the unwary. The harder you struggle, the farther you sink."

"Got it. I've seen every episode of *Gilligan's Island*, and I know all about the dangers of quicksand."

He looked off into the fog, scanning our surroundings as he spoke. "You do not have to make jokes to demonstrate that you're okay."

"Don't mind me, Crowley. It's how I deal when things go bad."

"I see." He continued scanning the foggy landscape around us, then started off in a new direction. "I recognize this area. Come, it's not far now."

"How you can recognize anything in this fog is a mystery to me."

"It's more of a feeling, really. As I said, the landscape conforms to its master. The qualities and characteristics of the land change as you enter a powerful fae's demesne."

He pointed at a faintly glowing patch of moss on a nearby stone, the first living plant life I'd seen since we'd left the mountain path. "That tells me we're close to Peg Powler's lair. Mother's magic is all about deception, death, and entropy. But Peg, for all her faults, is a creature of the swamps and wetlands, and therefore of life. A twisted representation of it, but life nonetheless."

I ventured a guess based on observation, more out of curiosity than anything else. "It sounds like you almost care about her."

He continued on in silence for a time before answering. "Peg is more a force of nature than a purposely evil being. She represents part of the cycle of life. The swamps and wetlands take life, true—but they also help sustain it in their own way. Peg kills, but only because it is in her nature. One does not hate the lion for killing to survive."

"I know you didn't grow up on earth, but we tend to take a dim view of drowning children and eating them."

"I'm aware, and in full agreement. But as I said, a predator is as a predator does. You cannot fault them for following their own nature."

Out of habit, I rested a hand lightly on the handle of my Glock. "No, but we still kill predators who develop a taste for human flesh."

Crowley chose to remain silent rather than respond, and we walked along in silence for some time, traversing an area that was not unlike the swamps surrounding Lugh's lands. It made me wonder what sort of messed up things had happened to Lugh, for his lands to be so ugly and dismal. He seemed a nice enough guy, but I supposed even Celtic deities got the blues.

I could so relate at the moment.

Crowley pulled up short as we exited a thick bank of fog. "Ah, here we are. Wait a moment for me, while I prepare a gift for Peg. Doing so will greatly facilitate our negotiations."

He set off into the fog bank, so I sat on a nearby rotten log and took in the surroundings. We'd exited the mists right on the edge of a large, swampy lake. Dark shadows moved just beneath the algae-covered surface in the murky waters below. Every so often I heard the *plop* of a toad jumping in the waters to avoid some larger predator. Besides the toads and the shadows that moved within the waters, nothing else stirred as far as the eye could see.

In the middle of the lake and several hundred yards distant, a ramshackle wattle hut sat on a low island that was surrounded by cattails and reeds. A thin wisp of smoke trailed from its thatch roof, and the scent of dried peat being burned hung thick in the air, melding with the rotten odors of swamp gas and stagnancy. I thought I saw a shadow pass behind the burlap curtain that covered the hut's window, but I couldn't be sure.

I busied myself with a weapons check while I waited for Crowley to return. I neither saw nor heard him until he stepped out of the fog again, carrying a six-foot crocodilian creature trussed over one shoulder, and a black silk bag that bulged and shifted over the other.

"Here, help me with one of these," he said.

I stood and considered my options, finally reaching for the sack.

"Mind the teeth. They're poisonous."

I didn't have to ask what was inside, because I recognized the musky, slightly uric odor. "Snakes? Really?"

He readjusted the crocodile-like creature on his shoulder, as it was wriggling around in an attempt to escape its bindings. "I told you, services in trade. Peg rarely leaves her island these days, but she still needs to eat. If you wish to cross her demesne, either you bring her food, or you are food."

"Okay, at least you're not sleeping with her." Crowley stiffened, and I raised a hand. "I kid, I kid—relax. I presume we're headed to that island? How the hell are we going to get over there?"

I could hear the smugness in his voice as he replied. "Oh, ye of little faith. Here comes our ride now."

I FOLLOWED the direction Crowley's hood was facing and observed as one of the underwater shadows headed toward us. The shadow gained speed, growing larger until whatever it was began creating a wake as it neared the shore. Finally, it broke the surface. I had to blink to assure myself that what I was seeing was legit. A rocky island floated through the murky lake at us, and it was closing in fast.

As it got closer, I recognized a familiar hexagonal pattern of horned plates on the creature's moss-covered back. That's when I knew what our "ride" was.

"Either that's the biggest turtle I've ever seen, or the swamp gas is getting to me," I remarked.

The living island neared us, stopping a few feet from dry land. The part we could see was easily twenty feet across, and I assumed at least one-third remained under water. The wake it made as it neared shore splashed beyond the lake's edge, forcing us to step back to avoid getting soaked.

Crowley adjusted his crocodile and took two quick steps to the water's edge, jumping lightly onto the creature's back. "Mind your step, and don't fall in the water," he said. "You'll be eaten before I could possibly pull you out."

"Wonderful."

I clutched my bag of snakes, holding it at arm's length as I leaped onto the algae and mud-covered shell. I nearly slipped as I landed, righting myself before I scrambled to the peak of the shell to take a spot next to the shadow wizard. No sooner had I come to a stop than the creature began making its way to the island.

On the way there, a smaller shadow approached us. I watched with interest as the turtle snatched an eight-foot eel from the water. The creature's huge beaked head broke the water with the eel in its mouth, biting down and snapping it up in two or three gulps. It turned to fix one reptilian eye on us for an instant, before lowering its head back beneath the surface with a splash.

We arrived at the island moments later. The turtle stopped a few meters from the island's edge, and we hopped off just as quickly as possible. The huge beast sank beneath the water, making nary a ripple as it disappeared into the unseen depths below.

A wheezy, gurgling voice called from within the hut. "Who dares venture on my island? Two humans, I smell. One with magic woven from shadow, the other with magic not his own. Interesting. Come closer, that I may see you both."

Crowley leaned over to whisper low in my ear. "Let me do the talking, unless you fancy drowning in that lake."

He stepped forward and dropped the croc on the damp earth in front of the hut, and motioned that I should do the same with the snakes.

"Mother Powler, do you not recognize me? The lad who dared traverse your lands, just to escape his guardian's wrath?"

A wet chuckle escaped from the shadows inside the hut. "Crowley. I should have known. And you bring gifts, I see. As always, a proper tribute from a proper child."

He nodded within his hood. "As always, Peg. I'd not forget the one who sheltered me so many times."

"But these days, lad, you've fallen out of favor with the sorceress. What's to keep me from drowning you and your companion, and eating the rotting flesh from your bones? You're not as tender and succulent as you once were, true, but from here it looks as though I could make several meals of you both."

"I'm not the same boy I once was, Peg—I believe you'd be hard-pressed to make an easy meal of me, even here in your own demesne. And my companion here is no slouch himself, of that I can assure you."

Peg took a long sniff of us while remaining hidden inside the hut. We heard a gurgling gasp. "Fomori? You bring a Fomórach to my home?"

Crowley took a step back. "We mean you no harm, Peg. We simply require passage through your lands."

"Ah, I know you now. Peg hears things, down here in her

boggy swamp. Plans, machinations, conspiracies." She coughed, making a wet, hacking noise. "Tell me, druid, do you intend the sorceress harm? Or does she have something you need? Two somethings, maybe?"

I looked at Crowley, and he shrugged.

"Both, actually," I replied. "I have business with the sorceress, that's a fact. But mostly I just want what she has."

The hag coughed again, in a fit that lasted a minute or more. "She has several things. Life. Magic. Power. Influence. Which of these would you gain for yourself?"

"Magic."

"Ah, the Treasures, then, as I thought." She remained silent for several seconds. I opened my mouth to speak, but Crowley nudged me and shook his head. Moments later, the hag continued. "I will allow you to pass, but only for a price."

"Name it," I said.

"A bowl from the Dagda's cauldron. That is my price. I know you have it on you. I can sense it, even inside Fionn's bag."

I looked at Crowley, who stood silent. "Give me a minute." I pulled Crowley away from the hut, leaning close to whisper to him. "What do you think?"

"She's fae, so she certainly has some ulterior motive. Of what, I can only guess. The broth from the Dagda's cauldron surely has properties of which we may only speculate. Peg is a skilled magician, so there's no telling what she might concoct from it."

"Harmful to us? Or to others?"

"It is difficult to say, but I doubt she could harm us, once bound to grant us safe passage through her demesne."

I thought about it for several seconds, then exhaled forcefully. "Fuck it. I need to get in that palace, so we really have no choice. What she does with the concoction once we're gone is none of our business."

I walked the few steps back to Peg's hut. "You agree to give us both safe passage through your demesne and back out again? All for one small bowl poured from the Dagda's Cauldron?"

I heard shuffling inside the cabin. "A few ladles of broth, no more."

"Deal."

A small wooden bowl clattered to our feet, although I didn't see where it'd come from. I dug inside my Craneskin Bag and pulled out the Cauldron, carefully filling the wooden bowl to its brim. I stepped back, replacing the Cauldron safely back into the depths of my Bag.

A pale, wrinkled hand, covered in algae and moss, appeared from behind the burlap curtain over the cabin doorway. Peg extended a long finger, displaying a sharp, blackened fingernail at the end. It pointed to the other side of the lake.

"Go. Leave the bowl where it sits. On your return, a way back will be provided."

A loud sucking noise emitted from the lake where she was pointing. A slick, muddy isthmus of land began to extend out from Peg's island. Mud and stones boiled to the surface of the water as Peg raised the path with will and magic, stretching to the far side of the lake.

I glanced at Crowley, who was once more inscrutably silent inside the shadows of his hood. Wondering whether I'd gotten the better part of my bargain with Peg, I headed for the path that would lead us to Fuamnach's back door.

15

As we crossed the lake on that thin stretch of land that Peg had conjured, I kept a close watch on the surrounding waters. Crowley seemed uninterested in what might or might not jump out of the water to eat us, so I assumed he'd done this before. Despite his apparent lack of concern, I maintained a certain wariness until we reached the opposite shore.

The terrain on the other side of the lake looked much as it had the way we'd come. Everything was covered in moss, including the dead-looking trees that created a canopy of twisted limbs and vines above us. Shadows flitted about in the foliage overhead and in the mists surrounding our position.

I massaged the partially-healed fingers on my hand, considering whether I wanted to continue while still gimped up. "Crowley, give me a minute to shift and heal this hand completely. Something tells me I'm going to need it when we go inside."

The wizard crossed his arms, cradling his chin in one hand. "Will you be able to shift again if we get into trouble in there?"

"Depends. How long will it take us to get through the tunnels?"

"Hours."

"Great. Yeah, I'll be ready by then." I shifted and focused my energies on healing my hand fully. Twenty minutes later, the task was done. "Ready as ever."

"The entrance isn't far now," Crowley said as he glanced around. "Come, we shouldn't tarry here—one of Mother's patrols might spot us."

"You won't hear me complain. Lead the way."

We marched a short distance, maybe a half-mile, before reaching our destination. One minute we were walking through a swampy, decaying forest, and the next the trail opened into a small clearing at the foot of a steep cliff. I'd never get used to traveling in Underhill. It often felt like you were walking on an invisible airport conveyor belt, the way the terrain changed so rapidly.

My eyes followed the cliff upward to the ridge above, maybe a hundred feet or more. Clouds of fog obscured the clifftop at intervals, but when they cleared I could just make out stone walls and parapets. Apparently, the Tuatha liked their castles.

"The entrance is over here, where the sewer empties into the swamp."

Something flew over my head and at Crowley—a shadowy mass moving at speed. I began to call out a warning, but it hit him before I could react, settling across his shoulders like a cloak.

He rolled his shoulders out like a fighter. "That's better. The troll must have made it to the summer lands while we were dealing with Peg. If we hurry, we can be in and out of Mother's lair before your friends have a chance to catch up with us."

"Sounds good to me. The last thing I want is for someone else to be hurt on my account."

"I won't bother telling you it wasn't your fault, because I know you won't listen." Crowley's head swiveled around as he searched for the entrance. "Once we enter the tunnels, we should remain as quiet as possible. Things lurk in the sewers that are best avoided."

I welcomed the change of topic. "What, like Rats of Unusual Size?"

He chuckled. "Worse—although there are some large nasty rats living down there. Mostly you'll find wights, the old-world kind that can chill you with a touch, giant spiders, and, in the upper levels, a tribe of feral red caps who guard the tunnels for Fuamnach."

"Sounds like a good warm-up for what lies ahead," I joked.

Crowley's head snapped around. "You aren't really thinking about taking on Fuamnach, are you? She'll crush you underfoot without thinking twice. Believe me when I say that it's best if we sneak in, get what you came here for, and sneak out unnoticed."

I took a deep breath and stretched my neck. "Alright—but only because I have people relying on me. If we run into her, I won't run. I'm done running."

He looked down, then back at me. "Fine. Just don't expect me to help you do battle. I've suffered enough at that woman's hands, and damned if I'll spend the rest of my life in her dungeons." He pointed to where a small stream of filthy water ran out from the cliff's base. "There it is, the entrance to the sewers."

The entrance was a stone tunnel perhaps thirty-six inches across, covered by a rusted grate. I looked at it and grimaced. "Gah, small spaces. I hope it opens up inside."

"It does. Give me a moment." Crowley fiddled with the stonework the grate was embedded in, and soon he had worked several stones loose, enough to allow us to pull the grate out of the way. "I removed the mortar from these stones when I was just a child, and hoped they were still loose. Thank goodness for the laziness of fae."

He ducked into the tunnel and I followed, casting a cantrip that would allow me to see in the near darkness of the sewers. I'd discovered that even minor spells like this one were nearly impossible to cast without both my hands. It made me wonder if I should find alternate methods of spell casting. It was something to consider, if I ever got back from Underhill.

Phosphorescent lichens covered parts of the tunnel, providing just enough light to allow me to see. My night vision spell wasn't perfect; if we hit an area of complete darkness, I'd be blind. I had some glow sticks and flashlights in my Craneskin Bag, but Crowley had warned against using them. Even the dimmest light would shine like a beacon to the denizens of these tunnels.

The passageway led on for no more than thirty feet before it opened into a large chamber that dropped off below us. The chamber was obviously a waste water collection area, and it had several larger tunnels leading out of it. It also had standing sewer water at the bottom. It looked like we were going to have to get wet.

The shadow wizard pointed across the chamber to one of the tunnels, before dropping down into the nasty water below with a splash. I cringed before following him, wishing I'd brought just one more pair of combat boots on this trip.

———

THE SEWER TUNNELS seemed to go on endlessly, and we took so many twists and turns that I doubted I could find my own way out again. In some sections, we had to crawl on our hands and knees through filth, while in others the tunnels arched several feet over our heads. I began to look forward to those sections that provided us with ample headroom, and soon gave up on wiping the muck from my hands.

As we progressed ever upward, I reflected on how horrible Crowley's childhood must have been for him to have braved these tunnels as a young kid. We'd run across numerous rats that would've given a German Shepherd a run for its money in the size department, and it was dark as hell in here. Plus, the creep factor was a ten-plus. I knew every geek's dream was to do a real-life dungeon crawl, but I had to say that the reality of it sucked.

And that was *before* we ran into the wights.

We were crawling through another narrow tunnel when Crowley hissed a warning to me.

"Back up, back up, back up, damn it!"

I heard him muttering a spell, and knew whatever was happening wasn't good. I scrambled in reverse as fast as I could, with Crowley kicking me in the face as he followed. I barely caught a glimpse of a thin dark membrane covering the tunnel ahead of the wizard, obviously a temporary magical barrier to facilitate our retreat. Something was trying desperately to punch through it, and I doubted it would hold for long.

I fell backward out of the tunnel due to a frenzied kick in the face from Crowley's booted foot, landing in a pile of something cold and mushy. My olfactory nerves had long since shut down from sensory overload, a fact for which I was grateful beyond belief at the moment.

"Stand and fight, or run?" I asked as I stood up and shook the shit, mud, and algae from my hands.

"Wights," he said, as he exited the tunnel. "No time to run, so ready yourself."

I pulled my Glock and screwed the suppressor to the barrel, just in time to greet the first wight as it exited the tunnel. It was albino white—hairless, eyeless, and crawling like a spider on limbs that bent at impossible angles. Despite those empty eye sockets, it "looked" straight at me and screeched as it exited the tunnel, baring a mouth full of sharp, crooked teeth.

I shot it between where its eyes should have been, and it fell limp with its upper torso hanging out of the tunnel.

"More coming!" Crowley exclaimed.

I moved into position directly in front of the tunnel and began blasting away, figuring I'd hit a few of them while they were lined up. Despite the suppressor on my pistol's barrel, the muzzle flash still did a number on my eyesight. I was seeing spots by the time I ran empty and switched out the magazine.

"How many?" I asked.

"Six... no, seven more. You killed another and injured two of them."

I blinked to clear my vision as I holstered my pistol and drew my sword. Shooting in random directions in these tight quarters might result in a friendly-fire injury, so it was swordplay from here on out.

I still couldn't see shit.

"Fuck it," I said, reaching into my pocket to grab a light stick. I cracked it on the wall and tossed it into the center of the chamber. "Aw, hell."

Two of them were closing in on me, while two more were engaged with Crowley. He was ripping them limb from limb with those shadow tentacles of his, but it was anyone's guess how long it would be before he got overrun. I needed to take my two out fast to give Crowley an assist.

I ducked a swipe at my head, stepping off the line as I cut one wight's leg off at the knee. I kicked it into the other wight's way, stabbing it through the eye while it was entangled with its companion's limbs. I beheaded the first wight as they both fell, then turned to help Crowley.

He was backed up into a corner, holding four of the bastards off. The wizard was working with at least eight shadow arms, two to each wight, but he appeared to be weakening. I took a step toward him, wondering where the other wight was, just as I got blindsided and tackled to the floor of the chamber.

Something blurred past me as I tumbled to the ground with a wight on top of me. It was clutching my bare wrist, which was already going numb. I shoved a forearm under its chin to keep it from biting me, because wight bites were bad news. The resulting infection could only be cured by a skilled healer, and failing that, you'd end up as one of the living dead within hours of being bitten. No *bueno*.

I looked past the wight's snapping jaws to see how Crowley was faring. That's when I realized that the blonde, furry blur that had run past was Sabine. She flanked Crowley's attackers, making quick work of two of them with that elven sword I'd loaned her. Once the pressure was off him, Crowley had no trouble dealing with the last two wights. He tore the head off one with a whiplash swipe of a shadow tentacle, and bashed the other into the ceiling a few times until it stopped moving.

As for me, I was having major difficulties. I couldn't shift yet, and didn't want to because I'd need it later if we ran into Fuamnach. I had one arm shoved under the wight's chin, and the other was numb to the elbow and locked in the wight's death grip. I kept trying to hook its leg so I could bridge my hips up and roll it off me. The damned thing must've been a collegiate wrestler in its previous existence, because it was maintaining top mounted position like a champ.

"Um, guys—a little help here?"

Sabine did a quick pivot and sliced the top of the wight's head off, just above the nostrils. It struggled for a few more seconds, still trying to take a bite out of me. Then, it seemed to lose steam, just before it collapsed in a heap on top of me, leaking brain fluid and gore all over my chest.

"Ugh. Well, it's not like any of this is going to wash out of these clothes anyway." I threw the thing off me, just as Sabine leaned over to offer me a hand.

"Miss me?"

"How in the hell did you find us so fast?"

She smirked. "Sympathetic magic, and a bit of the Dagda's traveling magic. I stole a lock of your hair while you were sleeping. I'm fae, remember? We're sneaky as all hell."

"And they say I'm a creeper," Crowley muttered, probably louder than he intended. Sabine blushed slightly, acting as if she hadn't heard. I wisely did the same.

WE SPENT the next few minutes making sure no more wights were coming, then Sabine insisted that I explain how Hemi had been killed. Apparently, Guts had tried to tell the tale and failed. His interpretation had been more an attempt at immortalizing Hemi for all eternity in a poetic troll epic than an accurate depiction of events. So, we rested for a few minutes while I shared the story with her.

I only choked up twice telling it.

Sabine rested a hand on my shoulder and squeezed gently. "Don't give up hope yet. You have two Celtic deities pulling for you. And besides that, don't you think there's a reason why Hemi insisted you bring him back from Underhill?"

I shrugged. "I just figured he wanted me to return his body to his family, so he could be buried with his ancestors."

Sabine stroked her chin. "Maybe... but Hemi has never been very forthcoming about his family roots. Call it a woman's intuition, but I suspect there's more there than anyone realizes."

I scratched the back of my head, scraping off something slimy and solid and tossing it away without bothering to see what it was. I didn't really want to know; some things were better left a mystery.

"I can't think about that right now, Sabine. I just need to focus on getting the final two Treasures and sneaking them back to Maeve."

"I understand." She gave me a concerned look, then turned to Crowley. "You know a way to sneak past all Fuamnach's security, that'll march us right into her treasure chamber?"

"I do. If it's where I left it."

Sabine crossed her arms, which only served to create a shelf for her ample cleavage. I gave points to Crowley for not tilting his head to look. Of course, he had the advantage of his hood and shadow magic to hide where his eyes went.

The half-fae girl arched an eyebrow. "Well, that's convenient. And please share with us, Crowley, just how you managed to build a tunnel to your adoptive mother's treasure room, right under her nose?"

"Hey, Sabine—ease up already. The guy has already saved my life more than once on this trip. He's earned our trust."

She turned and poked me in the chest, using her finger to emphasize each sentence. "You, Colin McCool, are way too trusting. I'm simply asking the questions you should be asking. Isn't losing one friend on this lunatic suicide mission enough?"

Sabine spun to face Crowley again. "So, mister—care to explain yourself?"

I was pretty sure I actually heard the guy sigh. "For starters, it's not a tunnel. And secondly, there were many times when I'd be left by myself in that great big castle, while Fuamnach ran off to who knows where. Believe me, I had plenty of time to scheme and plan my escape."

The fae girl narrowed her eyes. "Speaking of which, if your life was so horrible with Fuamnach, why didn't you escape?"

"I tried. I was beaten and starved. After a few cycles of that, I realized it was futile."

She tapped her cloven foot. "Convenient. Colin, I don't like this."

"You may not like it, but at the moment I'm your best bet for getting the Treasures and getting out of here alive," Crowley said.

I chopped my hand between them. "Enough with the arguing! What I want to know is, how are we getting into Fuamnach's treasure room?"

Crowley laughed. "It's simple, really. We're going to use a portal to get in and back out again... and no one will be the wiser."

16

Portal magic was serious, hardcore spell craft that was the sole territory of magic users who were either immortal or in possession of highly powerful magical artifacts. And not just any trinket would do. Such artifacts had to be specifically designed to create portals.

The only magic users I knew who could open portals to other places and dimensions were Finnegas, Maeve, The Dark Druid, and possibly Fuamnach. I'd seen Finnegas pull one off once, when he'd saved my ass by sending a headless horseman named the Dullahan to some random place in the Underrealms. That spell had wiped him out for days. Maeve cast portal spells like they were going out of style, but then again she could tap into Underhill's magic, so theoretically her power was pretty much limitless.

And the only time I'd seen the Dark Druid cast a portal spell was under duress. I'd gotten the impression that it took a lot out of him to pull one off. What Crowley had said, about his trip from Underhill to earth being a one-way ticket, only reinforced that assessment. As for Fuamnach, I had no idea. That being said, she was a sorceress both ancient and powerful, so I assumed it was within her purview.

But a mortal human, casting a portal spell? No way.

Crowley was a talented magician, that was a fact, and a hell of a lot better at using magic than I was. But he was human and not much older than me. There was no way he could cast a spell like that without help.

And, because of that, the whole thing sounded like a trap.

Crowley recognized our skepticism, and he began explaining himself with vigor. "I know this seems suspect, but hear me out. I didn't cast the portal myself. Instead, I bargained with Peg Powler for help. She provided the spell craft and wove it into a physical anchor for me. The idea was that I could use the portal to make my escape from Fuamnach's castle."

I looked at Sabine to gauge her reaction. She was testing the edge of her blade with her thumbnail. *Not good.* I turned back to Crowley.

"What went wrong?" I asked. "I mean, why didn't you just get the hell out of Dodge once the spell was in place?"

Crowley sat down on a nearby ledge that was mostly sewage-free. "Unfortunately, Fuamnach has her castle spelled and warded against entry or exit by portal. I suppose she's paranoid, after so many years of enmity with the more powerful of the Tuath Dé. And, Peg being Peg, she knew about it. She made it so that once I activated the portal, it couldn't be moved."

I sucked my teeth. "Typical fae, always giving people the raw end of the deal."

"Indeed," Crowley replied. "I set up the portal spell in my quarters, but quickly abandoned it after I discovered it was useless for its intended purpose. Admittedly, I failed to see the utility of the thing until much later. While the spell couldn't help me escape from Fuamnach, it *can* transport us anywhere within the castle walls. We just have to get to it."

Sabine sheathed her blade as she glanced in my direction. "I still don't like it, but what choice do you have?"

"Not much, at this point," I muttered. "How are the kids holding up?"

Her face lit up at the mere mention of the children. "Oh, they're having a grand old time. The Dagda is an old softy, as it turns out. Says it's been centuries since he heard the laughter of children in his lands. He's set up the world's biggest petting zoo on his farm to keep them entertained, and I think he's enjoying it as much as they are."

"Good to know. I guess that means we have some time to think this through?"

Sabine shook her head and grimaced. "Not so much. That's one of the reasons I hauled ass after you two. The Dagda says the longer the kids stay here, the more likely they are to suffer ill effects when they go back to earth."

I rubbed my temples and growled. "Damn it... can't anything go smoothly for a change? Alright, so how long do we have?"

"Depends. He told me he'd use his magical influence to keep them from acclimating to Underhill, but that we should get them back as soon as possible."

I looked at Crowley. "Why didn't you suffer any side effects when you left here? After spending your childhood in Underhill, it seems like going back to earth would've messed you up royal."

He fussed with his sleeve, covering up his scarred hand and arm as much as possible. "I was, for lack of a better term, 'altered' by Fuamnach's experiments. She's rather fond of using magic to experiment on human children. Since I was one of her successes, she allowed me to live."

Sabine snapped her fingers and pointed at Crowley. "That's how you got your magic. Holy shit, Crowley... what did she do to you?"

"I'd rather not discuss it. But I can assure you, the process was not pleasant."

Sabine's eyes softened, and doubt registered on her face. She wanted to believe him, but being fae, she was naturally suspicious.

"As far as I'm concerned, it's settled. We do it Crowley's way. Check your gear, and let's get moving." I turned my back on them and began to do an inventory of my equipment.

Sabine walked around me and got right in my face. "I don't trust him," she whispered. "He's spent too much time down here with that bitch of a sorceress, and there's no telling what she did to him. He could be under a geas, he could be brainwashed—hell, he could be the world's best con artist. We simply don't know."

I shrugged, resigned to my fate. "I've already thought of all that, but our options are limited. It's either this, or I go in there hulked out and guns blazing—and odds are I wouldn't make it out alive if it came to that. You, Guts, and the kids would be stuck here and up shit creek. I can't have that on my conscience."

She crossed her arms and cocked her hip. "Fine. But when this thing goes sideways, don't say I didn't warn you."

WE MADE our way through the remainder of the sewer system mostly unmolested. As we ascended the tunnels that led higher into the complex, the walls gradually became less damp and lichen-covered, and wooden roof supports appeared at regular intervals. Soon, we saw torchlight in the distance.

Crowley pulled us aside and whispered softly. "The next few levels are controlled by a very nasty clan of fear dearg who keep things from the lower levels from making their way up to the castle. The Grimknife Clan runs regular patrols, and while their technology is primitive, their fighting skills and tactics are not."

Fear dearg were red caps, nasty little dwarves with a fetish for using sharp pointy things on humans. "How do we get past them?" I asked.

"We'll wait for the first patrol to check the intersection ahead, then we'll backtrack their patrol route until we make it upstairs. Stay here until I give the signal to move."

Shadows enveloped Crowley, and he vanished into the dark of the tunnel ahead of us. Sabine and I crouched in a narrow alcove, peeking around the corner every now and again to make sure no one was coming.

"I still don't like this," she whispered.

"I still don't care," I whispered back.

She stuck her tongue out at me playfully, but I was in no mood for games or jokes. Waiting only gave me time to think about recent events, and that made me both angry and churlish. I ignored her and busied myself by draining the water from my shoes and wringing out my socks.

Minutes passed, then we heard footsteps and light chatter from down the tunnel. I peeked out, just as a group of maybe a half-dozen squat figures passed through the intersection ahead. They were easy to spot, since the first and last red cap carried torches to light their way. Knowing Crowley would return soon, I hurriedly put my shoes back on, hoping they wouldn't squelch and give us away.

Just as we were getting ready to bolt, Crowley's form materialized out of the shadows, just outside the alcove.

"That's creepy, dude," I whispered.

I thought I heard a quiet laugh, but I couldn't be sure. "Come. The patrol has passed and another won't be by for some time. Still, we need to move quickly. If you stay close, I can conceal your passage somewhat."

Sabine grunted. "Give me a second to get rid of these goat hooves and put some shoes back on. Cloven feet are too loud on these dry flagstones."

We both stood there watching until she gave us "the look" and spun her finger in circles like she was stirring a drink. "Duh, turn around, you imbeciles. I have to put my pants back on, too."

I winced, and Crowley cleared his throat. We gave her the privacy she requested, looking elsewhere until she cleared her throat.

"I'm done, knuckleheads. Now, let's get this over with."

Wispy shadows congealed around us, covering us in velvet darkness. It made it hard to see more than a few feet, but we were following Crowley anyway, so I didn't think it mattered. We headed down the hallway, moving swiftly and silently past every circle of torchlight. We paused in areas of darkness to listen for the approach of any patrols or lone wanderers.

Crowley whispered to us at one such interval. "We're almost to the stairs. Wait for me here while I check to see if it's clear above."

He vanished into the shadows again, leaving Sabine and I exposed, save for the natural darkness around us. I sat there watching for Crowley's return when Sabine poked me in the back.

"Company!" she hissed.

I turned and saw torchlight coming up the hallway toward us.

"Crap. There's nothing for it—we'll have to follow Crowley and hope for the best. C'mon."

I took off in a crouch, moving as fast as I could while keeping a low profile. We turned a corner and I saw stairs thirty feet down the corridor, but they were well-lit and exposed. The only consolation was that the landing above was cloaked in blessed, welcome darkness.

I searched for the shadow wizard, but Crowley was still nowhere to be seen. The sound of footsteps and approaching torchlight told us time was running out. If we were spotted, chances were good the red caps would alert their fellow clan members, and then we'd be really screwed.

"Shit, Sabine, we'll just have to make a run for it. Head up the stairs, now—I'll be right behind you."

Sabine did as I asked. I paused to gauge how close the patrol was to seeing us. Too late, I realized they were right on top of me.

I drew my blade and pistol, hoping the sound of suppressed fire wouldn't echo in the corridor. Then I backed against the wall, waiting until the last moment to spring my ambush.

———

I FELT SOMEONE BRUSH my shoulder, just as I was getting ready to pounce. It was Sabine. I scowled and held the gun barrel to my lips to caution her to silence. She narrowed her eyes and flipped me off as if to say, *You're the dumbass who didn't run.* Then, she drew her sword.

I wasn't sure if I liked the new, sassy Sabine who was showing her claws and teeth on this trip, but now wasn't the time to voice a protest. The footsteps and torchlight were getting closer, and the patrol was almost upon us. I plastered myself to the wall and counted down to contact.

3...2...1... Yahtzee!

I pivoted out from behind the wall, firing my pistol. Time slowed and my field of vision narrowed. The first red cap I hit was a squat little barrel of a dwarf wearing crude leather and bone armor. Human bones, or maybe fae. Two to the chest and one to the head, and I was pivoting to the next fighter as the first dropped.

I double-tapped two more red caps with shots to the chest and head, capitalizing on the "oh shit, we're being ambushed" response that caused most people to freeze during a surprise attack. I wasn't as good as Belladonna with a gun, but I could hit three steel plates at fifteen yards in under three seconds from a standing draw. Three seconds was an eternity in a fight, but it was all I needed to take them out before they could react.

After I dropped those two, it was bedlam. The other three members of the patrol charged me, and I found myself fighting two of them with my sword in my non-dominant hand. That was my first mistake.

They swung axes and clubs made from bone and volcanic glass, and I knew the edges on those things were razor sharp. I blocked one swing with my sword while stepping back... then tripped over Sabine as she was moving into position to help me.

Mistake two, always clear a line for the man behind you. Brother, but I was slipping. I hadn't practiced team tactics in a while, and I wasn't thinking about my other team member. Sabine went sprawling, her sword clattering across the floor. I fell on my ass with two red caps coming at me, and a third right behind them who was zoning in on Sabine.

I had ten rounds left in the magazine, and I used them all by shooting a classic El Presidente drill: two shots center mass on each target, with a repeat until the slide locked back. All hits. Unfortunately, people didn't always die the instant you shot them in the torso. Sometimes, it took the body a while to realize that it was dead.

Thus, one of the red caps was still charging me, yelling bloody murder and swinging at my head. Sabine was doing her best to crawl out from under me, because I'd pinned her legs when I'd fallen. I had my sword in my left hand, my pistol in my right, and this red cap was swinging for the fences with a huge razor-sharp axe made of volcanic glass.

Blocking one-handed with a sword against a heavier weapon was always going to end up badly. Nevertheless, I raised the flat of my blade, attempting to brace it with my pistol. Awkward, but it might have kept me from getting my head chopped off.

Time slowed as the red cap's attack sliced through the air at my head. It was funny what you noticed at times like these. The red cap was roaring his battle cry and baring his chompers as he attacked, and I noticed he had spinach or something stuck in his teeth. *How odd*, I thought. *I always assumed they only ate meat.*

Like I said, it was weird what you noticed and thought about right before you were going to die.

A split-second before impact—which would have likely resulted in a failed block and a loss of cranial attachment for yours truly—a huge shadowy arm flew overhead and punched the red cap in the chest, knocking him off his feet. Then, it grabbed the little guy and bounced him off the walls and floors until something went *crunch*.

I collapsed in relief, with Sabine still trying to squirm out from under me. Dead red caps were scattered all around. I looked behind me and, of course, Crowley stood there.

His hood swiveled back and forth at me, Sabine, and the red caps. Even upside down, I could tell he was at a loss. "What in the name of Ankou are you two doing? Stop fooling around—we have to go before more of them arrive."

With a flourish of shadow and his cloak, he disappeared around the corner.

"He might have saved my life, but he's still a pain in the ass," I muttered.

Sabine extracted her legs out from under me and reached for her sword. "Hey, don't look at me. I'm not the one who decided to befriend his arch-nemesis."

I holstered my pistol and wobbled my hand back and forth.

"Arch-nemesis? Naw. Maybe 'staunch antagonist' or 'dedicated rival.' But Crowley was never my arch-anything."

Crowley popped his head back around the corner. "Now, I said. Hurry!"

I sighed and looked at Sabine. "That being said, he's approaching frenemy status, real freaking quick."

17

W e spent the next thirty minutes or so playing hide and go seek with the Grimknife Clan, who came out in force after someone discovered the patrol we'd taken out. Between Crowley's shadow magic and Sabine's glamours, we managed to make it into the castle proper without being found out. But it was touch and go until we exited the dungeon.

The level above the dungeon looked exactly like what you'd expect a medieval castle to look like. Stone walls, vaulted chambers, arched doors, and tapestries everywhere. Plus, it was drafty as all hell.

The castle was much colder than the lower levels, whether from exposure to the elements or the elevation, I couldn't be certain. As soon as we found a decent hiding spot, I dug out my trench and threw it on. After the swamps, mists, and sewers, most of my clothing was soaked. I was soon shivering, even with the trench coat.

Crowley pulled us into an alcove behind a tapestry, where he muttered a short incantation and tapped the wall in an intricate pattern. The wall swung inward, opening the way to a dusty, cobwebbed passage. We ducked inside, and Crowley closed the hidden door behind us.

"Servant's passages and spy ways," he explained. "Hardly used anymore. Mother rarely entertains, and The Dark Druid prefers... alternative means of subsistence."

I shivered and pulled the trench coat tighter around me. "Is he here, Crowley? Do you think we'll run into him?"

The wizard brushed cobwebs off his chest. "I certainly hope not. While you may believe you have unfinished business with him, I am not as delusional. We should avoid him at all costs, else we may end up as corpses for his necromantic experiments."

My teeth started chattering as I spoke. "Y-yeah, well, if I s-see him, it's on."

The wizard pointed at me. "You're obviously freezing. Why don't you cast a warmth spell on yourself, instead of suffering?"

I shrugged. "Don't know that spell."

Crowley's hood turned to Sabine. "Is he serious?"

Sabine rolled her eyes. "He's human, and he sucks at magic. Don't ask me—I have no idea how they train druids these days. But his magical skills are limited to minor cantrips and the like."

Crowley shook his head. It was impossible to see his facial expression, but I could hear the contempt and disbelief in his voice. "I have no idea what Belladonna sees in you."

"You and me both," Sabine said as she crossed her arms.

"H-hey!" I protested.

The fae girl snorted and pointed a finger in my general direction, waving it around like a laser pointer. "Crowley, can you fix this?"

"Of course," he said, as if offended by the mere suggestion that he couldn't.

Crowley muttered a spell and waved a hand at me, and my clothing began to steam as it heated up. Within moments I was dry from head to toe and toasty warm. He stood back and placed his hands on his hips.

"Pretty useless druid, eh, Crowley?" Sabine teased.

"Useless? I would remind you both that I'm a reluctant druid, at best. And before you tell me that I need to learn more magic, let me stop you right there. It's already on the agenda."

Crowley headed down the tunnel. "I honestly do not understand Belladonna's obsession with you. A druid who can't work serious magic? It makes no sense."

I shook a fist at his retreating back. "You'll see how useless I am if we run into Fuamnach!"

Crowley dismissed my comment with a wave, not sparing me another glance.

Sabine chuckled as she walked past. "Oh, stop sulking. It just makes you look small. C'mon, my reluctant druid. The last thing we need is to get separated from Crowley in this castle. I may not completely trust him, but I sure as hell don't like the idea of making it back out of here without him."

Despite her admonishment, I sulked in silence as I followed behind, mostly because they were both right and I knew it. I'd been putting off continuing my studies with Finnegas since Jesse had died, and it had turned out to be a mistake on more than one occasion. Druids were known to be incredibly powerful healers. Maybe if I hadn't put it off, Hemi would still be alive— because I could've saved him.

But now, I'd never know.

If we got out of this mess and made it back to earth, I'd track Finnegas down and finish my training. Or maybe I'd find a way back and study with the Dagda, and get the knowledge from the source. Either way, recent events had shown that I needed to improve my magical abilities. It wasn't just a matter of personal survival; it was a matter of protecting my friends.

And damned if I was going to see another friend die because I couldn't save them.

WE FOLLOWED Crowley through those passageways for an interminable amount of time. He led us down a never-ending procession of winding, narrow corridors, up steep, rough-cut stairways, and through several partially-collapsed tunnels.

After who knew how long, he finally pulled to a stop and held up his fist. He gestured for us to come forward, and we gathered close behind him in the confines of a rough stone passage, barely as wide as my shoulders were broad.

Crowley leaned in and whispered. "Just ahead is the secret entrance to my quarters. There lies the portal, hopefully still hidden from prying eyes. We will not want to tarry there, as the living quarters are all in the same wing of the castle."

"Meaning that your adoptive mother and father might be nearby," I said.

"Just so. Be on your guard, and remain completely silent beyond this point." He pulled his hood up to hide his face deeper in shadow, if that was even possible. "Let's go."

"Should it go without saying that I have a bad feeling about this?" Sabine whispered.

"You and me both," I whispered back. "Just keep your eyes peeled, and if things go sideways, get back to the gateway. Tell Maeve that I'm coming right behind, as soon as the kids are safely through."

"You want me to lie to her?"

"No, because I know you can't. Instead, I want you to assume the best and stick with the plan. As far as you'll know, I might actually be right behind you. And I'm telling you now that if we run into Fuamnach, I intend to take care of business and then meet you back at the gateway."

Sabines mouth twisted in a wry grin. "You're learning, druid."

"I may be slow on the uptake, but eventually I get the punch-line. Now, let's get these items for Maeve and get the hell out of here." I pointed at Crowley's dwindling shadow down the corridor. "After you."

We caught up to Crowley, who was leaning against a section of wall that looked like any other. He had his ear pressed to it, along with both his hands. I glanced at the scars on his hand and winced, turning away before he saw me. I felt bad about how he'd suffered, but in truth, I'd caused none of it. Still, I wondered now how much he blamed me for his current state, and how much he blamed his adoptive parents.

I had a feeling I was about to find which of us was the object of his anger.

The wizard nodded once, then muttered a spell and pressed on the wall. A section of stones pivoted on center, becoming a revolving door of sorts. Beyond, faint light revealed a large bedchamber that contained a four-poster bed, thick fur rugs on the floor, an unlit fireplace, and various pieces of furniture. Bookshelves lined the walls, occupied with various magical texts and tomes. Through an arched doorway, I spied a workshop filled with tables, benches, alchemical equipment, and the like.

Despite the quality of the furnishings, the place was sparsely decorated, and almost Spartan in its character. Based on the wizard's dour personality, I had no doubt that we were entering his living quarters.

"Cozy place," I whispered.

Crowley turned sharply and placed a finger to his lips—or, rather, to his shadowed cowl. He snuck across the room to the laboratory-slash-workshop, and we followed close behind. The shadow wizard slid a bookshelf aside, revealing a large, twisted oval of vines and leaves growing out of the wall. The vegetation seemed to be alive, and moisture clung to the leaves and vines, despite the cool and dry air in the bedchamber and lab.

The wizard placed a hand in the center of the oval, gently touching the bricks of the wall on which it resided. He muttered a spell and the wall shimmered, disappearing into mists that swirled inside the oval of vines and leaves. The smell of rot and swamp gas suddenly filled the room, reminding me of Peg Powler's demesne.

Crowley whispered, almost too low to hear. "This will take us into the treasure room. I will leave the portal open, and if all goes well, it will then transport us to the farthest reaches of the sewers—where we entered from Peg's lands. Hopefully, we can make our escape before Mother can muster her forces to pursue. If we're lucky, Peg will take pity on us and use her powers to delay them in their pursuit."

"That's a lot of 'ifs,'" I whispered back.

"It is the best I can do. Let's go, before we are discovered." He ducked into the portal.

Sabine followed after him, but I grabbed her before she stepped through. "Remember what I said—if we run into Fuamnach, beat feet back through the portal and get the kids out safe. Promise me, Sabine."

"Look, if you think I'm going to leave you to face her alone—"

I gripped her arm, perhaps a little too tightly. "You know what I've lost, what I've suffered because of her. Do you really think I'm going to tuck my tail and run, if I get the chance to confront her? No offense, but you'll only be a distraction. And if I'm to survive a confrontation with Fuamnach, I can't afford to be distracted. As long as I know you're getting the kids home safe, I'll be able to do what needs to be done. Now, promise me you'll do what I asked."

Indecision played across her delicate features. Finally, she nodded. "I promise. But get yourself killed, and I swear I will find someone to resurrect you just so—"

"Just so you can kick my ass." I smiled. "I got it, Sabine."

"So long as we're clear on that." She winked and ducked through the portal.

I HALF EXPECTED to step through that portal and into the torture chambers in the dungeon. Although we hadn't actually seen any torture chambers on our way into the castle, I had no doubt they existed. So, I was mildly surprised when we exited into a huge stone room with arched ceilings. It was filled with gold and gems that glittered in the light cast from torches along the walls.

"What is it with fae having treasure chambers that are straight out of *The Hobbit*?" I asked.

Crowley shushed me. "Keep it down. Mother may have guards in here that are unseen. And touch nothing. Everything is coated in poison."

I stopped myself just as I was about to pick up a ruby the size of a robin's egg. "Thanks for the advance warning there."

"I didn't expect you to stoop to common thievery, Colin," he replied.

"What do you think we're doing by taking the Sword and the Stone?"

"That is not stealing, since technically the Treasures belong to Ireland as much as they do the Tuatha. Besides, the Dagda himself gave you his blessing to carry out this quest."

Sabine tilted her head and smirked. "Well, you can't argue with his logic."

"Semantics," I muttered. "That one ruby could've paid for my college tuition five times over."

"Should we live though this ill-fated mission, I'm sure you'll find other means of paying for your second-class education," the wizard remarked. "Now, follow me. The Treasures are most assuredly in an adjacent chamber."

"Second-class? I worked hard to get accepted to Texas!"

Crowley began walking to a doorway across the room. "If you say so. The Treasures should be in here." He muttered a few syllables, and the door swung open.

"It's not trapped?" Sabine asked.

The wizard stared at the open doorway. "Not that I can tell. I became well-acquainted with Mother's traps and wards during the years I spent here, and I see none."

He crossed his arms and cradled his chin in one hand as he contemplated the problem. I took a moment to look at the doorway and room beyond in the magical spectrum. I might not have had much magic, but I knew how to spot magical traps and wards. As far as I could tell, there were none in the room or on the doorway.

But I could see a sword and a flat, unassuming gray stone sitting on a pedestal in the center of the room.

"I don't see a thing, Crowley. This smells fishy."

"I don't like it either," Sabine remarked.

Crowley remained silent for a minute or more, then scratched his head through his hood. "Well, there's nothing for it. Either we take the items and attempt to escape, or we abandon the mission."

"Not a chance in hell," I said. "You sure there's nothing there?"

"As certain as I can be," he stated.

"Alright, then here goes nothing."

I walked through the door, expecting the ceiling to cave in on me, or to be struck by lightning or a meteor storm or a magic missile attack, or for a pair of stone elementals to spring from the floor and attack.

But instead, nothing happened.

"Huh." I walked to the pedestal and examined the items. They both shone brightly in the magical spectrum, almost blindingly. But again I detected no wards, weaves, or traps on the items or pedestal. So, I took a moment to examine the items more closely.

The blade of the Sword of Nuada was currently inside a plain but finely-crafted scabbard. I leaned in for a closer look at the hilt, which was the only part of the sword that was exposed. It was made from bronze—and was nothing much to look at, to be honest. The handle was wrapped in worn, deteriorating leather; the crossguard was notched and tarnished; the pommel was dented flat in several places, giving it a faceted appearance.

Other than a crude face on one side of the pommel, it otherwise free from embellishment. On further inspection, I realized that the handle, guard, and pommel were crafted to form the shape of a man, with the legs making up the crossguard, and the arms and head the pommel. The sword was shorter than I would have guessed, more the size and length of a gladius than a longsword.

If I hadn't looked at it with my second sight, I'd never have guessed it was one of the most powerful weapons ever crafted by the Tuatha.

I grabbed it off the pedestal, holding my breath.

Nothing happened.

I quickly tucked it into my belt and turned to the Stone of Fál. It looked like any stone you might see in a walkway or garden wall. The stone was free from decoration, mostly square in shape, and no bigger than a melon. It had been cut out of some sort of granite, and worn smooth from centuries of being carried and handled.

Legend had it that the *Lia Fáil*, or Stone of Destiny, stood on the Hill of Tara in County Meath, Ireland. That stone was a four and a half-foot-tall, rough-cut stone obelisk that was definitely *not* the Stone of Destiny. I was pretty sure some fae had placed the stone there as a joke, and started the whole legend about it being the real Stone of Fál.

At any rate, this Stone looked to be the real deal. Supposedly, when the true king of Ireland stood or sat on it, it would respond with a shout, proclaiming the validity of the would-be king's claim.

I leaned in and stared at it, suddenly unsure of myself. Something about it felt off, like the Stone was charged and waiting to be triggered.

"Crowley, you sure there are no traps around this thing?"

"Ninety-eight percent. I would suggest you grab it so we can leave posthaste. Mother may already have been alerted to our presence here."

"Colin, just grab the stupid thing already!" Sabine hissed.

"Well, it's now or never," I said as I grabbed the Stone.

As with the Sword, nothing happened. I stood up straight and wiped the sweat from my forehead.

"Well, that's a relief," I said, as I began to tuck the Stone into my Craneskin Bag.

That's when the Stone of Destiny began wailing in ancient Gaelic at about a hundred and twenty decibels... plenty loud enough to alert the entire castle to our presence.

Shit.

18

"**D**amn it! Turn it off, Colin!"

Both my companions had run inside the room when the Stone had started its shouting fit. Sabine was frantic, looking around in anticipation of Fuamnach's forces swooping down on us.

"I can't! I don't know how!"

"Then stuff it in that damned bag!"

"Oh." I put the Stone in the Bag, and immediately our ears were met with blessed silence.

"By the way, what was it saying?" I asked.

Crowley shook his head again. "Let me get this straight. You're descended from Finn McCool, you studied druidry under his mentor, who is perhaps the greatest druid the world has ever known, and you don't speak Gaelic?"

"Just enough to cast a few minor cantrips." They were both looking at me with their mouths agape. "What? It's not like I needed to learn to speak Gaelic. I mean, who speaks Gaelic anymore, anyway?"

Sabine threw her hands in the air. "Apparently, ancient magical rocks. By the way, it kept saying 'imposter' over and over again."

Crowley scratched his forehead inside his hood. "Hmmm... I suppose we should have anticipated that. But, there's nothing to do for it now. We'd better get moving before we're discovered." He headed out the door for the treasure chamber proper, where our escape portal awaited us.

I heard a woman's sandpaper-and-silk voice echo from outside the smaller treasure room. It was reminiscent of the voice some college girls earned after too many nights spent drinking hard liquor, smoking weed and cigs, and yelling to be heard over loud club music.

"Why, hello, darling. So kind of you to bring the Eye directly to my treasure room. It's almost as though you wanted to save me the trouble of retrieving it."

I pulled Sabine off to one side of the door and peeked around the doorframe. Crowley was frozen in place directly in front of the doorway—whether by fear or magic, I couldn't be certain. I couldn't see around him, but assumed Fuamnach was standing directly across the room from him.

Sabine grabbed my wrist and growled in my ear. "Ugh! I knew we couldn't trust him. He probably led us here knowing that you'd trigger the alarm on the Stone. Bastard!"

I glanced around the corner again. Crowley was still frozen in place.

"I don't think so, Sabine. At least, I don't think he did it intentionally. Look, we don't have time to discuss this. When I step through that door, you glamour yourself with the strongest see-me-not spell you have. When I have her distracted, make a beeline for that portal."

"Colin, damn it—"

"There's no time. Take Crowley with you if you can."

I took a moment to feel for my shifter magic, to see if it was fully charged up again. As far as I could tell, it was. I slipped out of my sneakers, stuffing them into the Bag along with my trench. Then I tossed in my tactical belt so I wouldn't lose it when I shifted, along with my sword, pistol, and the Sword of Nuada.

Fuamnach's voiced echoed once more from the treasure chamber. "You may as well come out. I know you're in there, both of you. Stalling will only delay the inevitable."

I took two deep breaths, then I strolled out from behind Crowley. Fuamnach stood across the room, and she looked nothing like I'd imagined. In my mind's eye, I had expected her to be either monstrously ugly or otherworldly beautiful. She was neither.

The sorceress was attractive in a sort of Claudia Black kind of way, with fair skin, piercing gray eyes, a prominent Romanesque nose, high cheek bones, and full lips. Her face was framed by shoulder-length brown hair that fell in lustrous waves, sufficient to put any L'Oréal spokeswoman to shame. But her strong, masculine jawline and her mouth, set in a permanent sneer, offset these features.

As far her figure went, she looked like she did a lot of obstacle course races or parkour. She was slender and flat-chested, tall at maybe five-ten, with that lean track and field look women got when they did a lot of cross-training. Rather than wearing a long flowing gown like a proper faery sorceress, she bucked convention in black gabardine trousers, sensible black leather boots, and a white funnel-neck cashmere sweater that reeked of entitlement and privilege. She wore a few ivory bangles on one wrist, but was otherwise unadorned with jewelry. As with most fae, she apparently had an aversion to metal.

I took in her appearance in a heartbeat, searing it in my memory. "I've waited a long time for this, Fuamnach."

She looked rather nonplussed by my presence, and stretched languidly against a nearby arched buttress as she watched me walk to the center of the room. There was something familiar in her movements, in the way she held herself and how she looked at me... I just couldn't quite place it.

"Oh, Colin McCool. You have ever been a melodramatic and whiny little bitch. Are you still pining for that trashy little hunter girl?"

I bristled at her tone. "Her name was Jesse, and on her worst day she had more class than you've probably had in your whole miserable existence."

Fuamnach struck a pose, leaning against the arched ceiling support with an almost lazy composure and exuding a smugness that only the ultra-wealthy and ultra-powerful could assume. She flashed me a smile that was pure sugar-sweet flirtation, which played counterpoint to the rattlesnake venom in her eyes.

"Oh, I doubt that entirely. And her worst day was her last, as I understand it. You can't show much class when you're dead, dear."

I held my tongue, promising myself I'd make her pay for that remark.

She paused and looked me up and down, barely wetting her lips with the tip of her tongue. "But you, Colin, you were much too good for her. You have the blood of Tuatha royalty in your veins, and it shows stronger in your genes than any human in generations."

As she spoke, my head began to feel muzzy. At the same time, I became utterly entranced by what she was saying. I was starting to like Fuamnach, and considered that maybe she wasn't as bad as I'd made her out to be.

"We could rule, you and I. You have so much untapped

potential. Finnegas has been holding you back, the fool. He saw a glimpse of what you could become, and it frightened him. Or perhaps he's as jealous of you as he was of Fionn. Regardless of his motivations, he's been keeping you in the dark."

Sabine yelled from somewhere distant. "Colin, no! She's trying to—"

"Quiet, girl!" Fuamnach snapped. And like that, she was.

I wondered if Fuamnach could teach me to do that to Sabine.

All at once, my thoughts were interrupted by an intense pain just behind my eyes, like the onset of a killer migraine. But compared to Fuamnach's voice it was merely a distraction, and one I chose to ignore. All I wanted to do was listen to her speak. I could have listened to her voice for hours on end. It was glorious.

The sorceress walked toward me, her hips swaying with a sinuous grace that made my knees weak and my groin swell. I wanted her. I wanted to worship her. I wanted to bed her and do her bidding, and I couldn't decide which I wanted to do first. For that reason, I secretly hoped they'd be one and the same thing.

The pain in my head grew worse, but I did my best to ignore it.

Fuamnach looked at my eyes, and an expression of concern flashed across her face. Then, she smiled and continued speaking.

"Colin, you might think that I'm the one at fault for the curse that caused you to kill your former girlfriend. However, nothing could be further from the truth. The fact is, Finnegas and the bitch queen both knew about your ríastrad, long before you ever entered that cave to fight the Caoranach."

My head was pounding, but all I wanted to do was hear Fuamnach speak. She sauntered up to me, brushing my cheek with her hand, then running it down my chest. It was exhilarating, feeling her this close to me. Yet, for some reason, I couldn't respond. I realized it was because she didn't want me to respond, not yet. I accepted that as a reflection of her will, and I was okay with it.

"You see, Colin, you were born with Cú Chulainn's curse, which was handed down to him from his half-Formorian father, Lugh. It's a genetic trait. I know something of such things, as I have long had an interest in the effects of magic on human genetics. It's quite fascinating, really, what you can do by changing a chromosome here, and adding a DNA strand there. Science can't make such changes—not easily, not yet. But I've had centuries to experiment on your kind, and I've achieved such wondrous results."

I was certain her work would be fascinating, and wondered how I might help her in her experiments. A sharp pain in my head caused me to wince, and Fuamnach flinched, almost imperceptibly. I kept my eyes on her, because I was enraptured by her presence. She continued to talk as she walked a slow circle around me.

"Finnegas, the fool, knew that eventually your curse would show itself. What he didn't realize was just how strongly it had expressed itself in your particular genetic make-up. And when you shifted that first, glorious time in your fight with the Caoranach, he was entirely unprepared for your complete loss of control."

My head was throbbing now—and hot, as if I was running a fever. Sweat dribbled down my forehead and into my eyes. I forced myself to concentrate on what Fuamnach was saying. The sorceress ran a finger over my shoulder as she came around to face me, then leaned close to whisper in my ear.

"What I'm saying, Colin, is that it wasn't my fault that you shifted. I never cursed you—in fact, I was unaware of your presence until you began dogging my adoptive son's footsteps. And it wasn't your fault, either. It was your mentor's fault, Finnegas. He knew you had inherited the curse of the ríastrad, and he knew if you were hard-pressed, you'd shift into that warped, beautiful, deadly other form of yours.

"He put you and Jesse in that cave with the Caoranach. He told you she'd been weakened, that she couldn't transform into her more powerful, dragoness form. He wanted to trigger your warp spasm, so he could use you as a weapon.

"Colin, Finnegas is the person responsible for Jesse's death." She placed her hands on either side of my face, and despite the searing pain in my head, I gazed deeply into her eyes. "Join me, and we'll rule together. We'll destroy Finnegas, and I'll make certain no one lies to you or hurts you, ever again."

I wanted to believe her. I needed to believe her, because she wanted me to do so. I opened my mouth to say yes, to agree to join her and serve her. To make my will subject to hers, forevermore.

But before I could speak, pain exploded behind my eyes. It was a searing, intense pain, the likes of which I'd never experienced. I shut my eyes, and heard a scream that was filled with shock, terror, and frustration. That scream wailed on and on, and as it did it deepened into a roar.

That's when I realized the scream was my own. I was the one screaming, because my head was on fire with burning, agonizing pain. Unable to think, unable to speak or form clear thoughts, I did the one thing that was a reflex for me in times of stress.

I shifted.

-I SEE *you're once more in full control of your faculties. Welcome back, Colin.-*

The Eye was speaking inside my head, which was still throbbing. It felt like someone had boiled my brains from the inside out.

What did you do to me? I asked. *That hurt like hell.*

-I apologize, but it was the only way to break the spell Fuamnach was casting over you. I began phase shifting from the alternate dimension where I normally reside, into this one. I couldn't fully phase into existence here, for fear of killing you. But a partial phase was enough to force you to shift into your Fomorian form. Shifting allowed you to shake off the effects of her spell.-

Let me get this straight... you nearly fried my brain in order to save my bacon?

-Yes.-

Good work. Now, let's fry this bitch too.

-Gladly. It is my life's purpose to do so.-

I looked around for her, but she was gone. *Shit!* Crowley and Sabine were more or less where they'd been when I'd confronted Fuamnach. Both appeared to be shaking off the effects of her spell.

"Where'd that fucking coward go?" I yelled.

-It appears she fled when she saw you shift. There are few things the Tuatha Dé Danann fear, and I am one of them.-

"Well, I doubt she's going to let us just prance right out of here with the Treasures, so I suggest we get going. Can you blast us a way out of here without blinding me?"

-Negative. In your current, inferior half-Fomorian form, the energies necessary to burn through solid stone will boil your eyes in their sockets.-

"I hate it when she does that, honestly I do." Crowley leaned over, hands on his knees. He looked up at me and raised a very shaky hand. "I'm sorry, Colin—were you speaking to me?"

Sabine rubbed her forehead with the palm of her hand. "No, Crowley. He's talking to that Eye thing inside his head. Sorry I doubted you, by the way."

"Don't mention it," he said as he stood up straighter. "We should get going."

"Good thinking." I searched the room for our planned exit. "Crowley, where's the portal?"

His hood swiveled back and forth. "Damn her! She must have closed it before she left."

Fuamnach's disembodied voice echoed inside the treasure chamber. "Indeed, I did. Nothing goes on inside my home without my knowledge, son. Colin, it's such a shame we couldn't come to some sort of arrangement. I've had my eye on you for quite some time, although the real Siobhan doesn't quite share my attraction to you."

In an instant, it all came together. Fuamnach's mannerisms, her haughty air, the way she spoke... it was classic Siobhan. At least, the Siobhan I knew.

"How long were you posing as her?" I asked.

"Oh, on and off for some time now," she replied. "I had to play it safe, in order to avoid arousing Maeve's suspicions. Siobhan's mind was pliable enough for me to leave her in place during my absences, although eventually Maeve figured it out. Speaking of whom, you really shouldn't trust her, you know. Maeve isn't even her real name. But that's all a moot point now, considering your current precipitous situation."

I whispered sidebar-style to Crowley. "Can you find us a way out of here?"

"Oh, there's no escape, dear. Didn't Crowley tell you? The only way in and out of that room is via magical portal."

Sabine drew her sword and shouted her response. "Why don't you come back and face us, bitch? Scared?"

"Hardly, child. I intend to keep throwing my pets at you until you're overwhelmed, or until Colin tires and shifts back into his human form. At which point I'll place you all under my spell again, remove the Eye and the Treasures from Colin's possession, and use them to wrest control of the gateway from Maeve. Once I'm in possession of her demesne, I'll use it to stage attacks on the other supernatural territories... at least, those who haven't made alliances with me."

"Crowley, any ideas?" I asked.

"Unfortunately, no. Fuamnach speaks the truth. This room is inescapable except via portal."

I looked around the place, and realized for the first time that there were no doors save the one that led to the smaller chamber. "Fuck it, then. I'm going to blast us a way out of here."

I was about to go Cyclops on a nearby wall when Sabine grabbed my arm. "Um, Colin? You might want to hold off on that plan. Fuamnach's pets have arrived, and they don't look friendly."

19

I spun around, and my jaw hit the floor.

"What the actual hell are those?"

Three portals had opened around the room at three of the four cardinal directions, each equidistant from us and each other. A motley assortment of incredibly grotesque creatures emerged from them.

Some looked similar to me in my current Fomorian form—humanoid, but deformed and twisted. Others looked like the Creature from the Black Lagoon, with dark scaly skin, webbed feet and hands, and spiny fins running down their backs. There were a couple of fachen—the one-legged, single-armed giants from Irish legend—and several anthropomorphic spider-like creatures that crawled on their bellies. Others resembled trolls or goblins, with rubbery, hairless skin, black eyes, and fingers that ended in long, sharp claws. There were men with canine heads, tiny red imps, and more, in a seemingly endless variety of freaks and aberrations.

Fuamnach's voice echoed around us. "As I mentioned earlier, I've long had a penchant for using magic to enhance the human physiology. You'd be amazed at what traits are lying dormant, just under the surface and waiting for the right magical nudge to emerge.

"And, Colin, you might be surprised to find that you're not the only human with latent Fomorian genes in their genetic make-up. Oh, certainly none of my creations are quite as majestic as you. However, they are perfectly suited to serve as shock troops for our impending attack on Maeve's gateway."

Well, this blows, I thought, mentally scrambling for a way out of the situation.

I turned to Crowley and Sabine. "Here's the plan. Crowley, you do whatever it takes to keep one of those portals open. Sabine, you watch his back, and I'll clear a path. As soon as I do, head through that portal. I'll be right behind you, making sure nothing follows us. Go!"

Eye, get ready to burn us a path.

Crowley began chanting and making arcane gestures with his hands. Several strands of shadow spun into being around him and whipped across the room to the nearest portal. The wizard's shadow arms grasped the edges of the portal like clawed tentacles, holding it open as the other portals snapped shut.

Alright, Eye. You cut loose, and let's sweep a path through this rabble.

-On your command.-

Now!

I opened my eyes wide, directing the Eye's magic heat vision at Fuamnach's freaks. My eyesight lasted long enough for me to see the first creature cut in two—a fachen that had stood out from the crowd due to its sheer size. Then, they charged us all at once, and I began sweeping my head left and right as my vision faded to black.

The pain I felt as my eyes boiled and burst in their sockets was excruciating, but I kept it up. The Eye told me where to point, and I did as it suggested.

-*That has disposed of approximately fifty percent of the Fomorian-human hybrids Fuamnach portaled into the chamber with us. The rest are sufficiently cowed to allow for our escape.*-

I felt someone grab my hand as Sabine shouted in my ear. "That's enough, Colin. C'mon, Crowley can't hold that thing open much longer."

I felt her pulling on my hand, and followed her as best I could, stumbling over what I assumed were corpses and body parts.

"Stop," Sabine commanded. "Now, pick your foot up and step forward."

"Where?" I was worried I'd step wrong and lose a foot; clumsiness and portals didn't mix. The edges of magical portals were notoriously unstable, and prone to clipping stray pieces of clothing or even limbs off, if you were so unlucky. One magician was said to have met his demise when he stepped through a portal and slipped. He fell backward with his head sticking out the portal, and *snikt*—instant headless magician.

"Right there, you clown!"

"Directions, Sabine! I'm blind right now, if you hadn't noticed."

Crowley's spoke from nearby, his voice strained. "I can't hold this open much longer, and Mother's shock troops are getting restless!"

"Oh, you big baby." She shoved me from behind, and I tumbled forward. Concerned that I might clip the edges of the portal, I turned my fall into an awkward shoulder roll, coming to a stop in a heap on the ground. I had no idea where I was, but the floor was cold, damp, and hard.

I heard light footsteps next to me, and Sabine's voice. "Crowley, get your ass in gear already!"

"Coming," he said, although his voice was muffled. I heard more footsteps, followed by the sound of a portal closing with a soft pop.

"Where are we?" I asked.

"Hmm... it appears we're in a dungeon of some kind. Perhaps a section I haven't seen before."

"I thought you knew this place like the back of your hand?"

"The parts I was allowed to see, yes. This place is massive, if you hadn't noticed. And Fuamnach hid much of her work from me. I had no idea she was building an army."

"Those things—they used to be human children, didn't they?" I asked as I sat up.

Crowley's voice was solemn. "I believe so, yes."

"Damn." I supposed there was no saving them, but knowing that didn't do much to blunt the guilt I felt at slaughtering them. They were victims, too.

"This is all fascinating," Sabine said. "But I think the more important question is whether or not Crowley knows a way out of here."

"Well, I haven't been to this section of the dungeons, but they're bound to be connected to the rest of the tunnels under the palace. If we just keep working our way to the lower levels, eventually we'll run into a section that's familiar to me."

"Down it is, then," the fae girl said. "Colin, how are your eyes?"

"I'll get a little eyesight back in a few minutes. Until then, I'm going to need some help."

"Alright. Crowley, you navigate, and I'll lead Mr. Magoo over here."

"Huh?" The confusion in the wizard's voice was evident.

"Damn, you *were* deprived as a child." I stood up and held out my hand. "Alright, Sabine... lead the way."

I MANAGED to stay in my Fomorian form long enough to restore part of my eyesight. Things were still blurry, but it was better than complete blindness. We found our way down to the sewers and made a beeline for the exit, with Fuamnach's freak army in hot pursuit.

We exited the sewer tunnels through the grated opening at the foot of the cliff, at the same spot we'd entered them hours before. Or perhaps it had been days ago—time was always a fluid thing here in Underhill. Crowley collapsed a few passages behind us as we fled, but he said our pursuers would just find another way around.

"We have to make it to Peg Powler's lands," he said. "She'll take any invasion of her demesne by Fuamnach's troops as a direct affront, and act accordingly."

"I thought Peg worked for Fuamnach," I said.

"Not quite. It's more like they have a truce. Fuamnach is certainly the more ancient and powerful of the two, but make no mistake, Peg is not to be trifled with in her own lands."

"And you think she'll grant us safe passage?" Sabine asked.

"We had a deal," the wizard said simply. "Plus, she doesn't care for Mother much."

"You keep calling Fuamnach that, but it doesn't seem like she was much of a mother to you," I remarked.

"It's habit, and nothing more," he said. "And perhaps one I should learn to break soon, even though she was the closest thing I had to a parent."

"Not the Dark Druid?"

"No, never him. He was my teacher, but his teaching methods were cruel and unforgiving. I never enjoyed my time with him, and would welcome his passing."

"Sounds like it sucked for you as a kid," Sabine said.

"It was unpleasant." Crowley's answer was short, his voice sharp. It was obvious he wanted to change the subject.

"I hear someone behind us—lots of someones," I said. It sounded like Fuamnach's freaks had found a way around the cave-ins.

"Come, it's not far now," Crowley said.

I was still stumbling around with blurry vision, and Sabine had to help me down the trail. But even with partial eyesight, I could see that the path we'd taken from Peg's island was gone.

"Ah, hell," I muttered. "Looks like we got double-crossed."

Crowley tsked. "Not likely. Just wait."

"We don't have time, Crowley," Sabine said. "Those things are right behind us, and I doubt that Colin can shift yet."

"You doubt right," I said. "I need more time to recharge—maybe a half-hour or so."

Crowley held up a hand. "Sshh. Listen."

I heard the hoots and strange catcalls of Fuamnach's experiments in the distance, but not much else. They'd obviously picked up our trail, and were headed our way.

"All I hear is the crazies behind us. What are we listening for, Crowley?"

He pointed out across the lake. "That."

I strained to see what he was pointing at, but couldn't quite make it out. All I saw was a huge *something* rising up from the water a hundred yards distant. It easily rose twenty-five feet from the water, and let out a mighty foghorn roar.

"What the hell is that thing?" I asked.

Sabine grabbed my arm. "Um, Colin? That's a cross between a dragon and a turtle, and it's headed this way."

"Crowley, is that Peg's pet turtle? Because I don't remember it being that big."

"It's our ride," Crowley said. "Apparently, Peg has been busy in our absence. I wondered what she wanted the Dagda's broth for—now it's quite obvious."

"Don't tell me... Miracle-Gro for turtles?"

"Indeed," he said, the admiration in his voice evident. "The beast is easily three times as large now."

"And it's a dragon," Sabine said. "Sort of."

"As long as it gets us across this lake without eating us, and before Fuamnach's experiments get here." The huge blurry outline got more distinct as it drew closer to shore. Soon, it towered over us. If I had to guess, its shell was now easily the length of a football field. Adding the tail and head, it was half-again as long.

It looked like Fuamnach wasn't the only one who could grow monsters.

A huge wake preceded the dragon-turtle as it neared the strip of shoreline where we stood. The wave splashed up over the edge of the lake, forcing us to step back several feet to avoid getting soaked. The monster turned away from us as it reached the shore, slapping its tail down on dry land with a *whoomp* that shook the earth.

"I believe that's our cue to get on," Crowley said.

Sabine glanced over her shoulder. "And just in time—run!"

SEVERAL MURKY, indistinct forms of various colors and sizes ran from the cover of the swamp vegetation around the clearing behind us. With no choice but to take Sabine's advice, I ran toward the huge blurry mound ahead. Crowley beat us there, and was climbing up the creature's shell by the time we reached the tail. Sabine climbed up in front of me and pulled me up, and once I was on the tail it was just a matter of scrambling higher to reach the apex of the turtle's back.

Within moments, all three of us were safely nestled in the valley-like depressions between the protective plates of the dragon-turtle's carapace. The beast swept its tail across the shore, knocking a half-dozen of Fuamnach's creatures into the swampy lake. Based on the screams and splashes, it appeared that the dragon-turtle's smaller siblings were making short work of the unlucky creatures who had been swept into the lake's murky depths.

Even so, some of Fuamnach's troops seemed determined to continue their pursuit. As we made our way across the lake, I heard the distinct sounds of falling trees.

"Sabine, what's happening?"

"It looks like Fuamnach's giants are building a raft."

"Peachy," I muttered.

"Not for long, I think." Crowley stood nearby, leaning on a spiny protuberance sticking out of the dragon-turtle's shell. "Watch."

The dragon-turtle craned its neck around to face the creatures along the shore. Its head was huge, and although I couldn't see very well, I was close enough to witness it belch a yellow-green cone of gas at Fuamnach's troops. The gas enveloped the shoreline completely, followed by a chorus of choking coughs and screams.

"Did what I think just happened, really happen?" I asked.

"Wow," Sabine said. "Yeah, most definitely. Poison breath weapon for the win, and it looks like Peg's dragon-turtle rolled a twenty. I can't see the results because the fog is still obscuring the view, but I doubt there's much left of Fuamnach's shock troops."

"At least, not the ones pursuing us," Crowley stated. "She will have many more in reserve. Fuamnach has spent centuries planning this, and likely has thousands of those creatures ready to assault Maeve's demesne."

I leaned back against the dragon-turtle's shell, and considered the potential repercussions. "Think they could make it past her guardians?"

"In great numbers, yes—and I believe that's the point."

"They'd still have to make it out of Maeve's house," Sabine countered. "And I'm pretty sure that's no mean feat."

I resisted the urge to rub my eyes. They always itched before they were fully healed. "Still, I don't want to run into those things on our way out of Underhill. And I sure don't want them anywhere near the children. Crowley, what's the quickest way back to the summer lands from here?"

"Most definitely by portal. Peg can do it, but knowing our predicament, she will bargain hard with us."

"Wait a minute," Sabine said. "Can't Fuamnach just portal her troops to the gateway back to earth?"

Crowley shook his head. "No, she can't. The Dagda controls those lands, and he'd simply close the portals as she opened them. She'll be forced to march her troops through his lands, forcing a confrontation with the other Tuatha."

"The Dagda told me that The Morrigan was preparing to wage war against Fuamnach," I said. "Maybe that's what she's doing, preventing Fuamnach from marching her creatures to the portal."

Sabine scratched her leg, peeling something dark and squirmy away from her skin and tossing it into the water. "It sounds like we're going to end up in the middle of a war, if we don't get back to earth soon. And you know Fuamnach is going to pull out all the stops to keep you from getting back with the Treasures."

I turned to the shadow wizard. "Crowley, what do you think it'll cost us to get Peg's help?"

"You needn't concern yourself with that. I've a feeling she'll want another helping of the Cauldron's brew, to grow more of these dragon-turtles. However, she may also try to convince you to give up one of the Treasures. No matter what, do not yield to her demands. Eventually, she'll cave and settle for lesser recompense."

"Good to know. Sabine, once we get back, you know the drill. You get the kids through, convince Maeve to send them somewhere safe, and then come back and get me."

Sabine's voice was low and strained as she replied. "I hope you're not thinking of double-crossing her, Colin. It would be a mistake."

"Trust me, I have a plan."

"And that's what worries me," she said.

20

Peg's price for providing a portal back to the summer lands was three bowls of the Dagda's magic stew, plus a promise of a future favor from each of us. It took us quite a while to hammer out all the caveats and stipulations, details that would ensure none of us would be forced to act against our own interests in fulfilling the bargain. Still, I was uneasy with the deal we'd agreed to.

After the pact had been made, Peg extended one gnarled, algae-ridden hand from behind the burlap drapes that covered the door to her shack. I realized she'd never revealed herself to us, the whole time I'd been in her presence. Crowley said she merely valued her privacy, but I personally suspected she was ashamed of her appearance.

Legend had it that she'd once been a beautiful fae maiden who was spurned by a lover. Overcome by grief and the bitter need for vengeance, she either drowned herself and came back as a water hag, or she became that way over time. Regardless of the validity of any origin story, I for one was glad we didn't have to see her face, because she was supposed to be hideous.

Peg pointed behind us. "Your way has been made. Go now, away from here, and remember our pact."

I looked to where she pointed, and there stood a roughly man-sized oval of vines. The space between the vines shimmered, and soon we were looking at the hillside path that led to the Dagda's farm.

"Right, will do," I said with a wave as I headed for the portal. "Have fun growing your giant swamp kaiju!"

Peg's shadow faded into the dark depths of her hut. After she was gone, Sabine punched me in the arm.

"It's not smart to provoke powerful fae," she whispered.

"What? I'm just showing my support for her hobby. I mean, what else does she have to do out here in the swamp, with no people to drown and eat?"

Sabine leaned in and hissed at me. "Don't give her any ideas!"

"Alright, already. Sheesh, I was just trying to lighten the mood. Don't have a cow."

In truth, I knew I was provoking Peg, and I didn't care. I'd been feeling a bit reckless since we'd lost Hemi, and felt the urge to take it out on someone, anyone. I wanted to break down and sob, or find a bunch of Fuamnach's stooges and rip through them like tissue paper. Or maybe I'd use the Eye's powers to melt the sorceress' castle to slag. Unfortunately, this was no time for me to have an emotional breakdown, because I had children to save.

Colin the savior. Right.

I still had a mission, and I was still determined to complete it, no matter how Hemi's death had affected me. And despite the self-pity and guilt I felt, I did have one saving grace left, one ace in the hole I'd yet to play. If events worked out as I'd planned, I'd avenge what the fae had done to Jesse, Hemi, the children —everyone.

Sure, it might just make me the most hated man in the supernatural underworld. But fuck it, I could live with that. I just needed to make sure the children were safe before I went through with it.

That was, if we could beat Fuamnach to the gateway.

One thing at a time, Colin. I realized Sabine was talking to me, and I snapped back to the present.

"What was that you were saying?"

"I said, we'd better get going before Peg changes her mind. C'mon, let's get out of here."

"Right behind you." Crowley stepped through the portal, and Sabine followed right after. I paused before stepping through and turned back toward the hut.

"In all seriousness, I hope you're done with drowning children. Because if I hear word that Peg Powler has harmed one hair on a child's head, I'll come back for you. And that visit won't be friendly."

The hag's laughter drifted from the shack. "Oh, you'll be back someday, druid. I can assure you of that."

WE STEPPED through the portal and into a somewhat chaotic situation. Fae soldiers were marching from the Dagda's farm toward the winter lands. From our perch on the hill above, I counted thousands. They trampled his fields as they passed, a sign that there was no time to waste. I doubted that the Dagda would sacrifice his crops without good reason.

We shared a look and ran down the hill to the farm. The Dagda was sitting in front of his cottage whittling on a large stick, his war club leaning against the bench beside him.

"How'd things go with Fuamnach?" he asked.

"Well," I replied, "we have the Treasures."

He continued whittling his stick. "But not without trading some of my broth to the hag, I see. Probably for the best. She'll be a thorn in Fuamnach's side now, that's for sure."

"It looks like you've been busy, too," I remarked. "Where'd all those soldiers come from?"

He held up his stick, eyeing it down its length and shaving it here and there to true it. From what I could tell, he was carving a flute. "Oh, them? Conscripts, every last one. They live in my lands, so they do my bidding. They'll hold Fuamnach's menagerie off until you get through the portal safely."

He stood and set his knife and stick down on the bench. Then, he picked up his club and swung it over his shoulder. "Now, we'd best be going. I've sent the children on ahead with the troll, the wisp, the wyvern, and your friend's body."

I nodded and swallowed hard. "You couldn't bring him back, then."

He rested a massive hand on my shoulder. "I'm genuinely sorry about that. I'd do it if I could, but his life force is not mine to command. The best I could do was to mend his body whole again and preserve it, so you can present him to his family with dignity."

"Th—I mean, that was kind of you."

He patted my shoulder and smiled kindly, but there was sadness in his eyes. "Wish I could do more, lad, I honestly do. At least I can escort you to the gateway. You'll get there faster that way, long before Fuamnach arrives with her army. Follow me."

The Dagda walked around the corner of his cottage without looking to see if we followed. Crowley and Sabine both looked at me.

"Don't worry, we can trust him," I said. "He's not about to let me die, because I think he has plans for me—just don't ask me what, because I haven't a clue. We'd better hurry, though. I don't think he's the type that's accustomed to waiting on humans."

Crowley remained silent. Sabine extended an arm as she bowed sarcastically. "Well, it's your shit-show," she said. "Lead the way."

Oh, you have no idea, I thought as I ran after the Dagda.

———

BEHIND THE COTTAGE was a small yard where child-sized chickens scratched in the dirt, pulling worms as big as snakes from the ground and gobbling them up. A split-rail fence bordered the yard, interrupted by a gate directly across from us. There was no sign of the Dagda, but the gate stood open, so we went through it to the narrow dirt path beyond. It meandered through a stretch of the giant mushroom forest that hadn't been visible from the front of the cottage.

Or, it simply hadn't been there before. I had learned to not trust my eyes here in Underhill, because nothing made sense under the traditional laws of physics in this realm. I set the weirdness of it all aside and hurried down the trail after the Dagda. I'd catch glimpses of him ahead at times—around a bend in the trail ahead, or disappearing behind a giant mushroom stalk. But no matter how hard I ran, I could never catch up to him.

On the way, I pondered what Fuamnach had said while she'd been enchanting me. Two things bothered me about it all. The first was that it made sense, and the second was that fae couldn't lie. I wondered if that rule extended to the Tuatha, since the fae were their offspring. If so, it meant that everything Fuamnach had said was true.

Could Finnegas and Maeve really have known I was born with Cú Chulainn's curse? That at some point, some stressor or danger would trigger it, making me a danger to the people around me? What did that say about Finnegas? Had he been using me all along, and had he sacrificed Jesse on purpose?

I doubted it. He'd loved Jesse, almost as much as I had. He must not have known I'd lose control in that manner. But what about Maeve's knowledge of my ríastrad? Had she and Finnegas been working together, preparing me so they could use me as some sort of weapon? If so, why had Finnegas warned me so many times not to trust her? Had they parted on unfriendly terms?

So many questions, and few answers to any of them. The only thing I did know was that I'd been used, badly—and mostly by the fae. I'd grown tired of being a pawn over these last few months, and now it was time to stop being a pawn and start being a player.

And to do that, I had to flip the script and turn the entire game on its head.

Lugh's plan was my best bet to get out from under Maeve's thumb *and* get back at Fuamnach. Now, it was just a matter of keeping Maeve in the dark, in order to get the kids safely away before I went through with it.

———

IT DIDN'T TAKE LONG for us to get from the Dagda's cottage to the portal. It was impossible to know how much time had actually passed, but it felt like we'd only walked a few miles at most. We emerged from the mushroom forest almost right at the cleft in the hill where the gateway was located. The Dagda was already waiting there for us, crawling on his hands and knees while six children rode him like a pony.

I looked at Sabine. "Told you we could trust him."

She sneered and rolled her eyes. "I'm fae, Colin. Believe me when I say that you can't trust any of us."

"Not even you?"

She opened her mouth as if to respond, then clamped her lips shut and looked away. I decided to leave it alone. I'd known all along that Sabine was working for Maeve on this mission. Soon, I'd find out where her loyalties resided.

The clearing in front of the gateway was filled with children, some looking anxious while others chattered with obvious excitement at the prospect of being returned to their families. Guts and Ollie had positioned themselves between the children and the forest. While Guts kept an eye out for potential threats, Ollie kept the children corralled near the gateway.

Jack was nowhere to be seen.

"Anyone seen the wisp?" I yelled over the din. All I got in response were shrugs and head shakes. "Fine, he can find his own way back. Let's start getting everyone ready to go. Sabine, you know what to do. Guts, I need you to get Hemi's body back safely. Wherever the kids go, you follow."

"I'll stay with you," Crowley said. "I'm less likely to be turned into a toad if I remain in your presence."

"Makes sense." I got the Dagda's attention and pointed at the arch. "Can you fire that thing up?"

He signaled to the children that the pony rides were over, which elicited a chorus of protests. The Dagda stood and grabbed his club. "I can, and will."

The gateway opened with a sound like rushing wind. I noted that the Dagda didn't need to be in contact with it, nor did he need to cast a spell to open it. It appeared that he had simply wished it to open, and it had.

"I'll take up a watch with the wyvern while you get the children through the portal," he said. The huge old man walked among the children, saying goodbye to some and admonishing others as he passed.

"Sabine, it's time," I said. She got the children lined up, while

Guts hefted Hemi's shrouded body over his shoulder. The troll led the way through the portal, with the children following him in single file. Sabine and I helped keep them organized, encouraging them to stay on the path and to keep their eyes on the child ahead of them.

Once the last child had walked through, Sabine and I paused at the gateway.

"Remember what I said, Sabine. Tell Maeve that I'll come through with the Treasures only after the children are safe."

"I hope you know what you're doing," she said.

I glanced at the Dagda, who stood watch with Crowley's wyvern. "I do. Now, get going. The longer you're gone, the more time Fuamnach has to show her face and screw things up. Go!" I shooed her through the portal.

"Now what?" Crowley asked.

"Now, we wa—" My response cut short as something knocked me off my feet. I fell in a tumble of arms and legs, grappling with an invisible opponent. I started throwing punches indiscriminately, connecting with a few, but getting the worst of the exchange. An invisible punch or kick stunned me, and I felt the strap of my Craneskin Bag being pulled over my head.

"I'll take that, thank you," Jack's voice whispered in my ear. I struggled to grab at my Bag, but he'd clipped me hard, giving me a hell of a rattling. The little fucker was a lot stronger than he looked. I watched as the Bag floated toward the portal with the Treasures.

A wall of shadow coalesced in front of the portal, blocking the wisp's path. "Are we really going to do this, wizard?" the wisp asked.

Crowley stepped out from his shadow barrier. "Yes, we are."

Shadow tentacles whipped out from Crowley's body in every direction, lashing at the seemingly empty air where the Bag floated. The shadowy arms wrapped tightly around something unseen, trapping it in place, and Jack's form shimmered into existence.

"Have it your way, then," Jack said. He didn't even bother to struggle against his bonds, and instead transformed into his wisp form with a bright flash of light. Crowley shied away, covering his eyes with his arm, but he didn't let go. Instead, it appeared as though the shadow wizard's tentacles split, multiplying into dozens of thinner strands that wrapped the wisp in a sphere of shadow. Sickly green light shone from within the sphere, piercing the cage in places as the ball of light expanded.

"Colin, I don't know how much longer I can hold him. If you're going to do something, do it now!"

I stumbled to my feet, spinning through my mental Rolodex of options, most of which involved pulling some magic trick or weapon from my Craneskin Bag. I staggered over to the wisp just as several more of Crowley's shadow strands snapped. The cage was getting weaker, and Crowley had fallen to one knee under the strain.

"I wonder what this will do," I said as I pulled my Glock and emptied the magazine, firing through one of the gaps in Crowley's shadow sphere. With every round I fired, the wisp's light became weaker, until it faded to a dim glow. I drew my sword and plunged it through the center of the ball of light, pinning it to the ground.

A bright blast of pale green light and energy burst from the wisp, throwing me on my ass and temporarily blinding me. I blinked several times until my vision returned. When it did, Jack was lying flat on his back in his human form, with my sword pinning him to the ground through his breastbone.

He coughed blood and looked over at me as I got to my feet. "You can't kill me, you know. Ol' Nick made certain of that."

"Maybe," I said. "But by the time you get that sword out of your chest, we'll be long gone." I snagged my Bag from the ground next to him and kicked him in the jaw to knock him unconscious.

Crowley was leaning against the rock wall nearby. "You alright?"

He nodded. "Just a little bruised, is all."

"Well, you saved my bacon again. I'm going to owe you some beers when we get back to earth." I gave him a hand and pulled him until he was standing up straight.

At that moment, Sabine stuck her head out of the portal. "If you two are done cementing your bromance, you might want to get a move on. The queen is waiting for Colin to show up with the Treasures, and she's not happy about it."

21

"Are the kids safe, Sabine?"

She walked out of the portal and stood in front of us, arms crossed.

"Safe as houses. Maeve contacted Detective Klein while we were gone, and had her waiting at a transition center where the children will be processed and returned to their parents. Maeve's healer is looking them over and mind-wiping them as we speak."

I exhaled and felt some of the tension leave my shoulders and neck. "Alright. You and Crowley go through before me and tell Maeve she's to portal you out of her house. Tell her if I see you there when I come through the portal, I'll turn right back around and give the Treasures to the Dagda."

"Colin, I don't think she'll go for that."

"Just do it. And tell her I'll be along shortly."

Sabine shook her head. "Fine. But when she turns you into a lampshade for her parlor, don't come crying to me. C'mon, Crowley. Let's leave the great hero be so he can face his doom alone."

Sabine walked back through the portal without another

word. Crowley ran to his wyvern, whispering words in his ear that only the wyvern could hear. The beast bellowed a piteous cry, and it nuzzled its master tenderly.

"I'll take care of him, don't you worry," the Dagda said.

Crowley nodded and patted the creature one last time, then ran toward the gateway. The wizard paused at the archway and pulled his hood back, again revealing the destruction that the Eye had caused. Half of his face was horribly disfigured and one eye wept constantly, probably because his eyelid on that side wouldn't fully close. His ear had melted off, leaving him with a small outcropping of cartilage and scars where it should've been. He was partially bald on that side of his head, and his mouth was pulled in a permanent rictus of pain.

"If you doubt that I am on your side, you have only to look at how my adoptive parents left me to assuage your fears. Either one of them could have easily healed me of my wounds, but instead, they left me this way to suffer the regret of my failure. I don't know what you have planned, but if you wish me to stand by your side when you face Maeve, I will."

"That... that won't be necessary, Crowley. I appreciate the sentiment, and I honestly don't doubt your sincerity. But I have to do this on my own."

He cleared his throat and nodded. "Then let's hope she doesn't turn me into a frog when I emerge from the portal. If you happen to see a toad sitting on the floor when you come through, do me a favor and put it in your pocket, just in case."

The wizard snapped his hood back up and ducked through the gateway before I could reply.

"A joke from Crowley. Wonders never cease."

I looked to my left and saw that the Dagda stood at my side. I was sure he hadn't been there a moment before. For a giant, he was damned stealthy.

"Are you ready to act on Lugh's plan?" he asked.

I took a few seconds to mentally and physically prepare myself and nodded.

"Yeah, I'm ready. I might be tough to kill when I shift, but there's no way I could take out Fuamnach or Maeve, even in my shifted form. In a fair fight, they'd squash me like a fire ant at an exterminator's convention. Naw, I have to settle the score and clear the board. This is the only way to do it."

"You need more training. Don't be too hard on Finnegas; you'll need his guidance soon. And when you return, speak to the trickster, the one who calls himself Click. He's no friend of Maeve's, and he's not beholden to her will. Tell him the Dagda sent you."

"Just what am I supposed to talk to him about? That guy kind of scares me, by the way. He's way too powerful, and the last thing I need is another ancient fae stirring things up in my life."

The Dagda chuckled. "Who said he was fae? Now, go. Maeve's anger will boil over if you tarry any longer. And when you're surrounded by enemies on all sides, without an ally to turn to or a place to rest your head, plant the acorn I gave you."

"Um, alright. But what does it do?"

The old Tuatha winked. "You'll see."

Then he pushed me through the gateway.

As soon as I realized what the Dagda was doing, I reached a hand underneath my tattered trench coat and inside my Crane-skin Bag. When I emerged from the gateway, Maeve was no more than a few feet in front of me, arms crossed and brow furrowed. She'd shed her human disguise, and was floating a few inches off the ground with her back to the misty pathway beyond. Fae magic and power pulsed off her in waves, buffeting me with such force that it shook me down to my bones.

And if I had any doubts as to how pissed she was, she was flanked by a half-dozen fae hunters, dressed in leather armor with bows drawn... and pointed at me.

"Hiya, Maeve. Nice to see you, too." I gestured at the fae death squad. "Don't you think the guys with the bows are overkill, maybe just a wee bit?"

She frowned, an expression that was altogether out of place on a face that beautiful. I'd only seen her in full-on faery queen mode once before, when I'd showed up drunk at her house throwing insults. She was even more frightening in her beauty at the moment, radiant with magic and barely restrained anger, golden hair flowing out from her like a great billowing halo. Her diaphanous gown barely concealed her figure as it snapped and whipped about, driven by the magic she emanated rather than natural winds.

Her eyes shone bright—first a brilliant sapphire blue, then a deep sea-foam green, of a shade fully befitting a daughter of the Celtic sea deity, Manannán mac Lir. I'd figured out who she was based on hints that the Dagda, Lugh, and Fuamnach had dropped while I'd been in Underhill. Like Queen Galadriel in that *Lord of the Rings* adaptation, she was both terrible and beautiful. I could easily see how my ancestor Oisín would have been absolutely gobsmacked by her.

I waited patiently as she attempted to intimidate me with her presence, yawning and scratching my balls. It was crude, but I was beyond caring about offending the fae queen. I was tired of being manipulated and used like a piece on a chessboard in the games she played with Fuamnach and the Dark Druid. Instead of focusing on her, I thought back to Jesse's death, and Hemi's. I did it to remind myself of why I'd chosen this path. While Maeve seethed I bided my time, heartbroken but full of resolve.

Maybe she saw that I'd been broken, or that a part of me

was, at least. Her eyes softened, and she motioned for the hunters to lower their bows.

The Dagda had been right. She *did* have a soft spot for the "Sons of Milesius," as he called us humans. And that was a weakness I'd use against her.

"Colin, I'm sorry for the loss of your friend. But no matter what happened while you were in Underhill, I can assure you that whatever plan you've devised is both ill-conceived and ill-timed..."

I cut her off, barking my response with a sneer. "Is it, Maeve? Or should I say, Niamh Golden-Hair?" I paused to see what her face might reveal. It may as well have been made of granite. "Guess you figured I'd find out during this little trip. Well, no one told me, not outright. But it wasn't hard to put two and two together, after what you'd told me and the way the other Tuatha spoke of you."

-Is it time, Colin?-

Almost, Eye. Be ready.

I knew that the glamour the Dagda had cast on me wouldn't last forever. Lugh had told me as much when he'd shared his plan with me. If Maeve saw through it and realized I'd shifted into my Fomorian form, I was screwed.

I just needed her concentration to falter for an instant. Then, I'd make my move.

"This changes nothing between us," she said. "I am still your ancestor and your benefactor. I've done as you asked, and sent the children and your friends away, somewhere safe."

"Are they free?"

"They remain unharmed, and are not under guard."

That could mean anything. Maeve might have been keeping them under lock and key in a dungeon somewhere, or in suspended animation for all I knew.

"Show me."

Maeve waved a hand, and an image shimmered into view on the wall of the cavern. First, I saw Guts, deep underground and back with his tribe. Then I saw Sabine and Crowley standing with Luther in his apartment. Hemi's shrouded body was laid out on Luther's dining room table, and they were staring at it, mourning his passing.

"As you can see, they are safe," she said. "What happened to Jack?"

I sniffed and scratched my nose with my free hand, keeping the other hand hidden inside my Craneskin Bag. "He's been delayed."

She pursed her lips into a moue of annoyance, or perhaps disappointment.

"Is he dead?"

I tongued a tooth, trying to look bored. "If I thought he could be killed, I'd have done it. Unfortunately, he's still alive."

"Did you happen to see my father?" she asked.

"No, he never showed his face. Why would he? To send a message to you?"

"Perhaps, but it is of no consequence."

Her gaze wavered for a second. She was genuinely hurt at that.

Oh, Maeve, you've become much too human over the centuries, I thought. *Now, Eye. Do it.*

-I am satisfied to comply with your request.-

The Eye unleashed the full force of its true power, releasing it in a cone of incendiary death that enveloped both Maeve and her hunters.

———

MY EYESIGHT HELD out long enough for me to see the kill squad burned to ash, and Maeve being blasted out of the small chamber and into the mists that shrouded the pathway beyond. I screamed in agony as my eyeballs boiled out of my head and incinerated. The pain was unreal, but I only had seconds to do what had to be done.

I turned and felt for the archway behind me.

Eye, help me out here. This has to be perfect.

-I will ensure the task is done correctly. Have no fear.-

I pulled the Spear of Lugh from my Craneskin Bag, thrusting it deep into the stone threshold of the archway at a slight angle.

Where's Maeve?

-Still recovering. Continue.-

I reached into the Bag and pulled out the Dagda's Cauldron, threading the handle over the Spear's shaft and holding it in place. Next, I drew the Sword of Nuada from the Bag, thrusting it into the stone floor next to the Spear, so both blade and shaft would create an "X" in the archway. Where they met, the Cauldron now hung suspended, as if hanging over a cooking fire.

Is it good, Eye? Will that do?

-Yes, but hurry. She will soon recover.-

Last of all, I grabbed the Stone of Fál out of the Bag, then I fumbled around until I found the lid and lip of the Cauldron.

-Hurry Colin! She approaches!-

I lifted the lid and tossed the Stone of Fál inside. It dropped into the Cauldron as if it had been made to fit.

Maeve's voice was a wail of fear and despair behind me. "Colin, no!"

Fuse it, Eye.

-Gladly.-

I FELT the Eye's power rocket out of my skull as it blasted the Four Treasures of the Tuatha Dé Danann with the heat of a hundred forges. I gripped the sides of the archway, staggering with the absolute agony I felt as the Eye heated the Treasures with enough magic and flame to weld them together for all eternity.

In an instant, it was done. A shockwave tossed me away from the gateway, and I was thrown across the cavern. I collided with the wall and bounced off, landing on my hands and knees. In my Fomorian form, the impact was a mere nuisance— although if I'd been in my human form, it would have crushed me.

All was still for a moment, then it felt and sounded as though a huge vault door to eternity had slammed shut.

The Eye's voice echoed in my head.

-*It is finished.*-

With that one, defiant act, the gateways to Underhill had been closed, permanently.

All of them.

Maeve's scream pierced my ears. "Fool! What have you done, Colin? What have you done?"

I placed one hand on the floor, and the other on the wall of the cavern, then pushed myself to my feet. Still blind, I swayed unsteadily.

"I evened the odds, Maeve, that's what. Now, you're just like the rest of us. No more drawing on Underhill's magic. No more unlimited power. No more treating humans like pawns. No more."

"You have no idea what you've done. You've destroyed us all."

I swung my head around to face the sound of her voice. My eyes were healing, but slowly. It'd take several cycles of shifting to repair the damage that had been done to my eyesight.

"All of us, Maeve? Or just the fae? We've been your play-things for millennia. Did you think I'd let that stand, after all that I've been through because of your stupid games and power plays? You, Fuamnach, the Rye Mother. Pfah! I'm done being your butt boy."

Her voice dripped with venom. "I'll kill you."

"Maybe. I mean, you could, right? But how much of your rapidly diminishing magical reserves would that use up? The dimensionally-displaced path that leads to this cavern alone must be eating up your power at a tremendous rate. Never mind all that crazy shit your house does. Oh, I'm sure you have some power sinks tucked away, just in case. But you sure in the hell don't have them on you, or I'd sense them. No, it never occurred to you, because you never saw this coming."

"Petulant child. My people will curse your name for centuries to come."

"Those who survive. Admit it, Maeve. I've bested you."

The anger in her voice gave way to despair and regret. "And to your own detriment. Nature abhors a vacuum, Colin. You've weakened a major power that has existed for millennia here on earth. Do you not think something else, something worse is waiting in the wings to fill that void?"

"Oh hell... really? You're still trying to make me believe that you've been protecting me? That you've only had my best interests at heart, all along? Please. Fucking assholes like you think you can do whatever you want to those weaker than you—you, the rest of the Tuatha, the Dark Druid, and even Finnegas. But that's going to change, from here on out."

I heard her gasp in pain. It appeared that healing magic was just as expensive for her to cast now as it was for human mages. "It was the Tuatha who helped you devise this plan. And they've betrayed you, although you fail to see it."

I laughed. "That has to sting, that they screwed you so badly. But you should have known that the Dagda, Lugh, and the others wouldn't allow you to steal every bit of magic that was keeping Underhill alive, any more than they'd allow Fuamnach to take it and invade earth. Now, all that magic is stuck on the other side. The Tuatha and fae in Underhill get to live, and they've no choice but to leave us alone. Those of you who remain on earth are weakened, and from here on out you have to scrape by like the rest of us mere mortals. Sounds like a win-win, to me."

Maeve's voice was thick with disappointment as she responded. "Gloat if you wish, but your monumentally foolish act has sealed your fate. The pathways back to my manse from here are closed, thanks to you. I'll leave you here to rot and consider your many mistakes."

I heard and felt a magical portal open and shut nearby, then all I heard was silence. When I was certain I was alone, I spoke aloud to my only remaining companion.

"Eye, what's on the other side of the door that leads out of this cavern?"

-Nothing but rock, Colin. The pathway beyond has disappeared. It now appears there's no escape from here.-

"Any chance of blasting us out?"

-None. From what I have determined via magical probes, this cavern is buried a thousand feet or more below the earth's surface. Doing so would drown you in molten rock. It appears we are trapped.-

I laughed and leaned back against the wall of the cave. I slid down the wall and fell hard on my rump.

"Well. Fuck me after all."

22

I spent the next several days shifting, healing, and resting. I'd brought enough food and water with me in my Craneskin Bag to keep me alive for weeks if I rationed it. While I healed, I conversed with the Eye, and it gave me some ideas on how to improve my ability to shift and stay shifted. After my eyes healed, I spent my time practicing using my shifter magic, mostly focusing on holding my shifted form for extended periods of time.

I became very good at controlling my ríastrad.

I also found a pack of playing cards inside the Bag and taught the Eye how to play Solitaire, then we moved to Blackjack. The Eye turned out to be a natural at counting cards, and since I always played as the house, I lost a lot. I devised elaborate plans for sneaking into Vegas casinos in my shifted form, so I could use the Eye to clean up at the tables.

On the fifth day, the magically-powered lights inside the cavern went out.

The light sticks and flashlights I'd brought with me provided light for a few more days. I lost track of time after that, and stopped asking the Eye what day it was, because that just made it worse. I slept; I meditated; I practiced what little magic I knew.

An indeterminate amount of time later, I got the bright idea to dig around inside the Bag for another source of light. I found a flaming sword, but it would only remain lit while it was in my hand. I ended up carrying it around like a torch, and nearly burned my eyebrows off a few times. I tried sleeping while holding it in my hand, extended away from my body, and caught my clothes on fire.

But it was better than being in the dark.

My food eventually ran out, and I was down to my last few bottles of water. The cavern smelled like a sewer, and so did I. I cut back my water rations to a few sips a day. Hunger gnawed at me like the monsters who haunted my dreams.

Dreams. I also dreamed of Jesse, Bells, and Hemi. In my nightmares, they died in a multitude of horrible, painful ways. The Dagda also came to me once in a dream—told me to hang in there, help was on its way. I was beyond caring at that point, because I was so weak from malnutrition. Plus, I kept getting sick due to the poor sanitary conditions, so I was dehydrated as all hell. I became plagued with infections and sores, both from poor nutrition and not bathing.

The only thing that saved me was shifting. It allowed me to talk to the Eye, who tried to keep me sane, and it helped my body heal so it didn't break down completely. But even the Fomorian metabolism needed calories, so the amount of healing I enjoyed when I shifted was limited.

I was dying, and at some point, I stopped caring. Thankfully, someone was still rooting for me.

"Hiya, slugger."

I cracked an eye open that had nearly become welded shut with pus. "Jesse? What're you doing here? Am I dead yet?"

She smiled and caressed my face. It felt like warm sunshine.

"Almost, which is why I'm able to talk to you like this. You're right on the edge of death, champ, but you need to hang on just a little longer. Finnegas is searching for you—and he's close, so close to finding you."

"Fuamnach said Finnegas knew about my ríastrad. He knew I was going to pop someday. And he still sent us into that cavern together to face the Caoranach."

"I know. He warned me it might happen."

I lapsed into a coughing fit, which wore me out. My voice was whisper as I replied. "You knew? Then why? Why didn't you run when it happened?"

She looked at me with sadness in her eyes. "I thought I could calm you down, bring you back from the edge. But I accidentally got in your way. Maybe I should have run, but I didn't. So don't blame it on Finnegas, and don't blame it on yourself. It was my choice to stick around, Colin. Mine and mine alone."

Hot tears ran down my cheeks. "I'm tired, Jesse."

She smiled sadly and kissed my forehead. "I know, but you can't give up yet. We still have shit to do, you and I. Sorry, but it looks like you're stuck with me."

"That's the hardest part. Knowing you're always near, and not being able to touch you or speak with you."

"It kills me, too, but that's just the way things have to be."

"It's lonely in here. Do you ever get lonely, Jess?"

"Not really. There are other ghosts to talk to when I need companionship. I've made friends."

"That's good. I worry about you, all the time."

"I know."

"I'd be with you if I could."

"I know that, too."

"I love you, Jesse."

"I love you too, Colin. Now and always. Go to sleep, my love. Help will be here soon."

It might have just been another fever dream, I wasn't sure. But sometime after that, a blinding light woke me. It shone into the cavern, so bright I had to shield my eyes.

"Found you," I heard Finnegas say.

I struggled to raise my head. "Finn, is that really you? Sorry for the mess. I haven't had time to clean lately."

"I've smelled worse. You look worse than this place smells, by the way."

I tried to laugh, but it turned into a coughing fit. "Can you turn the lights down? Hurts my eyes."

"Sorry, it's daylight. If I shut the portal, it'll be days before I gather enough energy to create another one."

"Ah, no worries. How long have I been down here?"

"About a six weeks, give or take. You ready to go home?"

I shrugged. "I guess. How bad is it?"

He paused, stroking his beard. "It's bad, son. I've had to double up on the wards at the junkyard, to protect the workers. Despite their lack of magic, the fae have been trying to cast curses on the place on almost a daily basis."

"Well, it's good to be loved. How's Ed?"

"They reattached his hand. He's been going to physical therapy. Look, we can discuss this when we get back to Éire Imports. Maureen is waiting for us."

"She's not in the 'fae who swore eternal enmity against Colin McCool' camp?"

Finnegas chuckled. "No, not at all. She said something to the effect of, 'those bloody cunts needed a good comeuppance.' Or something like that."

"Good old Maureen. Is she still hot?"

"You'll be happy to know that her beauty is one hundred percent natural."

I nodded as I struggled to pull myself upright. "I might need some help standing up. Hand me that sword, would you?"

He did, but not before eyeing it warily. I tossed it into the Bag.

"Sometimes I think you shit magical objects, kid."

"Hey, they find me. I'm just lucky that way, I guess."

He grabbed me under the arms and lifted me like a baby. I swung an arm around his neck, and we stumbled toward the portal.

"Finn, where's Bells?"

———

FINNEGAS TOOK me back to my hometown, back to where I'd first met him and where the whole sordid mess had begun. I spent a few weeks at Éire Imports, hiding out in the warehouse where Jesse and I had used to work and train, while Maureen and the old man nursed me back to health.

I was hiding out because, according to Finn and Maureen, half the fae wanted me dead. And the half who didn't? They'd likely turn me in to the half who did.

Finnegas had filled me in on what had happened after I'd closed off the gateways to Underhill. Without a virtually unlimited pool of magic to draw on, the fae who relied on glamours and illusions to blend in were forced to go underground. A few, those who looked more or less human, were rumored to be getting by with makeup and prosthetics. The Hollywood version of illusory magic, so to speak.

Lives were turned upside down and economies were disrupted as entire communities of fae went into hiding, away from prying human eyes. Magic became scarce amongst the fae, a commodity to be pooled and hoarded rather than thrown about indiscriminately. This forced some of the fae to go back to their old ways, preying on humans to survive.

It was said that Maeve tried to crack down on it, on the fae who were getting out of line. But her power was limited now, and her subjects knew it. It wasn't open rebellion, but it was close.

And if they blamed me for cutting the power off, they blamed her even more for giving me the means to do so.

As far as Belladonna was concerned, no one had seen her since the day faery magic had gone dark. I kept calling and texting her, but got no reply. Whether she'd been snagged by Maeve, or if she'd been sent somewhere on a deep cover assignment by the Circle, I had no idea. No one did. So, I sat around going nuts while I recovered from my ordeal, and busied myself studying magic with Finnegas.

Finally, I couldn't take it any longer. I used magic to get into the local police impound yard, where I hotwired a car. I picked one with dark limo tint on the windows—a late model Impala that was inconspicuous except for the tint. I rolled it out of the impound yard, locked the gate up behind me, and headed for Austin.

I pulled up to Belladonna's place at about one in the morning. I cased the place for a while, because I knew there'd be fae waiting for me. Finally, I decided that I didn't care. I hopped out of the car and made a beeline for the door, gathering power and preparing to shift.

I was halfway to her door when a dark figure stepped onto the sidewalk in front of me. I almost belted him out of the way, before realizing who it was.

Crowley.

"There's a fae death squad waiting for you to show up. You could take them, but more will come along shortly."

He shrouded us in shadow, grabbing my arm and pulling me

along beside him as he power-walked away from Belladonna's building. He guided me back to the car I'd borrowed and got inside. I took one wistful look back at Belladonna's apartment, then took his cue and got in the car with him.

"Crowley, where's Bells? Did the fae take her? And how's Sabine?"

"Just drive, before they see us. I'd rather avoid an incident if I could. I'm not exactly popular with the fae now, either."

I started the car and pulled out of the parking lot. When we were a few blocks away, he spoke.

"I went looking for Belladonna soon after we returned from Underhill, not long after I realized you weren't coming back. As soon as Sabine felt that she was cut off from Underhill's magic, she panicked, and I haven't seen her since."

"She'll be in hiding. She's an agoraphobe who hid behind that reverse glamour she always wore." I felt bad for Sabine, but I had to know what happened to Belladonna. "She'll be fine. Tell me what you know about Bells."

"I searched her apartment, and it looked as though she'd packed for a trip and left. There were no signs of struggle, and nothing was out of place. But I did find this." He held up a sealed envelope with my name on it.

I snagged it out of his hand and yanked the wheel, making a sharp right into a convenience store parking lot. I held the envelope up to my face; it smelled like Bells.

The note inside was short and sweet:

Colin,

I'm more than a little pissed that you left without telling me, but Luther explained why you did it. While you were gone, something happened and I had to use that ticket. I know I told you I wouldn't, but my mother needs me. Call me when you get back, and I'll explain everything.

-B

"Crowley, do you know when this was written?"

"I asked around her apartment building, and no one had seen her since about the time we headed to Underhill. Why, what does it say?"

"She went back home, to Spain. I don't know the whole story, but I do know that her family has ties to the fae in Galicia. Shit, maybe something happened to her as a consequence of what I did." I crumpled the note and held it to my chest.

"Are you going after her?"

To tell the truth, I was torn. I had made a promise to Hemi, to return his body to his homeland and family. I still hadn't followed through on that promise. His shrouded body remained in a magical suspended animation back at the warehouse, courtesy of the Dagda. How? I had no idea. But I owed my friend a responsibility, and I needed to see it through.

Bells was a big girl, and I knew she could handle herself. If she was in a pickle, she'd find a way to get herself out again. I just needed to have faith in her. At least, that's what I told myself.

I shook my head. "She made it pretty clear that she didn't want me getting involved in her family business. But she didn't say anything about you."

"You trust me to look into this?"

"Crowley, it seems crazy for me to say this—but right now, you're one of the few people I trust."

"Consider it done, then. I'll call you when I hit the ground in Spain, and keep you posted on what I find."

"Thanks, Crowley. And when you find her, send her my love."

"Make no mistake, I'm going to try to steal her back from you."

"I know." I laughed. "That's one of the reasons why I trust you to find out what's happened to her."

"You're a strange man, Colin McCool."

"Tell me something I don't know."

It took weeks for me to fully recuperate from the time I'd spent starving to death in that cavern. Crowley eventually found Bells —safe and sound, in fact. I also got Hemi back to his family, fulfilling my promise to him and then some.

Did I mention that Hemi's mom nearly killed me?

Meh, those are stories for another time.

Bells and Crowley were still in Spain wrapping up a few loose ends when I got an unexpected visit from an old acquaintance. I was up late, sipping tea and reading in the corner of the warehouse that I'd converted into my living quarters. I'd been reading a lot, trying to stay off social media because Crowley kept posting pics of him and Bells and it was pissing me off. My best frenemy was trying to make time with my girlfriend, while I was stuck in Texas and they were half a world away in Spain.

I had to admit, when Sal showed up at the front door of Éire Imports late one night, it was almost a welcome distraction.

Almost.

"Sal, how'd you find me?"

"It wasn't hard, druid. It's just that Maureen and the old man have this town locked up tighter than a nun's cunt. I played hell tryin' to get to you, let me tell you. Can I come in?"

"Naw, the place is warded nine ways to Sunday. You'd fry like a pigeon on a high-power line. You alone?"

He held his left hand up with two fingers extended, and placed his right over his heart. "Scout's honor, I swear. I owe you for saving Little Sal's life. This red cap remembers his debts."

"Fair enough. Give me a sec, Sal." I went back inside and grabbed a bottle of Irish whiskey and a couple of coffee mugs. I hadn't had many visitors lately, so I wanted to make the most of it—even if it was Sal.

We sat on the concrete steps in front of the office, sipping whiskey in the cool night air, making small talk for a while. Finally, I got tired of waiting and asked him point blank what was up.

"Well, druid, you gotta understand that I'm going against Maeve's wishes by coming here. So, youse didn't hear this from me, alright?"

"My lips are sealed, Sal. Besides, I doubt I'll be speaking with Maeve anytime soon. Talk."

He swirled his whiskey around in his mug, staring at it for a moment before downing it all. "It's the fae, Colin. They've been disappearing."

"What do you mean, disappearing? Like heading back to the old country? Have they found a way to go back to Underhill?"

He took a long swig straight out of the bottle and shook his head. "Nope. And trust me, if they did, there'd be fae lining up for miles to make that trip. Naw, I mean fae are getting disappeared. *Capisci*?"

"How many? And for how long?"

He took another long drink, forcing it down with a grimace and a shrug. "I dunno—weeks, maybe. It took a while for us to start noticing, what with everyone being forced underground." He flashed me a grim smile. "Kind of hard for a fae to get by these days, you know."

"I'm not going to apologize for that, Sal."

The little fae held up both hands, with the neck of the whiskey bottle suspended between two of his fat little fingers. "I'm not asking you to. All I'm asking is that you look into it, is all. Maeve... well, she's not quite up to keeping us safe these days. And some of these missing fae were heavy hitters. Even without a connection to Underhill, they could hold their own. It's got our people nervous, some of us enough to forgive the past... *indiscretions* of a certain druid. That is, if he were so inclined to step in and help."

I rubbed a hand across my three-day stubble and nodded. "I'm sick of hiding out here anyway." I grabbed the bottle from him and took a pull off it, savoring the burn as the whiskey went down.

"Does that mean you'll look into it?"

I handed the bottle back to him. "Sure, Sal, count me in. And tell everyone..."

"Yeah, druid? Whaddya want me to tell them?"

I flashed a grim smile. "Tell them the Junkyard Druid is back."

This concludes the first tetralogy in the Colin McCool series, but Colin's adventures will continue in Book 5, Druid Justice! Please leave a review for this book on Amazon or Goodreads, and be sure to sign up for my newsletter at http://MDMassey.com. Thanks for your support!

IRL RESOURCES

National Suicide Prevention Lifeline
Call 1-800-273-8255
Available 24 hours everyday

National Sexual Assault Hotline
Call 1-800-656-4673
Available 24 hours everyday

Veteran's Crisis Line
Call 1-800-273-8255 and press 1
Available 24 hours everyday